MYSTERIES *of* MARTHA'S VINEYARD

A Light in the Darkness
Like a Fish Out of Water

MYSTERIES *of* MARTHA'S VINEYARD

Like a Fish *Out of* Water

JANICE THOMPSON

New York

Mysteries of Martha's Vineyard is a trademark of Guideposts.

Published by Guideposts Books & Inspirational Media
110 William Street
New York, NY 10038
Guideposts.org

This is a work of fiction. Martha's Vineyard, Massachusetts, actually exists, and some characters are based on actual residents whose identities have been fictionalized to protect their privacy. Apart from the actual people, events, and locales that figure into the fiction narrative, all other names, characters, businesses, and events are the creation of the author's imagination or are used fictitiously.

Every attempt has been made to credit the sources of copyrighted material used in this book. If any such acknowledgment has been inadvertently omitted or miscredited, receipt of such information would be appreciated.

Cover and interior design by Müllerhaus
Cover illustration by Greg Copeland, represented by Deborah Wolfe, LTD.
Typeset by Aptara, Inc.

Printed and bound in the United States of America
10 9 8 7 6 5 4 3 2

Like a Fish *Out of* Water

CHAPTER ONE

Ready to head home, boy?" Priscilla Grant glanced over her shoulder at the dog in the backseat of her car. She grinned when Jake's tail thumped against the leather. "I'd say we've had quite enough adventure for one day, wouldn't you?"

Adventure, indeed. She and Jake had shared a wonderful day exploring Martha's Vineyard, her new home. Though she'd only been on the island a short time, Priscilla still couldn't get enough of the breathtaking scenery or the kindhearted people. She'd grown to love it here.

Jake seemed to agree. His energetic tail wagged in merry fashion as if to say, "I'd like to stay put too."

"Good boy." She reached back to pat him on the head, and he settled down, ready for the ride home.

Priscilla turned the key in the ignition and then pointed her car toward her cottage at Misty Harbor, her thoughts shifting back to the island and its colorful residents. Could she have landed in a more idyllic spot? To all who dreamed of white picket fences, American flags waving in the coastal breeze, and a quaint life along the 120 miles of exhilarating seashore, this was the place. One could scarcely find a fault with Martha's Vineyard, unless the cost of living was factored in. Owning a home on the island could squeeze the pocketbook, no doubt about that.

Not that Priscilla wanted to fret over finances—not after a day like today, when she'd enjoyed a blissful tour of the island's historic homes. She would ponder the cost of updates to her cottage later. Right now, basking in the glory of this peaceful, picture-perfect day took priority. And eating a crème horn she'd picked up at the local bakery, of course. The take-home bag sat in her passenger seat. The sugary goodness permeated the air around her even now, but she would have to wait until after dinner to enjoy her treat.

Priscilla followed the road past several luxurious homes, beyond a local bed-and-breakfast, and past one of the island's many graveyards with its sloped grounds and massive, overhanging trees. She kept her gaze on the road as she rounded the bend toward her cottage, which always reminded her of one she'd seen in a children's picture book. At certain points, gorgeous, expansive trees cocooned the street and seemed to swallow her whole. At other points, they disappeared altogether, and she caught a glimpse of the harbor in the distance, rippling under the late-afternoon sunlight.

Like most stretches of water on the island, the harbor still caught her by surprise. She could curl around a bend in the road to a sudden viewpoint that took her breath away. There in front of her, a glass-like sea in all its brilliance. What a magical experience, one that always made her want to hit the brakes.

When she did have a chance to stand at the water's edge, Priscilla always found herself captivated by the sheer number of boats. Everywhere, boats. Some to sail, others to fish, still others to impress folks with their sheer beauty.

Would she ever grow tired of her new home?

"Guess what, Jake?" she said as the revelation took hold. "I just called Martha's Vineyard *home.*" A contented sigh slipped out. With each day that passed, another piece of her heart took root on the island, and she didn't mind one bit.

When the cottage Aunt Marjorie had left her came into view, Priscilla eased the car into the drive and paused to give the magnificent adjoining lighthouse a closer look. The tower was a bright white, capped by its black lantern room and encircled by a railing. Her gaze traveled to the small window about halfway up the lighthouse, which was also trimmed in black.

Soon, if she had her way, the bottom floor would morph into a small museum, complete with the Latham family history. Perhaps by next spring or summer, if all went well.

She shifted her attention to the waters of the cove, giving them a closer look.

"We're not in Kansas anymore, Toto," she whispered. No, indeed. A far cry from it, in fact. She turned off the engine and basked in the beauty of it all.

A glance to Priscilla's right revealed sailboats, fishing boats, and ribbons of late-afternoon sunlight dancing on the waters. What a brilliant display of God's handiwork. She wished she could spend a few quiet moments on the dock with her legs hanging over its rickety wooden frame. In that quiet spot, she would find time to reflect, to ponder life's complexities. To pray.

Unfortunately, something distracted her from the beautiful view—Tommy Townsend, the handyman she'd hired to replace the cottage's windows. He stood to the side of her driveway, worry lines etched across his forehead.

She climbed out of the vehicle and then opened the back door to let Jake run free. The hyper pup bounded toward the water's edge, tail wagging.

"Careful, boy," she hollered. "Don't get..." She didn't have time to add the word *wet* before he dove headlong into the reeds.

Oh well. She'd just hose him down later.

Priscilla took several steps in the handyman's direction. "Everything okay, Tommy?"

He shook his head and shifted his weight from one foot to another. "I hate to break it to you, Mrs. Grant, but I've uncovered some problems with the cottage."

"Besides the floorboards and windows, you mean?"

"Yes. When we pulled out the old window frame, I noticed the clapboard underneath had rotted."

"Can't you just replace it?"

Her question garnered another look of concern from Tommy. "Sure, but the more I got to looking, the more I realized that whole section needs to be replaced. It's one of those things that you need to do all at once."

"I see." She swallowed hard.

"And once the new siding is up, it's got to be painted, which brings me to my second point."

"There's a second point?"

"Yes." His nose wrinkled, and he swiped at his forehead with the back of his hand. "The original clapboards have really weathered over the years. So if we replace a section of the siding and give it a fresh coat of paint, it won't match the rest of the house."

"Ah."

"Common problem here on the island. But if we're really going to do this, we might as well do it right. With your permission, I'll replace all of the rotting clapboard, give it a fresh coat of paint, and then paint the rest of the exterior of the cottage as well."

"Paint the whole house?" Priscilla could almost hear the dollar signs clicking.

He nodded. "Yes, but it's not really that simple. If we're going to go that route, I'll have to sand and scrape beforehand to get rid of a hundred years' worth of buildup. We're talking a pretty big prep job here, and a lot more money than just replacing windows and a few floorboards. I hope you don't mind, but I've put together an estimate." He passed a piece of paper her way, and she gasped as she read the number he'd scribbled down.

"Twelve thousand dollars?"

"Roughly. That's just an estimate."

She gripped the paper, her thoughts in a whirl. "Tommy, I thought this was just going to be the windows and some refurbishing of the living room floor. You know? I'm not sure my pocketbook is prepared for a full-on home renovation job."

"I know." He pulled off his ball cap and raked his fingers through his hair. "You don't have to give me an answer right away. But let me know when you can because the siding has to be brought over from the mainland. That cost is factored in, by the way."

Priscilla couldn't help herself. She groaned. "I'll think about it and let you know, I promise."

"Thanks. And sorry about the bad news."

"Me too." She sighed. "But thanks for your hard work on my behalf, Tommy."

"You're welcome."

He headed to his truck and pulled away moments later, his oversize tires turning up gravel in her driveway.

Priscilla turned to examine the sea-blue cottage with its weathered clapboard siding and trim. The white shutters gave the place a fairy-tale look, and the flower boxes underneath really brought life to the old place. How she adored those beautiful rose-colored geraniums, framed out by elephant ear and lobelia. If only the old home didn't require so much work.

"Thank you, Aunt Marjorie," she said. "Thank you for leaving this lovely home to me."

A lovely home in need of repair, but a treasure nonetheless.

Treasure.

She couldn't help but think of her recent find in the attic, a trunk filled with old diaries and journals. What mysteries they had unraveled. Did this old cottage hold even more stories? Perhaps they would reveal themselves in time.

Priscilla turned her full attention to the dog, who was chasing something around the side of the house. "Jake, get over here." When he refused to cooperate, she let out a piercing whistle. He bounded her way and jumped up on her, covering Priscilla's clothing in mud. Ugh. "Now look what you've done." She continued to scold him as she turned on the hose. "I can't very well hose off out here, but you? You're getting a bath, here and now."

She bathed the dog then watched as he rolled around in the grass to dry off. So much for keeping him tidy. Now he was covered in grass and dirt.

Priscilla clucked her tongue as he shook off some of the loose grasses. "I think you were meant to be a farm dog." She could almost picture him chasing the horses and bounding through the wheat fields. Right now, though, she needed to think about other things, like getting the rowdy pup cleaned up once again and then heading inside for a bath. Afterward she would take a closer look at Tommy's list and then brave a glance at her bank account balance to see where things stood.

Priscilla bathed Jake once again and then headed indoors. As she made her way through the bedroom, a framed piece of art on the west wall caught her attention. This wasn't the first time Priscilla had zeroed in on the odd painting of a battle sword, of course. She'd wondered about it from the first time she'd seen it. It wasn't her style, not even close. Still, removing her ancestor's cherished belongings just felt wrong. On the other hand, could she live with all of the cottage's knickknacks for the long haul? Something to think about.

She headed to the small bathroom. Minutes later, she settled into the bubbly waters of the claw-foot tub and leaned back to rest her head and neck. How many years had this old tub stood in this same spot? From the rust on the claw feet, too many. Longer than that old sword painting, maybe. But how could she trade in an antique for something shiny and new, especially one with so much history behind it? Seemed sacrilegious somehow.

A sigh wriggled its way out as Priscilla realized that was exactly what she'd done with the farm. She'd traded it in for a new home in Martha's Vineyard. Her daughter's words ran through her mind: *"Come home, Mom. Come back to Kansas where you belong."*

Did she really belong on the farm, or was this a new chapter in her life, one that only led to newer, different adventures? In such a short time, her affections for Martha's Vineyard had taken Priscilla by surprise. The island now felt as cozy and welcoming as this bubble bath. No wonder Aunt Marjorie had made the island her forever home. No wonder Joan, Gail, and Trudy chose to stay. Her cousins could have lived anywhere, but Martha's Vineyard held them in its comfortable embrace.

And now it held her too. This was home now. As it had been for many generations for the Latham family. This little cottage by the sea had provided shelter for her family for more than a hundred years and was starting to show the effects of that.

A dark cloud passed over her, one that troubled her heart and threatened to shift her mood. Though she tried to avoid dwelling on it, the reality of her situation took hold. Would repairs on the cottage continue to snowball, eventually bankrupting her and forcing her back to the farm in Kansas?

This, of course, would delight her overprotective daughter. How many times had Rachel uttered the words, "You're in over your head, Mom"? A dozen at least. Now with this repair bill looming, Rachel's words rang true. Still, every time Priscilla thought about going back to the family farm, a pang of grief pierced her heart. To leave now would be to admit defeat.

On the other hand, staying would require a financial commitment that could very well escalate even further once renovations got underway. Would this old cottage turn out to be a money pit? If so, could she really afford to keep it in shape?

"I don't want to go back to Kansas, Toto," she said to Jake, who'd curled up at the foot of the tub. "No matter how impossible this seems."

The dog opened his eyes, yawned, then dozed back off. Clearly he wasn't losing any sleep over this.

Perhaps she shouldn't either. Priscilla resolved to keep a positive outlook. No looking back. But how, with financial woes looming, could she possibly move forward from here?

CHAPTER TWO

If it hadn't been for the ringing of her cell phone, Priscilla might have dozed off surrounded by water and bubbles. Instead, she bounded from the porcelain tub, grabbed a towel, and then slipped and slid across the bathroom floor as she headed for the phone on her bedside table. She managed to reach it just before the call went to voice mail.

She was greeted by a familiar male voice on the other end of the line. "Mrs. Grant, this is Tommy Townsend again. Sorry to bother you, but I thought of something I left off the list."

"Really? There's something else?" She pulled the towel a bit tighter and sat on the edge of the bed, bubbles and tiny beads of water dribbling down both legs.

"Yes. I wondered if you might be interested in putting in storm windows. They'll hold up better during hurricane season."

"Hurricane season?"

"Sure. And you'll be better insulated in the winter, once the weather turns cold."

Priscilla shivered as cold water continued to dribble down her legs. "I assume we're talking more money?"

"Quite a bit, but most people on the island use heavy-duty windows. Those who've been here long enough to know why they need them, I mean."

"I see." She paused. "Can I think about this and call you in the morning?"

"Sure. And by the way, a couple of local craftsmen will be working alongside me. Just wanted you to know to expect unfamiliar faces."

"Thanks for the heads-up."

"You're welcome." Tommy cleared his throat. "You know, your aunt Marjorie talked to me a couple of times about tackling some of the smaller projects but never really got around to it. And Gail has told me quite a few tales about the creaky floorboards and window frames. I guess they assumed the rest of the place was in good shape."

Despite the bad news, Priscilla couldn't help but smile at the mention of her cousin. Gail and Tommy were sweet on each other, albeit secretly.

"I'm sure Aunt Marjorie had great intentions." Priscilla decided to ignore the plops of water puddling at her feet. "But I'm guessing she felt a little overwhelmed by it all. I know I do. This cottage has been here for generations and is showing its age."

"We'll get 'er done. I'll be ready to order that siding whenever you are. Just let me know."

"Thanks, Tommy. I'll connect with you sometime tomorrow, likely."

By the time she ended the call, Jake was lapping the soapy water from the floor. Priscilla scolded him and then toweled herself off. All the while, her gaze kept shifting back to that painting of the sword. Strange how it drew her in. Priscilla shook it off and slipped into her comfiest pajamas.

After donning her house shoes, Priscilla walked into the kitchen and scrounged around in the fridge for something to eat. Leftovers from the restaurant at Tisbury's historic inn greeted her. Shrimp salad. She dove in as if she hadn't eaten in days. Tilly's shrimp salad had that effect on people. The crème horn from Candy's bakery provided the perfect finish.

Priscilla grabbed her laptop and carried it to the living room sofa, where she settled in with throw pillows all around her. During the next half hour she went over her finances, adding up totals from checking and savings. She could manage the repairs, but then what? If she dug too deep into her savings, it would change the whole dynamic of her experience on the island. Priscilla's funds would dwindle fast if the cottage required even more work than anticipated.

A quick glance at the laptop's clock showed the time: 8:15. Not time for bed. On the other hand, she could curl up under the covers and finish reading that book she'd started a few days back. Something about the cozy mystery sent chills down her spine, even now. After brushing her teeth, Priscilla climbed into the four-poster bed and leaned back against her pillows.

She read until her eyes grew heavy. Just before nodding off, her gaze traveled to the sword painting on the west wall, the same one that had drawn her eye several times before. An odd picture, to be sure: a painting of an antique sword, along with a Scripture from the book of Genesis: *And by thy sword shalt thou live, and shalt serve thy brother; and it shall come to pass when thou shalt have the dominion, that thou shalt break his yoke from off thy neck.* Not the most peaceful thing to gaze at right before bed. Which of her relatives had placed the painting on the wall. . .and why? Maybe she would garner the courage to pull it down. Surely Aunt Marjorie would approve?

Before she could give it much thought, Priscilla dozed off. The most puzzling dreams greeted her—images of sword fights and bloodshed. At some point in the dream, she found herself holding the sword, fighting for her life against some unknown foe. On and on the battle went, exhausting her to the bone.

She awoke in a puddle of sweat, her thoughts in a whirl.

Off in the distance, Jake let out a little moan. He rose from his bed on the floor and sat at her bedside as if anticipating trouble.

"Easy, Jakey." Priscilla tried to still the quiver in her voice as she did her best to calm her nerves. "I'll be okay."

She hoped so anyway.

A quick trip to the bathroom gave her something to do while calming down. As she passed the mirror in the bathroom, her own reflection caused her to jump.

"Calm down, girl." Priscilla released a nervous laugh. "No enemies here." Not in the mirror anyway.

She walked back into the bedroom, her gaze now affixed to the picture of the sword on the wall. Had the painting triggered that awful dream? Probably. First thing in the morning she'd pull it down. No more nightmares for her.

Priscilla settled back in bed and tried to sleep. She tossed and turned for several minutes, images of the sword running through her mind. After nearly twenty minutes of wrestling with the sheets, she rose, determined to put the painting out of her mind once and for all. She walked toward the closet, stifling a yawn as she went. Once inside, she found an unopened box she'd brought from Kansas, one that contained a large framed photo of the old homestead. The farm. Her farm. Hers and Gary's.

Priscilla lifted the artwork from the box and wiped dust off of it. Though it brought back bittersweet memories, at least they didn't leave her with haunting dreams of sword fights and other such nonsense. She would replace that painting on the bedroom wall with this lovely framed photo from home.

Home.

This time the word led her back to Kansas.

"Guess I'm not as sure of myself as I thought, Jake," she said to the dog, who had wedged himself into the closet behind her.

She gazed at the framed photo and allowed herself to be transported back in time once more. How sweet life had been when she and Gary were together. How precious, those memories. Raising Rachel on the farm they loved. Singing in the church choir. Harvest season. She gripped the frame, and tears brimmed her lashes. After a few moments, Priscilla shook off her ponderings and forced herself to think about the present.

"No going back." She rose and carried the photo to the bed, where she set it down. "No going back."

But that wouldn't stop her from hanging the picture—right now—so she could sleep. Priscilla walked to the wall and reached for the large painting of the sword, determined to pull it down. Strangely, the task was harder than she'd expected.

She eased the bottom of the frame up and away from the wall, but the top part didn't want to give. After another upward motion, Priscilla heard a strange click, and the whole picture lifted like a trap door. She gazed behind it, more perplexed than ever as she noticed a deep compartment in the wall. Was the dream continuing, or was this real? It felt like a scene from an old Alfred Hitchcock movie.

She squinted to see inside the long, slender compartment. A sword lay inside it. Priscilla stared at it with more intensity.

No, not *a* sword. *The* sword. The very one in the painting she'd been staring at just moments before.

CHAPTER THREE

Priscilla awoke on Saturday morning after a near-sleepless night. The clock on the wall tick-tick-ticked as she tried to force herself back to sleep, this time praying for a calmer mind. But she couldn't stop thinking about the sword.

When the morning arrived, Priscilla pulled herself out of the bed and headed to the kitchen to make a pot of coffee. She'd need more than one cup this morning for sure. Maybe the whole pot.

With her first cup in hand, she walked back into the bedroom and straight to the dresser, where she'd laid the sword the night before.

"Who did you belong to?" she asked as if the crazy thing could answer her.

She sat on the edge of the bed and stared at the initials on the sword: JWL. Odd. And why hide a sword in the wall? That made no sense at all. Why not hang it in a place of prominence?

Then again, not much about this old cottage made sense, did it? First the mysterious tunnel in the cellar. Now hinged artwork hiding buried treasures from watchful eyes. Fascinating.

Priscilla felt the need to talk to someone about this, but who? She could take the sword to Mildred Pearson at the museum, but family members seemed like a better place to start.

She made a quick decision to call her cousin Joan. Priscilla felt a smile tug at the corners of her lips as she thought about her blossoming relationship with this particular cousin. Priscilla adored them all, but watching Joan on that funny little scooter of hers, the one with the sidecar, always made her smile. Joan was the sensible one in the bunch, known for her common sense and steady way. She'd be perfect to solve this mystery.

Just as she picked up the phone to punch in the number, it rang in her hand. Priscilla jumped, nearly flinging the phone across the room. She managed to catch it before it took flight. She answered on the fourth ring, just before voice mail kicked in.

"Priscilla, it's Joan." Her cousin's voice sounded calm and reassuring, something she needed right now.

"Hey, you," Priscilla responded. "How did you know I was thinking about you?"

"Really?"

"Yes. Just this minute in fact."

Joan laughed. "I didn't, but I must've had some sort of prompting from the Lord. You've been on my mind all morning. Started in the wee hours of the night actually. I had a particular burden to pray for you. Hope that doesn't sound too odd."

"Not at all. I'm grateful for those prayers." Priscilla leaned back against the pillows. "You have no idea how grateful."

"I understand from Gail that the repairs on the cottage are going to be a bit more extensive than you thought."

Boy, news sure traveled fast around here, even faster than in small-town Kansas.

"I see." Tommy must have told Gail. "That sure didn't take long."

"If there's one thing I can count on in life, it's my seven a.m. phone call from Gail."

"Well, she was right. Tommy gave me an estimate yesterday. Twelve thousand dollars, to be precise."

"Ugh." Joan released a sigh. "I'm so sorry to hear that, but I'm not really surprised. I've lived in the Vineyard all my life and know how costly renovations can be. It would be expensive enough on the mainland, but getting the materials to the island can be very costly. I spent a fortune last year renovating my master bedroom, and that was just one room. Brace yourself, Priscilla, and don't panic if the costs climb even higher."

Priscilla found little consolation in that warning.

"I'm sure I'll have a lot to think about." She paused, feeling a bit overwhelmed. "The farm was a lot of work, so I'm used to big projects, but I'm a little lost with this one."

"It's just because you've only been in the cottage a short time," Joan responded, her voice filled with empathy. "Doesn't truly feel like home yet, so you're probably wondering why you'd sink all your money into a place that doesn't have your stamp on it yet."

"You've nailed it." Priscilla shifted the phone to her other ear. "But on the other hand, if I go ahead and have the work done now, I can put my stamp on it. It will definitely feel more like home once I've boxed up some of the current decor and added my own flair." Her thoughts immediately shifted to the antique sword.

coming through every Saturday." Priscilla could almost hear the coins clicking and the dollar bills shuffling.

"I could do most of the work myself, but I'm juggling a couple of other projects right now. Folks on the island tend to get their repairs done before summer ends, so there's always a rush in August. But don't worry, I know just the people to send your way. Beau Ortmann is really great with shingles. He's a close friend, someone I can trust to do a good job. You okay with giving him a shot?"

"Sure. Wait... Ortmann? Isn't that the family that owns the grocery store?"

"One and the same. But Beau was always more interested in construction than in running the family store, so he set off on his own."

"Ah."

The conversation carried on for a few more minutes as they settled on the details. After wrapping up the plans for the house, Priscilla ended the call. Now to head to the bakery to meet her cousins. She slipped on her sandals and grabbed her handbag before heading toward the front door. She climbed into her car and waved goodbye to Jake, who peered out of the new living room window.

Priscilla started the engine and pulled away from the cottage. As she rounded the bend just west of her home, she caught a glimpse of the water. Several Windsurfers were out this morning, taking advantage of the early morning breeze. What would it be like to completely give yourself over to the wind, to let it pull you where it may across the rippling waters? In many ways, it must feel like trusting God to move you all the way from Kansas to Cape Cod.

As she made her way toward Tisbury, she found herself captivated by her surroundings, as always. Martha's Vineyard had won her over with its weathered buildings and winding roads, with its coastal views and delicious breeze. Most of all, she'd fallen in love with the water, that sparkling masterpiece. Depending on the time of day, she would often catch upside down glimpses of the trees along the shoreline, as if they were standing on their heads under the shimmering sea. Sometimes the sunlight hit the water with such intensity that she found herself blinded by a dazzling light display. Other times the tranquility served to calm her troubled nerves and remind her of the Scripture "Be still."

To her right, an old graveyard on sloped ground was dotted with massive pine trees. Just beyond the graveyard, everything seemed tight. Pressed together. The houses along this stretch of road were small, shingle-style homes with gingerbread trim. Many had white picket fences and shrubbery. Nothing at all like the farm, but oh, so quaint.

The road wound along like a tight, curvy maze. At one point, she found herself slowing almost to a halt to pass some cyclists. Trees canopied a couple of the streets just beyond them. Priscilla passed a local B & B, one with a fabulous front porch decorated with rocking chairs, and then the road seemed to swallow her whole again. The trees practically touched her car as they cocooned her path. Besides the water, she loved this spot best of all.

Moments later, she neared the ferry landing, where seagulls swarmed around an incoming batch of tourists, cameras in hand. Priscilla was reminded of her first trip over on the ferry, anxious but excited to begin her new life here on the island. Now it all seemed so comfortable, so familiar.

She passed the post office and decided to pull into the parking lot. Seconds later, she picked up a copy of the *Vineyard Gazette.* Priscilla could hardly wait to learn more about the upcoming fair, an annual tradition every August on the island. Most of the pages were dedicated to the event, but she found a reminder about the farmer's market in Tisbury next Saturday, one week from today. Perfect. She would stop in to pick up some fresh produce. She loved picking through the fresh vegetables in season. It reminded her so much of life on the farm.

Of course, she loved everything about her little corner of the Vineyard: the quaint gift shops, the eclectic mix of art galleries, and especially the cozy inns and yummy restaurants. Everything here seemed very... unspoiled.

She sat in the parking lot, looking over the paper. One particular article caught her eye. Looked like the upcoming fair boasted a dog show. Interesting. Maybe she could work with Jake this year and prepare him for next year's show. She skimmed another article that focused on draft horses and cattle then found herself reading an article about the annual lumberjack competition. She certainly wasn't in Kansas anymore, was she?

Priscilla tossed the paper aside and started the car. She'd best be on her way. Just a few more blocks, and she would reach the bakery—if she could keep her eyes on the road and not the sailboats dotting the coastline to her left.

Glancing at the sidewalk, she caught a glimpse of Mildred, resident historian. She gave Priscilla a smile and a wave as she passed by. How wonderful it felt to have new friends. Yes, Martha's Vineyard had welcomed her with open arms.

At five minutes to ten, Priscilla walked inside Candy's bakery. She sniffed the air, and the familiar scent of sugary goodness awakened her senses. Yum.

From her spot behind the counter, the owner gave her a wave. "I can't shake you," Candy called out with a hint of laughter in her sunny voice.

Priscilla laughed and took a few steps in her friend's direction. "I know. I'm like a bad cold. I just keep hanging around."

This got a chuckle out of Candy, who came around the counter and brushed her hands on her apron, leaving powdered-sugar handprints behind. She greeted Priscilla with a hug. "You hang around as much as you like. Always happy to have you."

"I'll know it's time to back off when my pants start getting tight." Priscilla tugged at her waistband and shrugged. "Might be too late."

Candy's lips curled up in a smile. "There's a fabulous boutique in Edgartown that I have to take you to. You can always buy new clothes, but giving up crème horns is unthinkable."

"True that."

"Can I get you something?" Candy asked as she led Priscilla to a nearby table.

"In a bit," Priscilla took the seat facing the window so that she could watch the sailboats in the harbor. "I'm meeting Trudy, Joan, and Gail, but I'm a few minutes early."

She smiled as she thought about her cousins. What wonderful friends they had become. Trudy, Joan, and Gail had made the transition to the island more than bearable; they'd become friends of the closest sort. Priscilla could hardly believe the kindred feelings that wrapped themselves around her heart—and in such a short time too.

"Trudy's already here." Candy pointed toward the restroom. "You know how she is. Smallest bladder in Tisbury."

Priscilla brushed a crumb off the table and grinned. "Yes, but she's quick on her feet. You've got to give her that."

"Indeed." Candy's bubbling personality radiated joy, not just today but every time they were fortunate enough to spend time together. Some people were just born with welcoming facial expressions. They didn't have to try hard to put you at ease.

Candy cleared her throat and gestured with her head to a woman entering the front door. "Sheila Weller," she whispered. "If she tries to sell you anything..."

"Like cranberries?" Priscilla asked.

"*Mm-hmm.*" Candy released a slow sigh. "Wouldn't be the first time, eh?"

"No. She harvests them, right?"

"Yep. Great at what she does, but she's always after me to add cranberries to all of my dishes: baked, dehydrated, doesn't matter.

Cranberries. In my now-famous orange-cranberry bread, really in everything."

"Not everyone likes cranberries," Priscilla said.

"Shh." Candy put a finger over her lips. "Don't let anyone in these parts hear you say that, okay? They're our bread and butter." She laughed. "They bring in a lot of income, especially in the fall." She leaned down to whisper, "And it's almost fall, so look out!"

Priscilla laughed.

Candy walked away to greet Sheila and a couple of other incoming customers, which left Priscilla alone at the table to peruse the menu hanging on the wall behind the pastry counter. What should she have today? Something more brunch-like would make sense at this time of day. Less sugary. A croissant, maybe? No, one of Candy's yummy muffins. On the other hand, the crullers sounded good. Nah, too sweet. She continued to look over the menu, having a harder time than ever.

Trudy emerged from the ladies' room moments later, brushing a loose strand of her platinum hair out of her face.

Watching the crooked grin appear on her cousin's face, Priscilla had a flashback to what Trudy looked like as a child—with hair the pale yellow of a field of grain. Her memories of her childhood visits to the island were fuzzy, but suddenly the image of young Trudy running with that gorgeous blonde hair in her face shone bright and clear.

Of course, these days Trudy's 'do wasn't quite as natural. Only a visit to the salon could achieve that particular shade of platinum. But it was delightful, and so was she. Priscilla returned Trudy's grin and then noticed someone had entered the bakery. A handful of *someones* actually.

Looked like the cousins were here. Now, to share the story about the sword she'd found in the wall.

CHAPTER FOUR

Oh boy." Trudy's brows arched as she glanced toward the bakery's door. "Looks like Gail brought Uncle Hugh along."

"Why, oh boy?" Priscilla asked.

Trudy lowered her voice. "You haven't had adequate time to get to know him, have you? Otherwise you'd know he's a bit of a curmudgeon."

"Awe, he's not so bad." Priscilla thought through what Trudy had said. "I expect I'd be much worse if I were in his shoes."

"I expect we'd all be. Still, it wears on the rest of us." Trudy sighed. "Let's just say if there's a flaw in his food, he'll find it. Too windy? He'll complain about it. Too hot? He'll whine until Candy turns on the AC. That sort of thing. We love him to pieces, but he can wear a person out in a hurry." She plastered on a smile and waved. "Over here, ladies. Hi, Uncle Hugh."

Joan's brown hair appeared a bit disheveled from the wind outside. She approached first and took her seat. "Thanks for waiting. Sorry we're late." A little eye roll followed, though Priscilla wasn't sure why.

"Just got here a few minutes ago," Priscilla responded. "And you're not late at all. I'm perpetually early."

"Like Trudy." Joan ran her fingers through her messy hair. "She's a half hour early everywhere she goes."

"It's better than having to make apologies all the time like some people I know." Trudy gave her a knowing look. "And it's done wonders for my blood pressure. Being late all the time ratchets up the tension, and we all know what happens when our tension is ratcheted."

Candy joined them, water glasses in hand. "What's ratcheted?"

"My nerves," Joan responded, "if we don't stop this conversation."

Priscilla glanced over as her uncle approached. His button-up shirt would've been fine had he put the buttons in the correct holes. Not that he seemed to notice.

"Just ignore his getup," Gail whispered as she approached the table. "I pick my battles."

Uncle Hugh raked his fingers through the fringe of gray-white hair that surrounded his balding scalp and then attempted to straighten his hunched back. Priscilla was pretty sure she heard his bones pop.

"We would've been here sooner," he mumbled, "but Gail's slower than a tortoise with a broken leg. You should see her behind the wheel. Thought we'd have to skip breakfast today."

"Thanks, Pop." Gail rolled her eyes. "I'm just careful, that's all."

"Careful, my eye." He gave Priscilla a playful wink. "Just like to give her a hard time, girlie. How are you today, Priscilla?"

"Fine. Hungry." She rose to give him a warm hug.

"I'm hungry too," he added. "And grateful for a chance for something tasty. You should've seen that sorry excuse for a waffle Gail fed me for breakfast yesterday. I've had shoe leather softer than that thing."

"It was a bagel, Pop." Gail sighed and took a seat at the table next to Priscilla.

"Whatever. Anyway, I hope you gals don't mind that I tagged along. My poor old tummy's so empty I can hear it begging for food." He rubbed his hand across his ample belly and then patted it.

"Good grief." Gail shook her head.

Uncle Hugh glanced around as if looking for something. "Anyway, I plan to find my own table and read the paper while you ladies gossip. Just act like I'm not here."

"What makes you think we're going to gossip, Uncle Hubert?" Trudy asked.

He snorted. "Really? Isn't that why everyone comes to the bakery?"

"There might be a bit of truth to that," Candy said. "Though it wasn't my intention, the bakery has become rather the rumor mill." Her gaze traveled across the room to an older woman seated alone at a table, nibbling on a croissant. "You might want to keep your voices down," Candy whispered. "Eldora's here this morning, and, well, you know how she is."

"That woman." Uncle Hugh glanced her way. "Always spreading stories. I'd like to give her a piece of my mind."

"She'd just twist it and spread it to others," Candy said, her voice still low. "So don't waste your time."

"Told you this place was a rumor mill." Uncle Hugh flinched as he shifted his weight to his left leg.

Gail looked perturbed as she turned her gaze from the bakery owner back to her father. "Dad, I'm not Eldora. I've told you a dozen times, just because I mention a person by name in a conversation doesn't mean I'm gossiping about them. If I've got a personal involvement in the story, it's not gossip. Right?"

His bushy brows arched. "Run that one by the pastor, and see what he says."

"I will." Gail grabbed a menu and opened it. "Tomorrow, in fact. How's a person supposed to resolve any of the situations in her life if she can't discuss them?"

Uncle Hugh quirked a brow. "If we're going with that theory, then I guess it would be okay to let you know that Jimmy Clayborn is leaving his wife. I was personally involved in that story, after all."

"Jimmy is leaving Hannah?" Trudy clasped a hand over her mouth and then pulled it away. "Really?"

"See?" Uncle Hugh pointed at Gail. "See what you've done? This is all your fault."

"Do I even want to know how you were involved in that story, Dad?" Gail pierced her father with a look.

"It's not what you think, though I have seen Hannah Clayborn give me more than a second glance over the years. No, it's because I slipped and almost fell on a floor she'd just mopped at their bait shop."

"They're divorcing because of a wet floor?"

"No. And who said they were divorcing? I just said he was leaving. That could mean any number of things. Maybe he's just taking a trip to the mainland for a few days to rest his ears. That woman can talk a mile a minute."

"I cannot believe you're telling us all of this." Gail groaned.

"It's your fault, really." Hugh shrugged. "You said if I was involved in the story, it was my story too. And actually their problems are much deeper than that, but I dare not say because they do not involve me. Point is, the day I almost fell, Jimmy ended up confiding in me, which—according to Gail's theory—puts me smack-dab in the middle of the tale. So going with her logic, what I'm doing now isn't gossiping at all. Because I'm involved, you see."

He walked to his table and took a seat.

"And *this* is my life." Gail groaned and rested her elbows on the table as if admitting defeat. "His clothes are crooked, his attitude debatable, and his stories in need of editing. And just for the record, he gossips all the time, far more than I do."

"But you gotta love him," Trudy said with a smile.

"Sure do. Bible says so." Joan gave Gail a wink. "But seriously, Gail. Don't get so worked up over him. People know Uncle Hugh for who he is and love him that way."

"True." Gail's nose wrinkled. "There's just a lot to wade through, that's all."

Candy showed up moments later to see if they'd had enough time with the menu.

"Don't really need it, Candy," Joan said. "We all know I'm going to have an orange-cranberry muffin and coffee."

"And I'm having a chocolate croissant." Gail glanced at the chalkboard as if to confirm her thoughts. "*Hmm*. Maybe two? They're small."

"What about you, Priscilla?" Candy looked her way. "The usual chocolate chip cookies?"

"A little sweet for this early in the day." Priscilla laughed. "I've got to make a few responsible choices. What about the blueberry muffin and some Earl Grey? That sounds good."

"You've got it." Candy smiled. "But speaking of cutting back, would you believe I've gained twenty pounds since I opened the bakery? It's shameful."

"Only twenty?" Trudy snorted. "I would've packed on quite a few more pounds than that with all this temptation surrounding me." Her gaze traveled to the pastry case. "Maybe I should just skip breakfast and go straight to the coconut cream pie."

"Not on my watch." Joan glanced over the menu. "She'll have the low-fat cranberry scone."

"Gee, thanks." Trudy's piercing gaze as she looked Joan's way spoke volumes. "You going to start paying my bills for me too? And chauffeuring me around the island?"

Joan shrugged. "Maybe. Depends on how you behave."

"Well, I like that. I might just let you pay my bill today, all things considered. I hardly think it's fair to pay for something I didn't order."

Uncle Hugh began to grumble from the next table. "Could you keep it down over there?" He shot Trudy a pointed look. "I can't even read the paper in peace."

Trudy grabbed her water glass and took a sip then released a slow breath. Afterward she turned Priscilla's way, her expression much calmer.

"I understand there are some rumors going around the island about you, Priscilla."

"Wow. Really? Rumors?" Priscilla leaned back in her chair and looked Trudy's way. "Like what?"

"Oh, just folks wondering if you're planning to stay on the island permanently or leave. Some are taking bets that you'll head out before winter hits. Others are adamant that you're hanging around forever and selling your farm back in Kansas."

"And why, pray tell, am I the topic of so many thrilling conversations?" Priscilla asked.

Trudy shrugged. "Folks around here are always suspicious of newcomers, especially those who live in a house riddled with mysteries."

"Riddled with mysteries." Priscilla laughed. "Only one mystery so far. And did anyone ever stop to think that my old cottage is just that—an old cottage? One in need of repair, I might add."

"Well, that's another reason folks are questioning whether or not you'll stay. They know the cost to renovate any building on the island is triple what it would be on the mainland." Trudy gave her a pensive look. "The cost of living is crazy here, so I share their concerns. Tell me you're staying."

"I'm staying." Priscilla swallowed hard. "The deed is done. Or at least it will be once I cut Tommy a check. He's got a full list of things to tackle on the exterior, and he's bringing in some locals to help."

"Wonderful." Gail clapped her hands together. "So you're a true islander now."

"I'm an islander." Joy filled Priscilla's heart as she spoke the words.

"I do feel for you though." Gail's expression soured a bit. "It's tough getting supplies to the island. They either have to be flown in, which isn't cheap, or brought over by ferry. And we all know how expensive the ferry is."

"True." Priscilla felt her excitement over the upcoming project waning.

Trudy's voice brought her back to the conversation at hand. "Okay, so what's the big secret, Priscilla? Joan said you found something in the cottage last night."

"Oh, I did." Out of the corner of her eye, Priscilla noticed an elderly man at the table next to them. While Uncle Hugh was round and soft, this man was wiry and thin. His silver-white moustache twitched as he set his cup of coffee down on his table. He had a nagging cough that irritated the folks at the table on his right. The cough also seemed to bother Uncle Hugh, who kept glaring at him. Odd.

And the stranger was glaring back at all of them.

The strangest sensation consumed Priscilla as she looked into his steel-blue eyes.

Why the accusatory look, sir? What have we done to you?

He dropped his napkin on the floor and then leaned down to pick it up. As he did, he nearly toppled from his chair. She bounded out of her seat to help him, but he managed to right himself, napkin in hand, just as she got to him.

Priscilla gave him a nod and sat back down. "Okay, what was I saying?"

"You were saying you found something in the cottage, but you didn't tell us what it was."

"Oh, it's the strangest thing. I kept staring at that picture on the bedroom wall, the one of the sword. Have you ever noticed it before?"

"I have." Trudy shivered. "Gives me the creeps. Never understood why it stayed. I'd have thought Aunt Marjorie would've stuck it in the attic years ago. She must've had some special attachment to it."

"Yes, I can't explain it, but it's always made me nervous too." Joan shrugged.

"What about it?" Gail asked.

"Well, I kept thinking about what you said, Joan, about putting my stamp on the cottage. That picture doesn't seem like something I'd have hanging in my bedroom, so I decided to change it. Mind you, this was all happening at three in the morning, so I was a little groggy at the time."

"I do my best decorating at three in the morning," Trudy said. "Painted my bedroom dark purple in the middle of the night once."

"And we all got together and painted it white a couple of days later." Gail rolled her eyes. "Sometimes those middle-of-the-night decisions aren't the best."

"Well, I think mine was." Priscilla leaned in close and lowered her voice. "I decided to replace that sword painting with a framed photograph of the farm."

"Wise choice." Gail offered a nod. "One needs to be comfortable in one's own bedroom."

"Which is why I repainted my bedroom dark purple as soon as you ladies left that day," Trudy added. "But never mind all that. Go ahead, Priscilla."

Uncle Hugh looked their way from his table and closed his newspaper. "All this talk of decorating is giving me a headache. I'm going to check out the pastry case." He rose, albeit slowly, and made his way to the counter.

Priscilla cleared her throat. "I got ready to pull the painting from the wall, and the strangest thing happened."

All three of the ladies said, "What?" at the same time.

"I couldn't pull it off in the usual way. But I did manage to get it to lift, like a trap door. When I did..." She lowered her voice to a whisper. "You won't believe what I found."

Trudy had apparently had enough of Priscilla's suspenseful approach. She hollered, "What did you find?" and then leaned forward with her elbows on the table.

"When the picture lifted, I realized there was an opening in the wall behind it. Inside the opening, I found a sword—a real one—that matched the one in the painting, with the initials JWL on it. Any idea what that means?"

"James Williams Latham." Joan seemed to lose herself in her thoughts. "Must be our great-grandfather's sword."

Priscilla nodded, her excitement growing. "I see. That makes it even more of a mystery. Why would our great-grandfather put his sword in the wall?"

"Maybe he didn't," Gail interjected. "Maybe someone else hid it from him."

"Seems like an odd place to hide something." Priscilla shrugged.

"I can't believe you found a sword in your wall." Trudy shook her head. "The only thing I ever found in my wall was a mouse. Cute little guy. I didn't have the heart to fumigate him."

"Trudy, please." Joan shook her head then turned to face Priscilla once again. "So much for redecorating. I'll bet that stopped you in your tracks."

"Sure did. I brought the sword with me. It's in the trunk of my car."

"*Ooh*, I can't wait to see it." Trudy clasped her hands together.

The wiry fellow with the cough rose and tossed his napkin on the table. He looked their way, his expression stern. "If I were you, I'd take that weapon straight to the police." His words came out gravelly and strained.

"What?" Priscilla could hardly imagine what he meant. "Why?"

"Because, Mrs. Grant"—he pointed an arthritic finger her direction—"whether you know it or not, you've just solved a hundred-year-old mystery. And I'm thrilled to hear the murder weapon has been located at last."

CHAPTER FIVE

A gasp went up from the table as the wiry man wagged his finger in their direction. Deep wrinkles formed between his brows, and hatred blazed in his eyes as he spoke. "And one more thing." His words trembled with obvious anger. "My uncle was a good man, not a coward or a traitor, despite what all of you have to say about him."

"Wait, what?" Priscilla hardly knew what to make of this. Had this poor man gone mad? "I don't know what you're talking about." She'd certainly never spoken a word against the man's uncle, whoever he was.

The stranger's gaze landed on her with such intensity that Priscilla began to sweat.

The lines in his wide forehead deepened. "I'll say it again, this time more slowly: my uncle David was a good man, not a coward or a traitor. It's about time everyone on the island realized that."

"Mr. Pearson, please." Trudy rose and took a few quick steps in his direction. "As we've told you so many times before, there's no reason to stir up trouble."

"You think I'm stirring up trouble?" His pensive stare was cold and hard. "It's you Lathams that did this, not me."

"Please, Mr. Pearson." Trudy eased up to his side. "You're interrupting everyone's breakfast. This isn't necessary."

Priscilla noticed that Eldora, the town gossip, seemed to be leaning their direction, taking in every word. Terrific.

"Isn't necessary?" His volume rose. "Isn't necessary? I'd say it's more than necessary." He turned his attention back to Priscilla as Trudy sat back down. "And now that the sword has been located, we can prove who the real traitor was once and for all." He extended his shaky hand in Priscilla's direction. "Give me that weapon. I'm taking it straight to the police."

"I... I'm not giving it to you." Priscilla shook her head and tried to squelch the trembling in her hands. "It belongs to our family."

"Your *family*." He spit out the word with such disdain that it caused other restaurant patrons to look their way. "Your high and mighty family has hidden this vicious secret for nearly a hundred years, and we'll finally be able to prove it."

Naturally, Candy chose to appear at this very moment with their sweets. She emptied her oversize tray of the goodies, setting them in front of the ladies, and faced them with a smile. "There you go, gals. Let me know if there's something else I can get you."

"Coconut cream pie," Trudy said, her gaze never leaving the silver-haired man. "Now."

"Before your scone?" Candy looked perplexed.

"Now." Trudy, Joan, and Gail spoke in perfect unison.

"Okay, okay. What the customer wants, the customer gets. Who am I to lecture about when and how you eat your pie?" Candy walked away, muttering under her breath.

Priscilla's gaze shifted back and forth between Mr. Pearson and her cousins, who all looked a bit pale.

Candy returned with a gigantic slice of coconut cream pie. "Here you go, ladies. Don't say I didn't try to warn you." She set the plate in the middle of the table then turned to wait on an incoming customer.

Priscilla still couldn't wrap her head around the conversation with the old man. She looked his way, more confused than ever.

"What's all this about a secret? Trudy? Joan? Gail?"

"The days of secrets are behind us now, thanks to that sword." Mr. Pearson rose and drew so close she could smell the coffee on his breath as he spewed a warning: "You'd better not bury the evidence like your relatives did, girlie, or I'll have the police on you faster than flies on honey. Got it? And don't think you've seen the last of me either. Our family has waited a hundred years to pinpoint the murderer. We don't want to wait any longer." He stormed away from his table then turned back to give Priscilla the evil eye before disappearing out the door.

Eldora rose from her table and bolted out of the door behind him, no doubt ready to get the full scoop.

Priscilla turned her attention to Trudy, Gail, and Joan, who had all taken to shoving Candy's latest offerings into their mouths. Gail had gone for the double-dark-chocolate brownie. Trudy dove into the coconut pie, and Joan grabbed a cream puff.

"Who was that?" A shiver ran down Priscilla's arms, and she released a slow breath to try to calm herself. "And why would he say all of that?"

Joan set her pastry down and sighed. "I guess we should have filled you in right away, Priscilla. When you first arrived on the island, I mean. But some stories are harder to tell than others." She looked around, as if worried that other guests might be listening in.

"Filled me in on what?"

Joan lowered her voice. "That man is Fred Pearson, Mildred's father."

"Mildred?" Priscilla spoke in a strained whisper. "I can see now why she runs a little on the brusque side. Her father is one tough bird."

"True." Gail shook her head. "If I'd grown up in a household with a dad who spoke with such venom, it would've affected me too."

"Would've affected any child." Priscilla shivered as she remembered how rude the man had been.

Joan didn't look convinced. "Mildred is pretty independent. In her heart of hearts, I think she wants to be the opposite of her father. He's from that old-school 'women, obey your masters' era, and she's, well, let's just say she's strong enough to stand on her own two feet."

"Still makes me sad," Trudy said.

"Yes." Joan brushed a few crumbs from her blouse. "And suffice it to say he's not keen on the Latham family."

"Clearly. But I haven't a clue what he was talking about. What was all that about a murderer?"

"Well, see . . ." Joan paused, and fine wrinkles formed around the edges of her eyes. "There's a story floating around about our great-grandfather, and it's not a good one. We don't like to speak of it."

"What about him?"

Gail's nose wrinkled. "Some folks say—and by some, I mean Fred Pearson—that our great-grandfather killed Fred's uncle, David Pearson."

"Whoa. What?" Priscilla could hardly catch her breath after that news. "Are you serious? Our great-grandfather killed someone? Mildred's"—she hesitated to ponder the relationship—"great-uncle?"

"He wasn't really a murderer, so don't pay any attention to all of that." Trudy took a bite of her low-fat scone. A delicious smile lit her face. "Yum!"

"Told you, Trudy. Those new scones are nothing to be afraid of." Joan returned her gaze to Priscilla. "No one seriously believes that great-grandpa did it, but the police weren't able to figure out who did, so Fred has kept this dark cloud hanging over our heads for as long as I can remember. The story got passed down from his parents, I believe."

"And now he thinks this sword I've found has something to do with the murder?"

Trudy nodded. "I can see why. Can't you, girls? I mean, David Pearson was stabbed to death, after all. And…" She paused and looked at the other cousins. "There was that one little issue of the police finding our great-grandfather's sword next to the body."

"What?" Priscilla looked at the sword in a new light. "You're telling me that our great-grandfather, James Latham, was accused of stabbing and killing Mildred Pearson's great-uncle with the very sword I found in the wall?"

Trudy shushed her as she took her by the arm. "Priscilla, please. We probably need to keep our voices down as much as possible. It's not common knowledge."

"Sounds like other folks are talking about it, and I think we've already established that word gets around quickly on the Vineyard."

"Just rumors. Gossip."

"Is it really gossip if we're a part of the story?" Priscilla asked.

Trudy sighed. "Our great-grandfather was not a murderer. He was never arrested, never placed at the scene of the crime, and his sword was eventually returned." She took another bite of her scone, and a look of contentment flooded her eyes. "I can't believe I've never ordered this before. It's marvelous."

Joan shook her head. "You didn't order it today, remember?"

"So we know for a fact that he didn't do it?" A wave of relief swept over Priscilla, and she leaned back in her chair. "Well, that's consoling. For a minute there, I was starting to doubt everything I knew about the Lathams."

"What about the Lathams?" Uncle Hubert's voice rang out from behind her. "Did I miss something?"

"You missed something, all right." Gail nibbled on her croissant. "But I'll tell you in the car, I promise. Do you want to go to Priscilla's place with us after we're done eating?"

Uncle Hubert shrugged. "And miss my midmorning nap? I guess. If you can promise me another cup of coffee to go with this crème horn." He lifted a pastry.

"I can definitely promise you that," Priscilla said.

Just when she thought their time together couldn't possibly get any more interesting, Sheila Weller strolled their way and greeted them with a bright, "Morning, ladies."

"Morning, Sheila." Trudy turned her attention back to her sweets.

"Just popped over to see if you've tasted Candy's new cranberry whipped cream. It's wonderful on her pound cake."

Priscilla bit back the temptation to say, "I eat my cranberry relish at Thanksgiving time" and simply said, "No."

"Well, you must try it next time you come. Promise? You'll fall head-over-heels in love with the stuff, that I can guarantee you." Her expression brightened. "I gave her the idea. Did you know that you can add cranberries to your yogurt too? Of course, I love cranberry relish on my toast. It's as yummy as jam. But the whipped cream idea is absolutely delightful. Turns the cream the prettiest shade of pink."

"Thanks for the suggestion, Sheila." Gail offered her a warm smile. "I'll have to give it a try next time around."

Sheila nodded and made her way to another table, greeting those guests as if they were old friends. Maybe they were. Who was Priscilla to judge? Maybe everyone around here expected this sort of behavior from the local cranberry queen.

They managed to finish their meal, but Priscilla couldn't stop thinking about everything she'd heard. Was her great-grandfather really a murderer? Did the sword she'd found hold secrets that the Lathams had been trying to keep hidden for over a century?

A shiver worked its way down her spine. She took another bite of her muffin, but it suddenly didn't taste very good.

Candy walked up with to-go containers in hand. "Had a feeling you might need these today, ladies. And what was up with Fred Pearson? Is he still harassing all of you?"

"You have no idea." Trudy dabbed at her lips with her napkin. "But I won't need a to-go container, Candy. That scone was divine, simply divine."

"I'll take one." Joan stretched out her hand for a container.

"Me too," Gail echoed.

"Me three." Priscilla snagged a to-go container and set her leftover muffin into it. Maybe it would taste better after dinner tonight. Until then, she had to get to the bottom of this mystery with her cousins' help.

"Let's go back to the cottage," she said.

"Yes." Gail put her leftovers into the to-go container and closed it. "We'll tell you anything you want to know. Well, whatever we happen to know about the ordeal anyway."

"Let me pack up a couple of these cute little pocket pies first." Priscilla reached for the plate in the middle of the table. "I have a feeling this is going to be a two-sweets tale."

"Better make it three." Trudy gave her a knowing look. "Or even four."

"Oh my." Priscilla grabbed a handful of pastries and pressed them into her takeaway box, more perplexed than ever.

CHAPTER SIX

Priscilla led the way back to the cottage with Gail, Joan, and Uncle Hubert in the car behind her and Trudy taking up the slack at the end of the line. Priscilla couldn't stop thinking about the strange man in the bakery. What an odd encounter. So unexpected too. Why had he lashed out at her in such public fashion? And what was up with all of those strange things he had to say about her great-grandfather's sword? Why would the police need to see it? Didn't make a bit of sense.

Sword. She'd been so badly shaken that she'd completely forgotten to show her cousins the sword before leaving the bakery. They would have to see it once they arrived at the cottage.

If they made it. The weather must have taken a turn during their time inside the bakery. The midmorning skies lurked misty and gray, and the wind blustered its way through the trees on both sides of the road.

Priscilla had no point of reference. Did the Vineyard always face these weather changes in the late summer? Should she really be concerned about hurricanes, as Tommy had suggested?

She kept a watchful eye on the road, feeling a bit of apprehension. The terrain wound this way and that, with gentle slopes up and down and never-ending shifts to the right and left. There was nothing straight about Tisbury.

Priscilla's gaze occasionally shifted to the homes on either side of the street. The charming shingle-style homes captivated her, as always. They definitely spoke of an earlier era, perhaps the day and age when Great-Grandpa Latham lived here. Did he return home from war and spend time admiring these same houses she looked at today? These lovely homes with their ornamented facades and oversize verandas? Did he thank the Lord that he'd come home to such an amazing place? Did men even notice such things?

She could almost see him now, welcomed home by friends and neighbors on one of these oversize porches or balconies. Did the guests shout in triumphant cheer as he approached? Did they celebrate his return to the island after the war with a parade perhaps? Did American flags wave in the breeze? Did shopkeepers put signs of welcome in their windows?

Another glance at the road revealed a particularly lovely seaside house, this one crafted of stone.

"Didn't you get the memo?" she said out loud to the house. "All the cool kids have shingles." In many ways, she was like that house, a stranger trying to fit in. Would this sword-find push her further to the outskirts or help her blend in with the locals? Only time would tell.

A thousand questions ran through her mind at once, capturing her imagination. Was Great-Grandpa Latham who he claimed to be, or was he someone far more sinister? Did he tuck himself away in the cottage all those years ago, much as the sword remained hidden until now, harboring a secret? If so, could she discover little-known facts about him and his mysterious sword? Did she want to?

When Priscilla pulled up to the cottage, her thoughts shifted at once. A sea of tourists filled her lawn in front of the lighthouse. Oh no. Looked like Teresa's Premium Lighthouse Tours were finally underway. Why had Priscilla agreed to allow her lighthouse to be an official stop?

It was good for the island to have tourists, she reminded herself, to let the lighthouses shine—pun intended—and to allow photographs to cover the pages of social media sites. But did they have to start today of all days, when she harbored a WWI sword in the trunk of her car?

She pulled her car into the drive, taking care not to hit a young boy who wasn't watching where he was going. Her cousins pulled in behind her, one of them honking repeatedly at the boy, who continued to dart a bit too close.

Priscilla watched as a young woman, probably about the age of her daughter, Rachel, snapped a photo of the lighthouse and then took a few steps toward the cottage.

"What have we here?" Trudy asked after they'd gotten out of their cars. "A welcome-home party?"

Priscilla shook her head. "No, but it's funny you should ask that. I was just thinking about Great-Grandpa and what it must've been like to return to the island after the war."

"A lot like this, I'd imagine." Joan clucked her tongue and then shooed off the boy, who tried to snap a picture of her. "Only with invited guests and not so many cameras."

"I'm guessing folks rolled out the red carpet for all of the war heroes." Priscilla turned to face her cousins. "The sword is in the car, but I'm a little nervous to get it out in front of all these watching eyes. You know? I guess we can go on inside, and I'll come get it later."

"Give it to me now, and I'll hoist it like a weapon. That'll send these folks running." Trudy laughed.

"Don't you dare give her that sword, Priscilla," Joan said. "Might not end well."

"Yes, on second thought, don't." Trudy's nose wrinkled, and the humor in her eyes faded. "I'm getting so clumsy in my old age, I'd probably trip and fall on it. And my eyes aren't what they used to be, which just ups the risk."

Something about her words caused Priscilla to pause. The moment she heard the words "old age," she thought of Gary. Her husband hadn't lived to see old age. Why had the Lord taken him so young? Seemed wholly unfair. Not that she was one to tell God how to run the universe, of course.

"I say you come back and get it later, after the crowd has thinned." Gail slung her arm over Priscilla's shoulders. "And thanks for having us over. I'm so glad we're able to spend so much time with you."

Priscilla couldn't help but smile. A feeling of contentment wrapped around her like a cozy blanket. "It's different from my days on the farm, for sure. We were so busy, I rarely had time for socializing. Other than Sundays at church, I mean." With her key fob in hand, she locked the doors of her car.

"Looks like you've got enough folks to socialize with now." Uncle Hugh's voice sounded from behind them. "Why is half the county traipsing over your lawn? Want me to send 'em running?"

"Well, actually, I..."

"I'd be reaching for a megaphone to shoo them away if they came on to my property like this. What do they think they're doing here anyway?"

"Taking a tour," she explained. "The lighthouse is an official stop on Teresa Claybrook's island tour now. Actually, this is the first group to come through since I gave her permission, but I'll be seeing plenty more each Saturday." Priscilla did her best not to sigh out loud as a little boy reached for her water hose. Thank goodness his mother stopped him before he turned on the water.

"Just saying, if this were my place, I'd send these people packing." Uncle Hugh huffed off, but not before hollering to the youngster's mother to keep a better eye on her rapscallion.

Maybe adding the lighthouse to the official tour stop wasn't her best idea. On the other hand, people were learning more of the island's history this way and, in a roundabout way, spreading the history of the Latham family at the same time. And once she opened the museum on the ground floor of the lighthouse, tourists would really have something to look at.

She approached the tour group, catching Teresa right in the middle of a speech. "This is one of the most beautiful lighthouses on the island," Teresa said as she pointed to the towering lighthouse that shadowed Priscilla's cottage. "It was built in 1852 and has been moved twice due to soil erosion. The original lens is still operable. However, the lighthouse is now fully automated on a dusk-to-dawn timer. It is managed/maintained by the Coast Guard, who leases it from the private owner."

Several of the tourists glanced upward. Priscilla found her gaze traveling up as well, though she knew the structure well.

"The original lightkeepers were paid a whopping salary of three hundred fifty dollars a year," Teresa added, "but considered the job a great honor." She paused and gestured to Priscilla's home. "The cottage you see to the left of the lighthouse is where the lightkeepers lived. It is a private residence to this day, so we won't be touring that."

Priscilla breathed a sigh of relief.

"Now, if you'll turn your attention to the shoreline..." Teresa turned to face the cliffs in the distance. "The island was known for its merchant ships back in the day," she continued, her eyes bright. "Often hundreds at a time. Whaling ships arrived in Edgartown, just a few miles up the road, for servicing. Supplies were bought and sold. And speaking of whales, the waters surrounding the island are teeming with life. Keep your eye on the coast just beyond this lovely cottage, and you might just catch a glimpse of a humpback or even a minke."

Many of the tourists reached for their cameras and headed toward Priscilla's garden, ready to plow through toward her backyard. "Please, Lord," she whispered. "Don't let them tear up my new gardens. Not after all of the work Ida and Joan did on them."

"Folks, not just yet," Teresa called out. "And stick to the path, if you will. I want to share some information about the whale-watching cruise we offer. For a small price, you can board our state-of-the-art vessel and head straight to the national marine sanctuary, where you can see these whales up close. We can promise you whale-watching adventures aplenty, should you choose to join us."

At this point Teresa slipped out of tour guide mode and walked Priscilla's way. "See? Isn't this wonderful? Can you even imagine how many more people are going to be intrigued by the island's history? Why, people will show up in droves to take the tour."

That's what I'm afraid of.

Priscilla didn't speak the words out loud but wanted to. Was she really psychologically prepared for throngs of people outside of her bedroom window?

"I don't know, Teresa. This is a little nerve-racking. And my gardens..."

"I'll make sure they don't create a mess." Teresa put her hand up. "I promise." She eyed the cottage. "I hear you're having renovations done."

"Yes. I gave Tommy Townsend the go-ahead."

"Excellent. I know his workers have been on standby, ready to begin the renovations. Tommy told Gail, and she told Mildred, who told me."

"Terrific. Glad to know my secrets are safe."

"Now don't accuse me of gossiping, Priscilla. I'm involved in this story too. Besides, renovating isn't exactly something you can keep secret. Anyone driving by will see for themselves."

Priscilla groaned out loud. She turned and gave her cousins a stern look. They shifted their gaze to the cottage.

Teresa slung her arm over Priscilla's shoulders. "Point is, we're all family now. You're one of us. Your news is our news. Your concerns are our concerns."

In that moment, all concerns vanished. Priscilla's heart flooded with emotion. "Thank you. That means a lot."

Teresa smiled. "We're all about legacy around here, so let's keep your family's memories alive through these tours, okay?"

"Aye-aye, Cap'n!" Priscilla offered a little salute.

Teresa gave her a hug and returned to the tour group, slipping easily into guide mode again.

In the meantime, the cousins had taken to examining the gardens.

"They're coming along so nicely," Gail said. "Do you mind if we walk around back to see the rest?"

"Please do. Make yourself at home."

"We'll just pretend we're part of the tour group." Trudy reached inside her purse and came out with a phone, which she used to snap pictures. "I'll put these on social media first thing."

"Good grief," Joan said.

"You might want to wait a few weeks," Priscilla said after a moment's thought. "Once the cottage is prettied up, you can post all the pictures you want. Deal?"

"Deal." Trudy snapped another photo, this time one of the lighthouse. "I think Joan and Ida have done a terrific job helping with these gardens though. They're postcard worthy."

"Oh, definitely." Priscilla looked at the garden, a feeling of pride rising up inside of her. "A proper cottage garden, as Ida Jones calls it."

"She's terrific, isn't she?" Trudy smiled. "I'll have her come to my place next."

"That dog of yours will tear the place up." Uncle Hugh reached down to pluck a weed from the pathway. "Watch and see."

"We've created cut throughs, Uncle Hugh," she explained. "So Jake and I can take walks to the water's edge without going through the flowers."

"Humph." He shifted his weight, and she thought she heard his joints pop again. "Are we going inside, or are we going to stand out on the lawn all day and let the winds pull us out to sea?"

"Keep buying all of that hummingbird cake from Candy up at the bakery, and we'll all be too heavy to be blown out to sea." Gail slipped her arm through her father's to keep him upright.

For the first time all day, a contented smile filled Hugh's face. "I knew there were health advantages to eating cake. Never dreamed it could actually save my life though. The heavier I get, the less chance I have of being pulled out to sea by these ridiculous winds. Really puts things in perspective." He grinned. "And makes me hungry. What did we do with those pastries?"

"I've got them in a bag, Dad." Gail lifted the bag and waved it. "Patience is a virtue."

"So is silence, but I don't see you gals taking advantage of that one. And besides, if I'd wanted patients, I would've been a doctor." He guffawed at his own joke.

Priscilla led the way to the house. She did her best to make light conversation, but Uncle Hugh's chatter made it difficult. For someone who feigned grumpiness, he was a real hoot.

They reached the stairs leading up to the cottage, and Priscilla paused when she saw her uncle's hesitation.

"These rickety old steps don't make it easy for an old arthritis sufferer like me." His gaze shifted to the little boy from the tour group, who paused to snap a photo of him. "Then again, watch me move like a gazelle." He bounded up the steps and disappeared inside the house, slamming the door behind him.

"Good grief." Trudy shook her head. "Some things never change, do they?"

Priscilla led the way inside and walked into the kitchen to fill the teakettle with water. While she worked, Gail gazed out of the window at the throng of people, who were now boarding the tour bus to move on to the next stop.

"Does it bother you to have so many strangers peeking through your curtains?" she asked.

"Ask me again in a week or two." Priscilla put the teapot on the stove and turned on the burner. "Everyone want a cup of tea?"

"Coffee, not tea." Uncle Hugh's voice sounded from the living room. "After that I'm up for a nap, and that's about it. Wake me when you ladies are done gossiping."

Priscilla and Gail walked into the living room, where they found him in the oversize wingback chair.

"Really, Dad?" Gail groaned. "Still accusing us of gossiping? We're here to talk about something important that involves our family's reputation, not to gossip."

"Are you a part of the story?" he asked.

Gail gave him a pensive look. "Dad, we're all part of the story. This is your grandfather we're talking about. If not for him, none of us would be here."

"Oh." Uncle Hugh shrugged and then relaxed in his seat. "Well, I guess it's okay then. If you have any questions, just ask. I actually knew him, you know."

"Good point." Trudy snapped her fingers. "Uncle Hugh should be able to answer a lot of our questions."

He leaned back against the chair, and his eyes fluttered closed. Just about the time it looked as if he'd dozed off, he mumbled, "Wake me when the coffee's ready."

Minutes later, Priscilla brought the tray filled with delicate teacups and a porcelain teapot, which she'd filled with boiling water. She'd prepared one cup of coffee for Uncle Hugh, but glanced over at his chair and found him snoozing. His gentle snores filled the room.

Joan was still gazing out of the back window, taking in the gardens behind the house, but the other cousins sat in their chairs, talking about the weather. Jake lay at their feet, seeming to be attentively following the conversation.

"Should we wake Uncle Hugh?" Priscilla whispered.

"No, let him sleep," Gail said. "He's not been sleeping well for the past few nights. I think his rheumatism is acting up. And he's still not fully recovered from his knee replacement surgery."

"That might explain why he's so..." Joan's words drifted off. "Well, you know."

Gail gave her a knowing look. "You're going to blame that on the meds? Dad has always been a little rough around the edges, but deep in his heart he's an old softy."

A snort sounded from Uncle Hugh, who shifted position in the chair.

This got a laugh out of all the ladies.

"I can relate to his grumbling." Trudy rubbed her left knee. "Getting old ain't for sissies. My husband says that I'm the only woman on the island whose back goes out more than she does."

Priscilla couldn't help herself. She laughed so hard she almost dropped the tray with the tea things. The clattering of cups against the tray woke up Uncle Hugh, who sat up in his chair as if the enemy had just barreled through the door.

"Who got shot?" he yelled.

"Um, no one, Dad. I think you must've been dreaming."

"I was wide awake." He yawned and leaned back in the chair, his eyes fluttering closed and his breathing now slow and steady.

"Why do you suppose people always deny falling sleeping?" Trudy asked. "Doesn't make a lick of sense to me. Why not just say, 'Leave me alone, I'm sleeping'?"

"Leave me alone. I'm sleeping." Uncle Hugh stirred in the chair, but his eyes never opened. "That good enough for you?"

Priscilla laughed again. The grumpier Uncle Hugh acted, the more she adored him. A few moments later, after a few sips of tea, Priscilla went back to the car to get the sword, which she carried into the living room to show the others. She pulled it from its protective sheath, and it shimmered as if they were standing in direct sunlight.

"*Ooh*, that's a beauty." Trudy ran her hand over the initials. "Doesn't it just give you chills to know that someone, a hundred years ago, took the time to engrave our great-grandfather's initials in this gorgeous thing?"

"Gorgeous thing or murder weapon?" Priscilla asked. "After what Mr. Pearson said today at the bakery, I'm not sure."

"We can assure you, our great-grandfather would never have hurt a flea." Trudy continued to gaze at the sword, her eyes flooding with tears.

Priscilla wanted to believe that. She really did. Still, she had one thing on her mind, and it wouldn't leave her alone. After taking another sip from her teacup, she turned to face her cousins. "Okay, ladies, spill the beans. Tell me what you know about our grandfather's story, and don't leave out a thing."

CHAPTER SEVEN

Priscilla waited for her cousins to respond, but answers were slow in coming. Joan poured extra cream into her tea and stirred it with a spoon. After a moment of hesitation, she spoke.

"It's not what you're thinking, Priscilla. We can tell you that, plain and simple."

"Oh?" Priscilla reached for one of the pastries she'd put on the tea tray. "How so?"

"Great-Grandpa Latham was a wonderful, godly man."

"Served in World War I and came back to the island a hero." Uncle Hugh spoke with his eyes closed. "That sword was the very one he used in battle."

"How do you know?" Priscilla asked.

"Grandpa bragged about that sword all the time." Uncle Hugh's eyes opened, and he sat straight up in the chair. "Who would blame him? Not everyone carried the Patton Saber, you know."

"Patton Saber?" Priscilla echoed. "As in General Patton?"

"The one and only." Uncle Hugh beamed. "And Grandpa was mighty proud of it, I'll tell you. That particular saber was designed by Patton for the US Army."

"You're telling me we have, right now, in this very house, a sword that George S. Patton designed?" Joan rose and walked over to the sword to give it an admiring look. "Seriously?"

"Seriously." Uncle Hugh nodded. "Unfortunately, many of the men who carried the Patton Saber never made it home. They were sent to the frontlines but were easy prey for the Germans, who came at them with machine guns."

"Wow." Priscilla did her best to take this in but could hardly dwell on something so difficult to imagine.

"Grandpa showed it to us kids too, so I can vouch for the fact that it's the real deal." He reached for his cup of coffee and took a swig then made a face.

"But?"

"It disappeared after he passed away. At least no one in the family could locate it. We often suspected it had been stolen because of its value. So kudos to you, girlie, for locating it." He gave Priscilla an admiring look. "Now, could you get me some sugar and cream for this coffee? Never could abide black coffee."

"That's admirable, but how did he go from hero to suspect?" Priscilla rose and grabbed the sugar bowl and creamer, which she passed Uncle Hugh's way. "Just explain that part. He served in France during World War I, right?"

"Right." Uncle Hugh nodded. "My grandmother left us grandkids some of the letters he sent her."

"This doesn't sound like a murder mystery at all." Priscilla put the sugar bowl back on to the platter and sat down once again.

"Well, there was a murder." Uncle Hugh stirred his coffee. "And maybe Grandpa had a role to play in the story, but it certainly wasn't the role of murderer."

"I'm so confused." Priscilla fought the temptation to reach for another sweet treat. No point in drowning her confusion in calories.

"Listen up, girlie, and I'll tell you a story." Uncle Hugh rose slowly and walked over to the coffee table, where he picked up the sword. "It's actually a story about *three* young men, all good friends. A trio of friends, if you will. Two of them went to war. One stayed home."

"We're up to three people now?" Priscilla asked. "The cast grows."

"Yes, but let's cover them one at a time." Uncle Hugh eyed the sword. "Grandpa Latham went to war. So did a friend of his named Chester."

"And David Pearson, Mildred's great-uncle?" Priscilla took a sip of her tea and then set the cup down. "He went too?"

"No." Uncle Hugh shook his head but never took his gaze off the sword. "David Pearson was part of the friendship trio, but he didn't go, and that's where things get twisted. He managed to avoid serving."

Trudy interrupted the story. "Rumor has it the local doctor was a friend of his family and exaggerated David's asthma condition."

"We've never disputed his asthma diagnosis," Joan added. "Just saying, perhaps he stretched the truth a bit to get the doctor's official letter. You see?"

"Okay." Priscilla shrugged. "So two local men came back as heroes, the other—who may or may not have had asthma—never served. Doesn't sound like much of a motivation for a murder. And they were all good friends?"

"They knew each other well." Uncle Hugh set down his coffee and assumed a fighting position with the sword. "But were they friends or foes? That is the question no one has been able to answer." He rested the sword at his side, and his gaze narrowed. "Many in the Pearson family—particularly Fred—would like folks to believe that my grandfather had some sort of grudge against David for weaseling out of serving."

"Again, we don't know for sure he weaseled out of serving," Gail added. "That's just speculation."

"All we do know for sure is that David Pearson was stabbed." Uncle Hugh assumed a fighting position once again, sword in hand. "And left to die alone on the cliffs in Aquinnah just a couple months after our grandfather got home from France."

"Stabbed." Priscilla paused to think through the word. "Whoa." Absentmindedly, she picked up a pastry from the tray and took a big bite.

"Right." Joan shrugged. "Horrible way to die. And like I said, he was found all alone out there. Such a tragic way to end your life."

"Is that the suspicion, that David took his own life?" Priscilla set her pastry down, feeling like she couldn't eat another bite.

"I guess some might argue that theory." Uncle Hugh wielded his sword against an imaginary foe. "Grandpa Latham's bloody sword was found next to his body."

"Not *in* his body though?" Priscilla asked.

"Nope. Beside." Uncle Hugh took a quick swig of his coffee and set the mug back down.

"The wounds were deep," Gail added. "Very deep."

"Like, sword deep?" Priscilla asked.

Uncle Hugh swung around so fast, he almost took a tumble. The sword wavered in his hand. "Now you're catching on, girl." He extended the weapon once again. "*Sword* deep."

"Dad, you could have fallen. I almost had a heart attack." Gail clutched her hand to her chest.

"Nothing a crème horn won't cure." He winked and reached for his mug to take another swig of his coffee.

"Police concluded he'd been stabbed clean through," Joan explained.

"And Great-Grandpa Latham was the logical suspect because his sword was next to the body?"

"Bloody sword," Gail echoed.

"A lot of it came from rumors that Grandpa never forgave David for lying about neglecting his obligation to serve his country." Joan shrugged. "Who knows."

Uncle Hugh examined the sword more closely. "You know, back in those days, swords were more a ceremonial item for military officers."

"So our great-grandfather was an officer?" Priscilla asked.

"A lieutenant, to be precise." Hugh set the sword down on the coffee table and eased back into his chair. "And much more inclined to use a gun than a sword, I dare say. But military officers often appeared in full regalia at parades, reviews, and, of course, rank-and-file situations."

"*Ooh*, I have an idea." Joan's eyes lit up. "We should look for photos of Great-Grandpa at his wedding. Maybe he wore it then."

"Probably." Uncle Hugh settled against the back of the chair and reached for his coffee cup.

"And if he did, we can probably conclude that he wasn't the murderer," Joan added.

"How did you arrive at that conclusion?" Uncle Hugh took a big swig of his coffee and set the cup down with a clatter, a disgusted look on his face. "This stuff is cold."

"Just saying a groom wouldn't turn up in a public place wearing a sword he'd just used to kill someone. Right? If he's wearing the sword in his wedding pictures, he's off the hook."

Uncle Hugh shrugged.

"You might be right, Joan," Trudy said. "But I have my own theory, one I've been working on for ages. Anyone interested?"

"I am," Priscilla responded. "What kind of theory?"

"Remember the third man in the friendship trio—Chester Snyder?"

"Snyder?" Priscilla paused. "Where have I heard that name before?"

"Tilly Snyder," Trudy said. "Runs the Colonial Inn and Restaurant. Shrimp salad extraordinaire."

"Right." Priscilla gave a nod.

"Love that place." Uncle Hugh rubbed his extended belly. "Not a fan of the watermelon pickles though. Everyone says they're the best, but I think they taste like deep-fried pieces of rubber."

"Tilly attends Faith Fellowship as well." Priscilla reached for her teacup. "I've seen her there. But how does she figure into all of this?"

"Tilly is Chester Snyder's granddaughter," Trudy explained.

Priscilla took a little sip of her tea. "This story has so many layers."

"Boy, does it ever. Kind of like all those pastries." Uncle Hubert laughed.

"So why do we suspect Chester?" Priscilla asked.

Joan gave Trudy a knowing look. "Well, we can't prove it..."

"Yes we can, Joan, and you know it," Trudy said. "Chester Snyder was in love with a local girl named Josie."

Priscilla shrugged. "And?"

"And David Pearson had a fling with Chester's girlfriend while Chester was off fighting for his country."

Priscilla gasped. "Are you sure?"

"Yep." Trudy nodded.

After grabbing a napkin, Priscilla wiped the sugar from her fingers. "Well now, that's a horse of a different color. This is starting to make sense. Chester killed David to get revenge for stealing his girl, plain and simple."

"Except Chester didn't have a sword," Uncle Hubert said.

"Maybe he stole Great-Grandpa Latham's?" Priscilla surmised. "Who knows?"

"Could be," Uncle Hugh responded. "The police confiscated it after the murder but eventually returned it. That's all I know from the story. And that, my friends, is why this story doesn't have an ending. A hundred years come and gone, and we can't prove a thing." Uncle Hugh's eyes fluttered closed once again.

"Only we have the sword now. We don't know for sure if it was ever used to murder anyone, but we've certainly got what could be a piece of evidence." Priscilla stared at the sword, seeing it in a whole new light.

"You can see why Fred Pearson was in such an uproar over you finding it. For years folks all across this island have wondered where it went after the police returned it to Grandpa Latham."

"They returned it." Priscilla found that interesting. "So he wasn't seen as a suspect for long then."

"Doesn't seem like it. But after that, no one knew what happened to it. The saber disappeared, never to be seen again."

"And here it was the whole time." Priscilla felt a little nauseated. She couldn't tell if the squeamish sensation came from the sugar or the story.

"Was it the murder weapon, or wasn't it?" Uncle Hugh spoke with his eyes firmly shut. "Only my grandfather knows for sure."

"Wow. So if we find out the sword was used, then we're likely incriminating our own family." Priscilla sighed. "That's a double-edged sword." She clasped a hand to her mouth then pulled it away and laughed. "My wording was completely coincidental, I promise."

The wording was coincidental, but was the fact that her great-grandfather's sword had gone missing for nearly a century? Only time would tell.

CHAPTER EIGHT

Monday morning rushed in with a blustery vengeance. Priscilla had seen her fair share of winds whipping across the plains in Kansas, but this took things to a whole new level. Coastal breezes turned to hurricane-force winds without warning here, and one could barely stand up straight to face them.

But face them, she must. Priscilla's focus remained on the mystery of the family sword. A visit with Mildred Pearson at the museum was in order. Perhaps the town's favorite historian could be of help. And it wouldn't hurt to get her perspective, what with her family's involvement in the story.

Priscilla made her way to the car then did her best to steer the vehicle toward town. All the while her thoughts tumbled. How would Mildred react to her questions about her great-uncle? Would she balk or answer freely?

As Priscilla pulled out on to the road, the wind caught several leaves from the trees and sent them hurling across her windshield. They took to flight in the breeze once again. To the right, tree limbs bowed in submission to the mighty force of the wind. Her eye had so many things to take in, she almost found herself driving off the road.

No, that was the wind, trying to pull her off the road. Priscilla was suddenly very grateful she'd opted for storm windows.

She caught a glimpse of an elderly neighbor's home—a shingle-style beauty in varying shades of gray and white. Though tucked away in the trees, she wondered if the shingles would survive this windy onslaught. On any other day, the neutral color of the house brought a sense of peace. Calm. On a day like today, however? She had to wonder if the trees would come crashing down on top of the home, or if the wind would carry it off to Oz.

By the time she arrived in town the winds had calmed a bit. The gnarled oaks that lined Main Street were still upright, a fact that brought great relief. She found herself settling in as she eased her way down the quaint boulevard, surrounded by shops of every kind. It felt very much like old-fashioned middle America here, where folks took great pride in their love of country and sense of community.

She didn't like to compare the people in the Vineyard to what she'd known in Kansas. There was no comparison, really. Both places prided themselves on welcoming folks in to their midst, but something about the layout of the buildings on the island reminded one of a picture postcard.

She parked outside the museum and checked her appearance in the rearview mirror. After touching up her lipstick, Priscilla gave her windswept hair a closer look.

"Good grief." She reached inside the glove box for her spare hairbrush and pulled it through her messy locks. Seemed rather pointless, but she gave it the old college try. Finally content, she put the brush away and reached for her purse from the passenger seat. Just as she grabbed it, the phone inside rang. She answered it on the third ring.

"Mom?"

A wave of joy washed over her at the sound of her daughter's voice. "Hey, Rachel. Glad to hear from you." Priscilla switched the phone to her other ear to get more comfortable.

"Good to hear your voice." Rachel paused. "I miss you, Mom."

Bittersweet feelings enveloped Priscilla. If she could click her heels and send herself back to Kansas, if only for a hug, she would do it right this instant.

But life was more complicated than that.

"I miss you too, baby." Perhaps a change of direction was called for, to ensure the conversation wouldn't turn into a guilt trip. "You on a break from work?"

"*Mm-hmm*. Eating my lunch. What about you?"

"I'm hoping to eat in town later, at the inn. I need to talk to Tilly Snyder. But first I have to talk to Mildred Pearson at the museum."

"I don't remember meeting either of them when I was there."

"We'll remedy that next time." Priscilla spoke with as much positivity as she could muster. "Hey, guess what? I found something that belonged to your great-great-grandfather."

"What? That's cool."

"A World War I sword. Actually, I think it's called a saber."

"Whoa. Where did you find it?"

"In the wall." Priscilla caught a glimpse of local businesswoman Katie Ortmann walking into her family's grocery store to her right. Funny, she'd never noticed that Katie walked with a cane before.

"Wait... in the wall?" Rachel paused. "That's going to require a bit of explanation."

"We're still not sure who put it in the wall... or why. But it's been quite the find." Priscilla spent the next few minutes filling her daughter in on the details.

"Wow, Mom, that's some story," Rachel said when she'd finished. "So Great-Great Grandpa might've been a murderer?"

"Not likely. But a few of the locals seem to think so. If anyone can help me work through this story, it's Mildred Pearson. I can't imagine she believes our family had anything to do with her great-uncle's death. If she did, she would have shunned me from the moment I arrived on the island."

"Because of something your great-grandfather might have done to her great-uncle? Why would she even care?"

"The people here care a lot about their family history," Priscilla explained. "And Mildred's a historian, so she probably cares even more."

"*Hmm.*" Rachel sounded skeptical.

Before Priscilla could explain further, her daughter said, "Hey, Mom, I have to go. I've got to be back at my desk in less than five minutes. Just wanted to hear your voice."

"Good to hear yours too. I should get inside the museum before the winds pick up again."

"If they do, I still hope they blow you back home." Rachel's voice carried a hint of sadness. "But I do understand. You're happy there."

"I am. I miss you though."

"That feeling is mutual, Mom."

As Rachel disappeared from the other end of the line, Priscilla found herself feeling a little bittersweet. And intrigued. For the first time in ages, Rachel hadn't given her the Big Speech, the one that always ended with, "You need to come back home where you belong, Mom." She'd simply called to talk. Fascinating.

Unfortunately, the wind chose that moment to return. A second later, just as Priscilla was shoving her phone back into her purse, a rap on the window startled her. She turned to see Gerald O'Bannon on the other side, looking as if he might get blown away at any moment.

She rolled the window down and hollered to be heard above the whistling wind. "You scared me to death!"

"Sorry. Just being nosy. Kind of looked like you were sitting there talking to yourself."

"Oh, funny. I was talking to my daughter."

Pricilla braved the winds and got out of the car, taking time to close the window first. She could feel her hair getting messier by the moment. Oh well. She could also sense Gerald's curiosity as she opened the back door of her car and reached inside to grab the sword, which she'd carefully wrapped in a soft throw. She tried to close the door, but with her hands full and the winds working against her, she couldn't manage it.

Gerald closed it for her then crossed his arms. "Not trying to be nosy, but inquiring minds want to know what you've got wrapped up in that blanket. Or is it some big secret? Lots of those on the island, in case you haven't already figured that out."

"I'm learning. But I won't keep this one from you." She unwrapped one end and revealed the tip of the sword, though the wind threatened to pull it out of her hands altogether. A ray of sunlight chose that moment to peek through the clouds overhead and caused the end of the sword to shimmer like Excalibur. Priscilla uncovered the rest of the sword, being careful not to let any passersby see.

Gerald let out a whistle as he gazed downward. "She's a beauty. But that's something I never expected to see." He leaned in and gave the sword a once-over.

"What? Women don't walk through the streets of Martha's Vineyard carrying World War I swords every day?"

"Maybe out west, but not around these here parts." He spoke in a slow drawl and then laughed. "Do you mind if I ask *why* you're carrying a sword?"

"It belonged to my great-grandfather. I'm taking it to Mildred so she can help me figure out where it was made, how it was used, and so on. Oh, and I guess we'll have to turn it over to the police because there's some speculation it was used in a crime."

His eyes widened at this news. "I'm surprised I haven't heard about that. When? Where?"

"1919. Aquinnah."

"That might explain why I haven't heard about it." Gerald's expression shifted from concern to confusion. "But what makes you think your grandfather's sword was used in a crime?"

With a wave of a hand, she attempted to dismiss that idea. "Oh, I don't believe it. And he was my great-grandfather. A true upstanding citizen of Martha's Vineyard, I've been informed, who served his country during World War I. Not the sort to pierce someone clean through. Then again, I might just feel this way because he's my relative, you know? Folks never like to see their family incriminated in major crimes, even if the bloody sword was located next to the body."

"You're telling me someone—not your great-grandfather, but someone else—used this sword to stab someone in 1919?"

"That's what we're trying to figure out." She offered Gerald a broad smile. "See?"

"Um, not at all, to be honest. But if you need my help with anything, just let me know."

"I will. Maybe you could check around with your police friends to see if we could have DNA testing done."

"I work for the Coast Guard, not the police."

"But you know people, right? What about that lovely police officer, April?"

"I'll ask around."

"Great." She covered the sword back up as the winds died down. "My great-grandfather thanks you."

Gerald coughed, and Priscilla suspected it was to cover a laugh. "Well, good luck figuring out whatever it is you're trying to figure out."

They said goodbye, and she walked toward the front door of the museum, the wrapped sword nestled in her arms like a long, skinny baby.

Once inside, Priscilla tried to get her bearings. Where would she find Mildred? She walked through the front room and into a nineteenth-century parlor. She thought she saw a shadow to her left, but when she turned to look, there was nothing there.

"Mildred?"

No one responded, but Priscilla felt sure she heard footsteps and then the creak of the wooden floor.

"Is someone there?" she called out.

No response.

Must be her overactive imagination at work. Priscilla walked into the 1850s dining room, pausing only to examine the intricate wooden table and lovely antique dishes. The floor creaked again, and she cast her gaze to the left, only to see a shadow disappearing behind a bookshelf. She frowned for a moment then shook her head and continued deeper into the museum.

She walked toward the 1790s pantry, and Mildred popped up from behind it, giving Priscilla quite the start. The sword tumbled from the throw in Priscilla's hands and clattered to the ground, making all sorts of racket.

Priscilla knelt down and quickly rewrapped the sword then rose as Mildred came out from behind the pantry shelf.

"Mildred, you scared me to death!" Priscilla's hands trembled as she gripped the bundle in her arms.

"I'm sorry. I was working back here and heard a noise. Guess it was you." Mildred cast a curious look at the bundle in Priscilla's arms. "Did you need me for something?"

"Yes, actually. I brought something for you to look at."

"I knew you'd turn up with that sword sooner or later." The gruff male voice sounded from behind her, along with another creak of the wooden floor.

Priscilla turned to discover Fred Pearson standing directly behind her with a scowl on his face.

"What? I... well..."

His eyes narrowed, and his hand shot out in the direction of the sword. "Now hand it over, girl, before someone else gets hurt."

CHAPTER NINE

Dad!" Mildred frowned at her father. "Why are you talking to Priscilla like that?"

"She knows why." Mr. Pearson gave Priscilla a fierce look. "Now, are you going to hand over that sword, or am I going to call the police?"

"Sword? Police?" Mildred took a step in their direction. "Dad, what are you talking about? Have you been watching those detective shows again?"

His moustache twitched. "She knows what I'm talking about. She's got the proof right there in her hands."

Mildred gave her father a curious look then turned to face Priscilla, zeroing in on her hair. "Wow, must be really windy out there."

"Very. I'm not used to this."

"Stick-to-It hair spray. You'll find it at Ortmann's. All the women on the island use it. It's the only product firm enough to hold hair in place on windy days like today."

"Good to know, thanks."

"You're welcome. I thought I heard someone come in, but I've been engrossed in a project, so my thoughts were elsewhere."

"I've been engrossed in a little project too."

"Something to do with that long object in your hands, perhaps? The one Dad's so interested in?"

"Are we going to stand here all day and gab or get to the point?" Fred put his hands on his hips. "The sword, if you please."

Priscilla looked around to make sure there were no other patrons about. "Is there someplace private where we can talk? The three of us, I mean."

"Private?" Mildred's eyebrows arched. "Is this a top-secret conversation?"

"Yes, if you don't mind."

"Not at all. The museum doesn't have any scheduled tours today, and locals rarely stop by when the weather's being ornery. I think we'll be alone for a while."

"Perfect."

Mildred led the way to the kitchen and turned to face Priscilla. "Before you show me what's in the blanket, I want to make a speculation. And, Dad, give me a chance to say it before you interrupt, please."

He grunted.

Mildred faced Priscilla. "I'm pretty sure I'm right when I say that you've heard the story about your great-grandfather and my great-uncle."

Priscilla breathed a sigh of relief. "Well, that was easy. You didn't even make me say it."

Mildred groaned. "I wondered how long it would take before someone told you. Dad?" She turned to face her father. "Should I pin this on you?"

"There's nothing to pin on me. I heard her with my own ears. She's got the proof in that blanket right there."

Mildred looked Priscilla's way. "There's really a sword in that blanket?"

"Yes. See, the whole thing started when I found my great-grandfather's sword in the wall." Priscilla unwrapped the sword and laid it on the table. It gleamed underneath the overhead light.

"You found it?" Mildred's eyes widened, and she leaned down to give it a closer look. "But how did you know, Dad? I don't understand that part."

"He overheard me telling Joan, Trudy, and Gail," Priscilla explained.

"Oh my." Mildred glanced her father's way. "Let me guess. You decided this was a matter for the local police."

"Haven't called 'em yet, but I plan to."

Priscilla sighed. "Does it really have to come to that?"

Mildred shook her head at her father. "They could hardly charge anyone with a crime that took place a hundred years ago, you know."

"That sword is evidence," Fred responded. "No doubt about it."

Mildred looked at him for a moment then shrugged. "Who knows? Stranger things have happened."

"And you think my great-grandfather was responsible?" Priscilla ran her finger along the sword's grip.

"Think?" Fred gave her a pensive look. "We don't think it, we *know* it."

Mildred shook her head. "Don't let him sway you, Priscilla. He has no proof. It's just a story passed down through the family. Maybe the police would be the best to advise us after all. Wouldn't hurt to ask."

"I've asked Gerald to ask around, to get their thoughts."

"Perfect. And thank you for bringing it with you." Mildred reached for the sword then paused. "Do you mind if I look it over? Guess I'd better wear gloves though. Don't need to add my fingerprints to the mix."

She put on gloves and gave the sword a solid examination then let out a whistle. "Priscilla, do you realize what you have here?"

"The Patton Saber."

"*Mm-hmm.*" Mildred ran her finger along the engraving.

Fred put gloves on as well, picked up the sword, and held it under the light. "And what a beauty she is too." He examined it from both sides.

"I don't know, Dad. It's not very worn, which makes me wonder if this sword was actually used in battle or just carried for ceremonial purposes. Take a look at this basket-shaped hilt." Mildred tapped it with her finger.

"Easy access," Fred added. "And the blade is double-edged, meant for thrusting."

Priscilla shivered. "Doesn't sound pleasant."

"But necessary in war, nonetheless," he said. "The men underwent training to use the sword both on foot and mounted."

Mildred leaned in to examine the sword then gave another little whistle. "I think the scabbard is remarkable. The leather is in mint condition."

"Scabbard?" Priscilla asked. "I thought it was called a sheath."

"Same thing." Mildred gave her a knowing look. "Point is, it's in remarkable shape. This is probably worth a pretty penny, Priscilla. You've got quite a jewel on your hands."

"I had no idea. I mean, I knew it had a lot of sentimental value, but hadn't given much thought to dollars and cents."

"Sentimental value, my eye." Fred's gaze narrowed. "If you want to call a murder weapon sentimental. And don't go selling it until after the police have done their work."

"It never crossed my mind." Though the idea of easy money to cover the repairs on the cottage did sound appealing, come to think of it.

Mildred paused a moment. "Dad, it sounds like you've made up your mind that Priscilla's great-granddad used this sword to kill Uncle David, but personally, I've always felt there were more suspects than that."

"I've drawn the same conclusion." Priscilla nodded. "I assume you mean Chester Snyder, right?"

"Chester Snyder? Tilly's grandfather?" Mildred's eyes widened. "Never thought of him."

"Really? Because Joan, Gail, and Trudy..." Priscilla let her words trail off. No point in giving away her cousins' suspicions.

"No, not Chester." Mildred shook her head. "I've always wondered if perhaps Harrison Ortmann was to blame."

"Ortmann? The family that runs the grocery store?"

"Right. A hundred years ago it was the island's only big mercantile. I've always thought that perhaps Harrison Ortmann—he was the owner at the time—might've played a role in my great-uncle's death." Mildred took a seat at the table and gestured for her father and Priscilla to do the same.

"No idea where you're going with this, Mildred," Fred argued as he took a seat.

"I'm a little confused myself," Priscilla added. She sat next to Fred, but the tension coming off the elderly man was pretty thick.

"This is a hard thing to say out loud." Mildred's cheeks flushed pink. "But I've long suspected Harrison Ortmann took Uncle David's life over an unpaid gambling debt."

"Gambling debt? Really?" Fred crossed his arms over his chest. "So now my uncle David is the bad guy? Isn't it bad enough that someone got away with killing him? Now we have to make him out to be flawed as well?"

"Not at all, Dad. Just working on a hunch here."

"What makes you think that, Mildred?" Priscilla asked. "Did you read something to that effect?"

"An old article, yes. And just for the record, I'm piecing this together in my imagination. Dad, you told me yourself that Uncle David was in despair when his friends went off to war and he had to stay home."

"That's one way to put it." Fred seemed to soften a bit then turned to face Priscilla. "Uncle David was very ill, did you know?"

"Oh, well . . ." Priscilla's words drifted off.

"Folks said he was a coward, but they're wrong. The service wouldn't have him, and that fact caused him great anguish."

"It's the truth, Priscilla," Mildred said. "I have medical records on microfiche. He had asthma, but his heart was also weakened from a bout with scarlet fever as a child. He would never have survived on the battlefield, that I know for sure."

"Wow." Well, that cleared that up anyway.

Fred raked his fingers through his thinning hair. "Uncle David always felt guilty about his inability to serve his country. It really haunted him, and the comments from locals—like your great-grandfather—only made things worse."

"Poor guy turned to drinking and gambling while his buddies were away fighting on his behalf," Mildred added.

"Don't share family secrets with the enemy!" Fred turned his glare on his daughter.

"I'm not the enemy," Priscilla said. "I promise. If we work together, we can get to the bottom of this."

Mildred rolled her eyes. "It was common knowledge among the townspeople and hardly a family secret, Dad. I remember hearing the story whispered by aunts and uncles, even when I was a kid. Many speculated his drinking must've played a role."

"I never took to that notion. And how will incriminating the deceased help?"

Priscilla rested her hand on Fred's arm. "You have my sympathies, Mr. Pearson, now that I've heard all of this." She turned to face Mildred. "And I'm extremely relieved that you have information that dates back to that time period."

"There's more than one benefit to running the museum. I can research almost anything about the island I like. That's how I came to the conclusion that Harrison Ortmann might be involved."

"This I have to hear." Fred leaned back in his chair, his hands cupped behind his head.

"In researching, I stumbled across an old article from a newspaper dated 1919. Harrison Ortmann might've been seen as a fine, upstanding fellow in the community, but a reporter had suspicions he was leading a double life."

"What do you mean?" Fred and Priscilla asked in unison.

"Well, it appears Harrison kept a ledger of folks who owed him money."

Priscilla could hardly see what this had to do with anything. "For merchandise they bought at his store?" she asked.

"Yes."

Fred shrugged. "All store owners did that. Lots of folks bought on credit back then."

"Right, but the reporter had a lot of suspicions. He felt sure the ledger held proof that several locals had gambling debts. He surmised that the whole thing was written in some sort of code."

"Where can I find this article?" Priscilla asked.

"We have a copy on microfiche."

"And the ledger?"

Mildred shook her head. "Who knows if it even still exists?" She paused and appeared to be thinking. "Now you've heard my speculations. Time for you to share yours. What makes you think Chester Snyder had something to do with my great-uncle's murder?"

"Oh, I think he's a suspect, no doubt about that."

At that moment someone outside of the kitchen coughed. And then coughed again. Priscilla put her finger over her lips and motioned for Mildred to stop asking questions. Whoever happened to be on the other side of that door didn't need to hear their speculations about Chester Snyder.

She quickly wrapped the sword in the throw and cleared her throat. "Want to skip my speculations and show me the article about the gambling parlor?" she whispered.

Mildred nodded and walked to the door. As she opened it, Tilly Snyder almost tumbled into the room. The petite woman crossed her arms, and her gaze traveled back and forth between Mildred and Priscilla. "Friends." She spoke the word more as an accusation than anything.

Fred put his hand over his heart. "Tilly, you scared me half to death. What are you doing out there?"

"Just stopped by to tell you that shrimp scampi is the special of the day at the restaurant, Fred. I know it's your favorite." Tilly coughed. "Just thought you'd want to know."

The wrinkles on Fred's forehead seemed to relax. "Wonderful. Thanks so much for thinking of me."

"It's what I do... think of others. And I guard what I say about them too. Not everyone shares that trait." Tilly's gaze narrowed, and she glanced Priscilla's way. "Anyway, got to get back. Just wanted you to know, Fred." She turned and marched away as if on a mission.

"Whoa." Priscilla turned to face Fred and Mildred. "Do you think she overheard our conversation?"

"Maybe." He grunted. "If so, I'll hear about it later."

Mildred nodded. "She's been fighting speculations about her grandfather for years, and it's a bit of a sore subject."

"No doubt." Priscilla paused. "Did you still want to show me that article?"

"Sure." Mildred led the way to the microfiche machine and pulled up the article in question. "See here?" She pointed at a headline that read, "Local Grocer Stocks More Than Produce."

"*Hmm.*" Priscilla skimmed the article, which aired the reporter's suspicions about Harrison Ortmann running a gambling den in the back room of his store. "Interesting."

"So you see now why I think there might be more to this story?" Mildred asked.

"For sure. Looks like an investigation of Ortmann's is in order."

"Indeed."

"Just don't get so caught up in pointing the finger at everyone else in town that you forget your own great-grandfather," Fred said. "Remember, someone hid that sword in your wall, and it wasn't the townspeople. Had to have been someone in your own family."

"We don't know that for sure, Dad." Mildred shook her head then turned her gaze to Priscilla. "But he does have a point. If we can figure out who hid the sword, it would be helpful."

"Right."

Mildred scrolled to the top of the article. "You'll notice this piece is dated July 2, 1919, just a couple weeks before Uncle David was killed. If I'm remembering correctly, he died on the fifteenth. Hang on a second, and I'll double-check that date." She did a bit of scrolling until another article opened up, this one titled, "Local Man Murdered on Cliffs at Aquinnah."

"Whoa. I'd like to read that one top to bottom." Priscilla spent the next few minutes doing just that then turned to face Mildred. "So the sword really was found next to his body, and he was pierced clean through."

Fred's expression tightened. "Told you."

"But it was returned to the family later on."

"And then hidden," Fred countered. "That's what folks do with murder weapons. They hide them."

With nothing to say in response, Priscilla turned her attention back to the article. "He died on the evening of July fifteenth, just after sunset." A shiver ran down her spine. "Horrible."

"And this article is just the first of many," Mildred said. "There are a couple more during the weeks that follow, but the police were never able to pinpoint their man."

"I see." Priscilla shook her head, suddenly feeling overwhelmed with so much information at once.

"I'm still of the opinion that Harrison Ortmann is our man though," Mildred added. "Call it a hunch, but that's where I'd start."

As she headed out of the museum a few minutes later, Priscilla gave Mildred's words a great deal of thought, especially as they pertained to Harrison Ortmann. All store owners kept ledgers, but the notion that a written document of gambling debts might have once existed set Priscilla's imagination on fire. If she and Mildred could prove that David had gambling debts, then a case could be made against Harrison for sure.

Of course, all of this would take work. The mystery of David Pearson's death wouldn't be solved overnight, especially not with a new suspect adding his name to Priscilla's ever-growing list.

CHAPTER TEN

The following Sunday morning, Priscilla awoke earlier than usual. She took the opportunity to spend time reading her Bible and praying about the day ahead. After breakfast she fed Jake and then dressed for church, opting for her favorite pink blouse and black slacks. Folks on the island didn't go much for fancy church clothes, a notion that made her very happy. Still, Priscilla wanted to look her best, and that applied to her hair as well. She'd have to remember to pick up some Stick-to-It hair spray when she was at Ortmann's.

Her dog wound his way between her legs, nearly causing her to topple.

"I know, Jakie. I know. You want to go with me. You always want to go with me." She lifted his chin and stared into his deep brown eyes. "I would take you too, but they frown on dogs in church."

He wagged his tail as if he could change her mind.

"For today you'll have to trust that I'll be praying for you." She paused and added, "Praying that you'll eventually turn from your wicked ways and stop digging in my gardens and that you'll mind your manners around water snakes."

She gave him a rubber bone to chew on and then walked out to the car. She turned the key, and the engine sputtered. "Oh no you don't." She tried again, and this time the car started with ease. "Whew."

She pulled away from the house and drove to Faith Fellowship just a few miles away. She pulled into the parking lot moments later and paused to give the familiar building a closer look. Unlike the other churches on the island, the place she'd recently decided to call home was a simple red brick building, well-kept but in no way fancy or ornamental. It had a high-pitched roof and stairs leading up to wide doors that beckoned people to enter. She'd been drawn to these things at first glance, and the people inside had sealed the deal. They'd welcomed her with open arms.

She climbed out of the car and slung her purse strap onto her shoulder, then waved to an older gentleman who was walking toward the front steps with a grandchild in tow. What would it be like to attend church with a grandchild? Would she ever know?

Her attention shifted to the tall white columns that framed out the verandas of the church. They offered a place for parishioners to gather and catch up before they headed into the service.

To the right of the church, twisted, gnarled oaks, their branches curling this way and that, begged to be photographed. Everything in Tisbury had a quaint feel about it—the layout of the buildings, the way things were nestled together, the soft colors, the business names.

Priscilla was greeted at the door by a gentleman wearing a red bow tie. He handed her a bulletin and pointed her toward the sanctuary. As she entered the spacious room, Priscilla almost ran into Tilly Snyder, who greeted her with a scowl. She stood with her arms crossed, her tight gray bun as stern looking as her jutted chin.

"Tilly, good morning." Priscilla offered a friendly smile. "Happy Sunday."

"Hardly."

"I beg your pardon?" As Priscilla shifted her purse strap to her other shoulder, Tilly seemed to watch her every move.

"Why are you snooping around, asking Mildred questions about my grandfather?" Tilly put her fists against her hips.

"Oh, I . . ." Priscilla swallowed the lump in her throat.

"You can just stop right now because he was a good man. A Christian man. Served his country without shame while others refused to go."

Priscilla took a moment to gather her thoughts before speaking. "I never said Chester Snyder was anything but a good man, Tilly."

"Didn't you?" The irritated woman lowered her voice and leaned toward Priscilla. "You found the missing sword and came to the same conclusion the rest of your family members had already drawn, didn't you? Now you're spreading false rumors that Grandpa Chester took David Pearson's life because David was fooling around with Josie Bingham!"

Priscilla shook her head. "Well, not exactly. Just trying to get to the bottom of things."

"I know what you're trying to get to the bottom of. I heard enough of your conversation to draw my own conclusions. It's what all of you Lathams have been saying for years. Admit it.

You're too prideful to admit the truth about your own relative, so you go around the island pointing the finger. Now please, just leave my family alone. Okay?"

"Of course. I never meant to cause a rift between the two of us, Tilly."

"Humph."

A couple of the other parishioners, including the man in the red bow tie, tried to scoot past them to get to the pews. Priscilla stepped aside to make room and lowered her voice before speaking again. "Tilly, I'm sure you can understand that we're all just trying to solve the same mystery. I'm trying to look at all of the evidence as it presents itself."

"Evidence." Tilly stood her ground as a woman with two children tried to figure out how to get around her. "Show me one bit of it, and I'll hush up and go away. Truth is, you have none. Just speculation and hearsay."

"Excuse me," the woman with children said. "I just want to..."

"Here's a piece of news for you," Tilly said without moving. "Did you know that Josie Bingham was in the family way when David Pearson died?"

The woman with children paled and then guided the youngsters in a different direction altogether.

"No." Priscilla swallowed hard and tried to absorb this news. "Are you sure?"

"Am I sure?" Tilly laughed. "Oh yes. The only lingering question is, 'Whose baby?' We've all come to our separate conclusions, of course, but if you're looking for suspects, spend a few hours scoping out Josie Bingham's brother, Edward. From what I hear, he really had it out for whoever compromised his sister."

"Bingham? Edward?" Boy was her suspect list growing or what? Narrowing down persons of interest was turning out to be more trouble than keeping up with Jake's holes in her garden.

At the front of the sanctuary, the song leader took his spot at the podium. The musicians began to play the opening to a familiar song.

This didn't deter Tilly one bit. "And by the way..." She gave Priscilla a searing gaze. "You sat in my pew last Sunday."

"Excuse me?" Priscilla didn't even try to lower her voice this time.

"You sat in the Snyder pew last week. I didn't say anything because you're new here. But if you plan to stick around, and it looks like you do, best stick to your own pew from now on. That's how we do it here."

"I...well, I never dreamed we had assigned seating at church."

Tilly lowered her voice as the pastor walked by on his way to the front of the room. "Not assigned. Just...*understood*. And the same goes for the inn."

"You have assigned rooms at the inn?"

"No, assigned tables for guests who frequent the restaurant. I'm sure you understand."

"Are you telling me I'm not welcome at the restaurant, Tilly?"

"Never said any such thing. But your chances of getting a good table will go way up once you Lathams apologize for muddying my grandfather's name." She stormed away to her self-proclaimed family pew, muttering to herself all the while.

"What was all that about?" Gerald's voice sounded from behind Priscilla.

She tried to speak above the music intro. "I have absolutely no idea. But she made it pretty clear I'm not welcome."

"In church?" He looked flabbergasted by this notion. "It's a church. Everyone's welcome."

"Well, don't sit in the Synder family pew, whatever you do." She pointed to the spot where Tilly had planted herself.

"Huh?"

"Trust me, okay?" Priscilla fought the temptation to roll her eyes. "And for pity's sake, don't mention the name Josie Bingham."

"Josie Bingham?" He spoke above the music. "Don't think I know her. Does she live on the island?"

"A hundred years ago. And apparently she had secrets. Lots of secrets."

"I see." He leaned in close. "I love a good secret. And I've got a doozy myself. Did you know that the youth group is selling cupcakes after the service to raise funds for their mission trip?"

"That's no secret."

His eyes sparkled as he responded. "No, but I happen to be a cupcake connoisseur. I'm gifted in the art of telling the good ones from the bad. If you'd like to join me, I'll show you which ones to buy."

"Oh, I'm doing the buying, am I?" She laughed. "Did you forget the part where I have to pay for renovations on the cottage?"

"This one's on me." He offered a smile so bright it caused her to lose focus on the song leader, who spoke above the music welcoming everyone to the service.

She watched in amazement as Gerald headed straight for Tilly Snyder's pew and took a seat then looked back at her with a smile as if daring her to do the same.

No, thank you.

Priscilla eased into a different pew on the opposite side of the aisle. No point in agitating Tilly any more than necessary. But she'd better tread carefully from now on. Any suspicions about the murder would have to go unspoken—outside of the family anyway. If she kept slipping up, she might get even more townspeople riled. And right now Priscilla simply couldn't afford that, not with so many questions left unanswered.

CHAPTER ELEVEN

The following morning Priscilla headed out to the garden to pluck weeds. Jake followed, her ever-present companion.

"What did I ever do without you, Jake?" she asked.

He drew near, and she rubbed his ears.

"You're a good friend."

He responded by almost knocking her down as he took off toward the water's edge.

"Don't get w—" Priscilla called as he bounded into the reeds. "Ah, never mind."

She picked a spot where the weeds were starting to poke through then knelt down and put on her gardening gloves. Before diving into her work, she paused for a moment to listen to the sound of the waves as they lapped the shore, just yards away. Nothing compared to that sound, majestic and holy. It took her back to childhood summers staying with Aunt Marjorie. In those days, she could almost picture the Lord Himself strolling along, His gaze on the waters below.

"Stay away from the drop-off," Aunt Marjorie would say. *"It's beautiful to look at, but we don't want to lose you over the edge."*

Even now Priscilla kept a healthy distance from the rocky shore. Braver souls might climb those rocks, but not her. "Stay away from the water!" she called out once more to the dog. This time he bounded her way and disappeared into the garden. "And don't tear up my garden."

Priscilla gave the landscaping an admiring look as she reached for her gardening tools. Things were really coming along, thanks to Joan and Ida. It was looking like a proper English garden.

Working with the soil caused her thoughts to drift back to Wheatfield. How comfortable and familiar the farmhouse had felt. To live in the same home for so many years? Not everyone had that blessing. Kansas held a piece of her heart, even now. Some days it tugged at her, encouraging her to return to her roots. Other days it drifted through her memories, a place of the distant past, not the hopeful present.

She worked for some time, pulling weeds and rearranging some flowers that were a bit too close together. After a while, she stretched her back and then gave the side yard a closer look. She gasped when she saw a small section of the garden upturned. Plants were out of their bed, flipped upside down. Mulch and dirt were scattered like rubbish on the side of the driveway. Just as she wondered if someone had taken a hoe to her beautiful patch of land, she saw paw prints.

"Jake! How many times have I told you not to dig in my garden?"

The dog bounded her way, his legs and underbelly soaked with water and mud.

"What in the world? Did you tear up my gardenias again?" Priscilla continued to scold the dog as she looked over his mess. "Remember the day I found you roaming the streets? Remember how I took you in and gave you a comfortable house to live in and food to eat?"

He wagged his tail.

"And this is how you repay me, by digging up my garden?"

The back-and-forth motion of his tail increased. He yapped and tried to jump on her, but she dodged his muddy paws.

"Oh no. Not this time. I'll love on you later. Right now I've got to clean up your mess."

He ran in the opposite direction.

"Rotten pooch!" she called out. "You're supposed to take the path, remember? Cutting through the flowers isn't in the plan."

Then again, how could she convince a dog to stick to a path when she was so inclined to wander from the beaten path these days? Indeed, she'd taken full advantage of being on Martha's Vineyard, hiking to places she'd only ever dreamed of, far from where a street map could take her.

Suddenly the dog's indiscretions didn't seem as bad.

"I'll forgive you this time," she hollered, "but the next time I have to replant, you're going to help."

Priscilla knelt down, knees in the dirt, and plucked up the mashed flowers. As she worked, her thoughts drifted to Tilly Snyder. The woman had given her quite the welcome, hadn't she?

What was up with hogging the pews? A person couldn't own a pew, could they? Was that even legal?

Priscilla continued to fume as her workload with the flowers increased. She straightened to relieve the ache in her shoulders and decided to stretch her legs a bit too. Kneeling for so long had left them feeling stiff and sore. A few paces around the garden path seemed to relieve the stiffness, but it also served to confuse the poor dog.

"No, boy, we're not going in. I'm just stiff, that's all."

He jumped up on her and licked her arm.

"That's not helping, Jake. You're going to knock me down. Then I'll really be aching tomorrow."

The crunch of tires against her gravel driveway alerted her to the fact that someone had arrived. Jake stood at attention in full guard-dog mode.

"Good boy, Jake."

A low growl in the back of his throat made her wonder if he sensed trouble. The morning sun made it difficult to make out the vehicle, but it looked like a truck.

Jake's growl morphed into a full bark, and he bounded in the direction of the vehicle.

"Back down, boy," Priscilla called out.

A young man who looked to be in his early thirties stepped out of the truck. She took in his appearance. Tall. Whiskery. A little on the wiry side. Work clothes. Ball cap. Looked like a nice-enough fellow. Jake continued to bark until the visitor reached down to pat him on the head. Then Jake jumped up to greet the young man with a slobbery kiss, leaving muddy paw prints all over his shirt.

"That's quite a welcome." The stranger laughed and wiped his hand across his wet cheek then brushed the mud from his shirt. He took a few steps toward her. "Mrs. Grant, I'm Beau Ortmann. I'd shake your hand, but it's a bit muddy."

"Oh, that's right. You're going to help with repairs on the cottage."

"Yep." Beau offered a wide smile. "Tommy brings me onboard when we're looking at bigger cases, and..." His words drifted off as he stared at the cottage. "From what he told me, this is turning into a bigger case than anticipated."

Priscilla bit back the sigh that wanted to frame her next words. "Unfortunately. Didn't start out that way, but I suppose it is now."

"Tackling the storm windows first. That's my plan for the day." He went into detail, but she didn't hear much of it. Priscilla was far too distracted thinking through what Mildred had said about Harrison Ortmann and that betting parlor in the back of the family store. That was a hundred years ago, but still...

Harrison would be Beau's...what? Great-grandfather? No, probably great-great-grandfather. Did he realize his own family's history? Would she be the one to tell him?

"Mrs. Grant? You still with me?"

"*Hmm?*" She startled to attention. "Oh yes. Just thinking."

"I understand." Compassion filled his eyes. "It's a lot to think about. Renovating is a big job."

"Yes." And so was this mystery. And to think, the Lord had brought an Ortmann straight to her door.

Sometimes you had to lead the cat to the cream. Other times? Well, other times the cream came straight to the cat.

She would befriend Beau Ortmann and see if she could get some answers about that infamous gambling hall once and for all.

CHAPTER TWELVE

Beau went to work replacing the windows, and Priscilla continued to work in the garden, her thoughts in a whirl. How could she approach the young man and ask some pointed questions about the gambling hall?

Just before noon, Joan arrived with flower clippings in hand. She took one look at Priscilla and began to scold.

"You look worn out, girl."

"Well, thanks."

Joan laughed. "I didn't mean it like that. But you're covered in dirt, and you look a little…stiff. Did you start without me or something? I thought we were going to work together in the garden this afternoon."

"Jake gave me no choice. He tore up my gardenias, and I needed to get busy fixing up his mess."

Joan looked down at the dog. "Bad boy, messing up Priscilla's garden. You've got this whole yard to play in. Why tear up the one patch you're not allowed to touch?"

"Sounds like Adam and Eve and that tree with the forbidden fruit." Priscilla felt the edges of her lips curl up in a smile. "They just couldn't stay away." She glanced Joan's way. "Would you mind terribly if we skipped the gardening and just had lunch together? I've got the makings for sandwiches, and I squeezed lemons for some homemade lemonade earlier this morning."

"Sounds perfect." Joan followed her as they walked into the house and headed straight for the kitchen.

"Let me offer Beau a sandwich," Priscilla added. She walked over to the young man, who pulled off his ball cap and swiped his damp forehead with the back of his hand.

"Everything okay?" he asked.

"Oh yes. Just thought you might be hungry. Can I bring you a sandwich? Lemonade?"

"Is it lunchtime already?" He stared up at the sky as if examining the sun. "I brought my own, thanks, but I'll take you up on the lemonade for sure. It's a hot one out here today."

She headed inside with Joan on her heels then fixed a glass of lemonade for Beau.

"Let me take that out to him," Joan said. "You stay in here where it's cool."

Priscilla nodded and then pulled out the lunch meats, cheeses, and bread. When Joan returned, they put together a quick but lovely meal. The time slipped by as they nibbled on ham sandwiches, sipped lemonade, and talked. After a while they grew silent, both of them staring out of the newly installed kitchen window at the beautiful gardens.

"I love the island in the summer," Joan said after a few moments of quiet bliss. "It's impossible to describe just how lush and green everything looks."

"I've tried to describe it to friends back home in Kansas, but only a picture will do." Priscilla paused. "Did I say 'back home in Kansas'?"

"You did, but I won't hold it against you." Joan smiled. "The best part of summer for me is that rare moment when you capture the sun just over the water's edge and the colors of the trees reflect in the water. It's as if they want to dive in for a swim but don't quite have the courage."

"I've already discovered it. I spend a lot of time at the end of the dock in the late afternoons." Priscilla took another sip of her lemonade. "Gorgeous."

"You're going to love the Vineyard in the autumn. You'll see. It's remarkable to watch those trees give themselves over to the necessary change."

"I can't even imagine. I was only here in the fall once as a child, and I certainly didn't pay attention to the trees."

"Well, brace yourself. The evergreens hang on, determined to prove that life continues. They refuse to give in." Joan paused, and her eyes grew misty. "Call me an old softy, but I sometimes take that as a sign for those who are nearing the giving-up point. It's like the trees are saying: 'Stay green. Stand tall.'"

"Wow." Priscilla smiled at her cousin. "You're quite the nature lover, aren't you, Joan?"

"I am. Always have been. Others find it strange, I suppose, but in the fall when everyone else is glorying in the changing of the leaves, I look for that random green tree, holding on for dear life. I admire the hangers-on."

Priscilla looked at the large pine tree just beyond the garden. She could almost picture it hanging on, unwilling to release its needles to the ground below.

Joan interrupted her ponderings with a question. "How's the mystery solving coming along? Any news?"

Priscilla didn't mean to groan out loud, but there it was. "Other than the part where Tilly Snyder almost took my head off in the sanctuary of Faith Fellowship yesterday, you mean?"

"Whoa."

"Yeah. Especially since she chose to lash out at me in a public place where others could hear."

"Are you serious?"

"I wish I wasn't. *So* awkward and embarrassing."

"I can't believe she would do that. She's such a tiny little thing. And so prim and proper. I wouldn't think her fierce manners would allow a public spectacle like that."

"I'm not saying I blame her. Imagine being in her shoes. This whole thing is awkward, frankly, especially since one of our relatives was involved—or seemingly involved—and the other families are mostly people we know. Or at least I'm getting to know them. Not that anyone really wants to get to know me if they think I'm accusing their long-lost relatives of murder."

"Goodness." Joan took a sip of her lemonade.

The pinging of a hammer on the far side of the cottage alerted Priscilla to the fact that Beau must've finished his lunch and started working on window installation once again. Hopefully the noise wouldn't be a bother while she and her cousin visited.

After a couple of moments, Joan looked Priscilla's way. "So where do things stand overall?" She raised her voice to be heard above the hammering. "I mean, have you drawn any conclusions?"

"No. I'm just trying to put all of the puzzle pieces into the right place. It's been a lot to absorb in such a short amount of time. It hasn't been that long since I learned that everyone thinks our great-grandfather was a murderer."

"Well, some people. Not all." Joan shrugged. "Mostly Mildred Pearson's father."

"And some people in *our* family believe Chester Snyder killed his friend David when he learned of David's, um, indiscretions with Josie Bingham."

Joan shrugged. "We have no proof, of course."

"And Tilly has other suspicions altogether. She suspects Edward Bingham, Josie's brother, because someone—and I think we can all guess who—got Josie pregnant while two of the three men were off to war."

Joan's eyes widened. "Well, that's a new one to me."

"I'm surprised Tilly shared that information with myself, but I think she wants to clear her grandfather's name."

"Understandable."

"And by the way, I'm not allowed to sit in the second pew on the left at church anymore." Priscilla sighed. "It's the Snyder pew."

"Good grief. People and their pews." Joan released a sigh. "But what were we talking about?" She paused. "You were saying that

Josie Bingham was expecting a child when Chester returned from war. Is that right?"

"Not sure of the timing, but I guess we could figure all of that out. I wish I knew more about all the players, to be honest."

"This calls for research. I have an account on an ancestry site, so maybe I can help with that part." Joan rose from the table, suddenly looking very excited about the possibilities. "If you'll let me log on to your computer, I can tell you anything you want to know about the Latham family. I've researched for the past two years, so I really do know a lot."

"Except where our great-grandfather, James Latham, was on the night David Pearson was murdered. Bet you can't tell me that."

"Except that. But let's give the rest a try, shall we?"

"Sure." Priscilla led the way to her desk, where her laptop sat.

Joan pulled up the ancestry site then signed in with her username and password. "I have access to birth records, death records, and so on. Not just for our family, but anyone. All we have to do is type in a name"—she typed in the name Josie Bingham then leaned back in her chair—"and, in theory, we can find out anything."

It took more than a few tries to find the right Josie Bingham, but in the end they learned her date and county of birth and also discovered that she had passed away almost six months after David Pearson's death. Very odd.

Priscilla stared at the date of her death: January 2, 1920. "Do you think she died in childbirth?" she asked. "That's the only thing that comes to mind."

"Likely. Or shortly thereafter. But the question we haven't fully answered is, how do we prove there was a baby? And how do we know for sure if Josie was expecting before Chester returned? If so, how far along was she? Two months? Three?" Joan slipped her hands behind her head and leaned back in her chair.

"Back in those days, women didn't find out as early. If she was, say, three or four months pregnant when Chester returned, this would all make sense, time-wise." Of course, this was a speculation on Priscilla's part, but she felt that voicing the idea out loud made it feel more believable. "Or maybe the baby was a preemie."

"Who might or might not have lived." Joan shrugged.

"Right. So we've got to find out what happened to the baby. Can you see if there's anything else in there about the child?"

Joan did a bit of digging but came up with nothing. "If I had to guess, I'd say that Josie was pregnant before Chester came back and that she went away to have the baby. Otherwise the locals would already know what happened to her and the baby. It's sad that she died though. Such a somber ending to an already difficult story."

"Right, but I wish we knew for sure. Things are getting so confusing." Priscilla shook her head. "Can we go over the facts again?"

"Sure." Joan never turned her gaze from the computer.

"Josie was dating Chester."

"Who remains on our suspect list."

"But she was secretly having a fling with David."

"Who turned up dead."

"And who might have had a drinking and gambling problem."

"Gambling problem?" Joan swung her gaze to Priscilla.

"Yes, he frequented the gambling parlor at Ortmann's."

"Gambling parlor at the grocery story?" Joan looked flabbergasted. "What?"

Priscilla put her finger over her lips, suddenly realizing that Beau Ortmann's hammering had stopped. Perhaps he was listening through an open window at this very moment. "That's a story for another day. But back to Josie. She had a brother who somehow figures into this story. Let's not forget that."

"Edward Bingham. But I don't really see him as much of a suspect, at least not yet. Do you?"

"No." Priscilla reached down to pet Jake, who had curled up at her feet.

"And Josie died around six months after David Pearson's body was found on the cliffs with our great-grandfather's sword at his side."

"Yes, but we have no clue what happened to her baby, if there even was a baby. For all we know, the Snyder family might've made up that story to cast a shadow on Josie Bingham."

"Right. Which means we're back to square one."

"Great-Grandpa James?" Priscilla sighed. "But why in the world would people think that he killed David Pearson?"

"His sword was found next to the body."

"And later returned by the police. It still seems most likely to me that Chester Snyder stole grandpa's sword to divert the police's attention then killed David in revenge for cheating with his girl. I'm more convinced than ever now that we know—or suspect—Josie was pregnant with David Pearson's child."

"But Chester Snyder and Grandpa were close, right? Would he try to frame a friend? For that matter, he and David Pearson were close too. Before, I mean." Joan thought a moment. "Show me the sword again, Priscilla."

Priscilla led the way into the bedroom and pointed to the painting on the wall. "I didn't have the heart to take it down, not after everything I learned." Lifting the trap door, she revealed the opening in the wall. "Hang on just a second." She shoved her hand into the opening and came out with the sword.

"I can't get over it." Joan ran her finger along the letters JWL. "These are our great-grandpa's initials. He held this very sword in his hand and used it to . . ." Her words drifted off.

"I don't like to think about that part," Priscilla said. "He used it in battle against the Germans."

"True. Maybe some poor young German soldier died on the end of this thing." Joan pushed the sword back into Priscilla's hands. "It's possible."

"Let's not think about who died at the end of this sword, okay?" Priscilla wrapped it back up. "Just makes things more complicated."

"I think it's time to call for a meeting of the cousins again," Joan said. "And maybe it would be wise to get Mildred involved too. What do you think?"

"As long as she doesn't end up mad at me like Tilly is, that would be fine. I don't want to end up with all of Tisbury in a tizzy."

"I can't guarantee that," Joan said. "All we can do is ask for her help and see if she plays along. She loves to research. We have that on our side."

"True. So when will this meeting be held?"

"Tomorrow at the museum?" Joan suggested. "Does that work for you?"

"Yes. Now that repairs are underway, it's going to be pretty loud around here." As if to emphasize the point, the hammering started again.

"Perfect time to get away then." Joan closed the laptop and leaned back in the chair. "Maybe we can finally get to the bottom of this."

Priscilla nodded and prayed her cousin was right.

CHAPTER THIRTEEN

The following day, just before the noon hour, Priscilla carried lemonade and homemade chocolate chip cookies out to Tommy and Beau and the two other workers who'd joined them. She wanted to stand in the yard and watch them work but knew it would probably make them feel uncomfortable.

Gail arrived promptly at noon with a sack lunch in hand.

"Brought this for Thomas," she whispered. "Do you mind if I steal him away for a few minutes? It's been ages since we've had time together."

"Of course I don't mind. Use my kitchen if you like or the picnic table on the waterfront."

"Thanks." Gail offered her a warm smile. "At the water's edge will be just fine with me. That way the other guys won't give him a hard time."

Priscilla still thought it sad that Gail and Tommy felt they had to hide their blossoming romance. They really were quite the couple, weren't they? In a romance novel, their parents would marry each other and free up their stepchildren to do the same. Then they could all live happily ever after in one big house.

Priscilla sighed. For some reason, Tommy and Gail were nervous about upsetting the apple cart. Or, in this case, their elderly parents. What was wrong with people on this island anyway? Swords fell out of walls. People had designated pews. General stores were betting parlors. And now this? The golden-years folks got to call the shots when it came to whom the young people fell in love with?

Sometime later, after Gail and Tommy finished their secret lunch, Priscilla walked their way to ask her cousin a question. "Want to ride into town with me? We're seeing Mildred this afternoon, but I need to stop by the grocery store on my way."

Gail shrugged. "I've got a couple of errands to run. I'll just meet you at the museum at two o'clock like we said."

"Okay. There's lemonade in the fridge. Help yourself, and make sure the guys have what they need."

"Oh, I will." Gail's gaze shifted back to Tommy, who'd climbed a ladder to remove some shingles.

Priscilla grabbed her purse and climbed into the car then headed to Ortmann's, where she planned to pick up a can of Stick-to-It hair spray. According to the ad sheet, Ortmann's was having a two-for-one special. Perfect timing to browse the store's layout and possibly get a look at where the betting parlor used to be. Maybe if things went her way, she'd walk out of the store with more than a great hair product. Hopefully she would obtain additional clues to help her solve this mystery.

The sunny afternoon made for a beautiful drive. It didn't take long to arrive at the grocery store. Priscilla parked and walked inside then grabbed a shopping cart. She was anxious to collect the items on her list so that she could spend a bit of time chatting with

Katie Ortmann. Up and down the various aisles she went, tossing things into her cart. Along the way, Priscilla tried to imagine what this place looked like a hundred years ago. No shopping carts back then. How did patrons lift and lug their groceries? With assistance from Harrison Ortmann, no doubt.

When she reached the back of the store, Priscilla noticed a door with a sign above it that read Employees Only.

"*Hmm.*" She rose to her tiptoes to see through the tiny window in the door. Typical storeroom on the other side.

"Can I help you?" A woman's voice sounded from behind her.

Priscilla turned around to face Katie Ortmann. "I, um..."

"Looking for something?" Fine lines formed between the heavyset woman's brows, and her jaw tightened as she leaned against the cane in her right hand.

"Could you tell me where the restroom is, please?" Priscilla forced a strained smile.

"It's at the front of the store, Mrs. Grant. Clearly marked."

"Right. Front of the store." She grabbed her cart and pushed it along with Katie walking next to her, her gait a bit off. "While I have you, I wonder if I could ask a question."

Katie froze in her tracks, her gaze narrowed. "About my great-grandfather, you mean?"

"Oh, um..." Priscilla fought hard to come up with something to say. It looked like this wasn't a great time for a conversation about the betting parlor, judging from the tight expression on the store owner's face. "I'd like to talk to you about Stick-to-It hair spray."

"Hair spray?" Katie's hardened features softened.

"Yes, the ad sheet says you've got a two-for-one special going, but I didn't see the particular brand in question."

"Ah." Katie relaxed completely and offered a nod. "We're out of it, but we'll honor your coupon when our new shipment comes in. Anything else I can help you with?"

"No, I..."

"Because I'd hate to think you'd left Ortmann's with any sort of ill will against us." Her stare bored a hole through Priscilla. "Or any of our deceased relatives."

"No ill will."

"Good to hear."

"But since you brought it up..." Priscilla paused and then dove right in. "I'd like to ask a couple of questions about your grandfather's...interests."

"Interests?" Katie's gaze narrowed.

"I'm not asking you to betray your relatives." Priscilla lowered her voice as a customer passed by. "I'm sure you realize that. I'm just curious."

"I know what folks have said about my great-grandfather. They muddied his name and didn't give a rip how that would affect our family, but trust me when I say it has affected all of us."

"Are you saying your great-grandfather didn't have a betting parlor in the back room?"

Katie's cheeks turned red. "Well, I wouldn't go that far. There has been some...evidence to that end. But he was a good man, a godly man who gave much to many during his lifetime. If you're going to stand here and accuse him of taking another person's life, then I might have a few issues with you. I'm sure you understand."

"I've drawn no such conclusion."

"Well, Mildred Pearson has." Katie put her balled-up fist on her ample hip. "And just for the record, my great-grandfather was in no way connected to her great-uncle's death. Do your research. The police never even questioned my great-grandfather."

"As I said, I've not let my thoughts go too far in that direction. Just looking at all the evidence."

"It was your own great-grandfather's sword that was found next to the body, you know, so while you're pointing the finger at me, remember there are several more fingers pointed right back at your family."

"From what I understand, the police returned the sword to Grandpa Latham and cleared his name."

"And they never questioned my great-grandfather at all. That should be all the proof you need."

"So neither of us has any reason to worry." Priscilla released a slow breath and lowered her voice even more. "I was just wondering if perhaps you had his ledgers from back then. I would love to see them, if so. It would be an easy way to eliminate him as a suspect."

"What I have—or don't have—is my own business. Mine and my family's." Katie leaned forward and whispered the rest. "Now if you would be so kind as to leave my shop, I've got customers—real customers—who are here to do business." She cleared her throat. "And just for the record, the room behind the store is currently being used for storage, nothing more."

"Thanks for the information." Priscilla pushed her cart to the front of the store, paid for her items, and left in a hurry. So much for getting information about Harrison Ortmann.

"Now what?" She sat in her car, staring at the digital clock. With thirty minutes before their scheduled meeting at the museum, she had little to do. On the other hand, if she arrived ahead of her cousins, maybe she could bend Mildred's ear a bit. Their conversation might prove helpful.

Priscilla arrived at the museum just as a senior citizens' tour left. When she found Mildred inside the nineteenth-century room, the poor woman looked exhausted.

"You okay?" Priscilla asked.

"Oh yes." Mildred stretched her back. "Didn't sleep well last night, and I've had nonstop tours through this place today. And to top things off, I just had a run-in with Alma Whitaker."

"Alma Whitaker?"

"Yes, I know you two have also had your differences."

"You're right," Priscilla explained. "Poor Alma. She always seems to be angry at someone."

"That's the one. She's one of the old set, completely against any sort of change on the island."

"Not that it's any of my business, but why is she upset at you? You're the resident historian, for heaven's sake, keeper of the island's legacies. You're not changing anything."

"Right." Mildred sighed. "Problem is, she thinks I'm in cahoots with you to hurt the reputations of some of the others in town."

"Seriously?" Priscilla crossed her arms at her chest. "She's upset at you because of me?"

"That's only part of it, but yes." Mildred glanced at her watch. "Hey, aren't you early?"

"Yes, but I was hoping you had a little free time. I don't want to wear you out, though, and certainly don't want to add to the Alma drama. Sounds like you're ready for a break."

"I am. Haven't even had lunch. Follow me into the kitchen, and I'll eat while we visit."

"Perfect." Priscilla followed the curator into the kitchen at the back of the museum and had a seat at the table.

Mildred pulled a to-go container out of the refrigerator and opened it, revealing a lovely salad. "So what's on your mind?" she asked as she reached for a fork.

"I've just been thinking."

"That's dangerous." Mildred took a bite of salad, and a contented look came over her.

"I know, right?" Priscilla paused. "Mildred, why do you think that fellow at the newspaper was so keen on exposing the betting parlor?"

"Ah." Her friend took another bite of the salad, and then a thoughtful expression settled on her face. After a moment, she spoke. "To put things in perspective, the newspaper was brand new in 1919. And the editor, in a former life, had worked for Hearst at the *Boston American*, a daily tabloid."

"Whoa. The original gossip rag."

"I guess you could call it that." Mildred pulled out a chair and sat at the table next to Priscilla. "And we all know about the Pulitzer-Hearst headline war."

"Right. I remember studying that in school." Priscilla reached deep in her memory bank. "The various newspapers were out for blood, one always trying to outdo the other with sensational headlines. Is that right?"

"Yes. I believe the editor, a Mr. Jordan Kramer, came to the island with that same spirit very much intact. He wanted headlines—and the bigger, the better." Mildred rose and walked to the refrigerator then returned with a bottle of water. "Would you like one?"

"No, thanks." Priscilla shook her head. "Guess that reporter found what he was looking for with Ortmann's. I'm sure it was quite the tale back in the day."

"Indeed. Poor Harrison—if one can call him that—never saw Jordan coming. Of course, the paper covered many other events as well: the welcoming of the soldiers back to the island that same year, incoming storms, those sorts of things."

"Interesting."

"Problem was, the paper didn't have a press of its own, so the pages were sent out for printing. You can imagine how cost exorbitant that was." Mildred ate another bite of her salad.

"No idea how they stayed in business."

"They didn't. Or, rather, they did, but Jordan ended up selling to another buyer, someone with a lesser taste for blood."

"And what happened to Jordan Kramer?" Priscilla's lips felt dry, and she found herself wishing she'd said yes to that bottle of water.

Mildred paused, fork halfway between the container and her mouth, lettuce dangling. "If I recall, he moved back to Boston, where printing was as cheap as the stories." A dribble of ranch dressing plopped on to her blouse, and she wiped it off with her fingertip.

"Ah."

"Not to knock the city of Boston, you understand. Just knocking that particular brand of journalism." Mildred scooped the bite into her mouth. "And I'm not saying journalism has changed much over the years either. Folks are still far too interested in sensationalism. The Internet has fed right into this problem."

"Agreed." Priscilla paused. "At any rate, I would imagine the Ortmann family has been carrying the very public shame of those betting parlor stories for a couple of generations now."

"And had done a pretty good job of burying them and moving on."

"Until I came along." Priscilla dropped her head into her hands and muttered, "What have I done?"

"Stirred up a bit of animosity? Caused a wee bit of division?" Mildred laughed and then pushed the container of salad aside. She took a swig of water from the bottle.

"But my intentions were good. I'm not out for a big story, at least not one I'll splash across the headlines. I'm no journalist. Not even close."

"Pretty sure the Ortmanns can't tell the difference. All they see is someone else trying to make their long-lost relative look bad. And by the way, just so you know, Harrison Ortmann completely turned his life around after the betting parlor shut down. From what I've read, a great revival swept the island in the thirties. One of the saved and sanctified was Harrison Ortmann. Pretty sure he took to preaching after God got ahold of him."

"Oh boy."

"Yes, so you can see why his great-granddaughter Katie, a religious woman, would want to keep those memories alive instead of the negative ones. We're talking about a family with strong Christian convictions." She grabbed a piece of carrot and then nibbled on it.

"One more question before the others arrive." Priscilla rose and paced the room. "What do you know about the Bingham family?"

"I had a feeling you would ask." Mildred picked up another carrot. "Josie had one brother, Edward. A short time after David passed away, Edward moved from the island to Falmouth."

"Falmouth? Interesting."

"He had a son, Edward Jr., who's still living in Falmouth. Quite elderly now. He runs an inn on the square. Bingham Inn." She popped the carrot into her mouth.

Priscilla plopped back down into the chair. "I'm so sorry I've taken up your lunchtime with this. The least I could've done was bring you a pastry from the bakery."

"Trust me, I have a steady supply." Mildred stood and opened the refrigerator again. "Cheesecake?"

"I'd love some."

They spent the next several minutes gabbing about current events on the island, including the upcoming fair and dog show.

"I guess the Vineyard is quite different from what you're used to," Mildred said after the conversation took yet another turn. "Do you see it as staid? Conventional?"

"I never thought to use those words, but I guess they fit." Priscilla took a bite of her cheesecake.

"We like to say, 'You can get your kicks on Route 66, but not on Martha's Vineyard.'" Mildred slapped her knee. "I've always loved that line. Point is, we do our best to avoid looking and feeling like every other town in America, even the quaint small ones. You'll notice we're not big on things like fast-food joints or strip malls, that sort of thing."

"Yep. Noticed that."

"People don't come to the Vineyard—whether it's to live or to vacation—to get the same old, same old they can get elsewhere. We move at a much slower pace."

"Noticed that too, but it really suits me, especially at this stage of life." Priscilla finished her cheesecake and pushed the empty plate back a few inches.

When Joan, Gail, and Trudy arrived at two o'clock, Mildred was just wrapping up a story about a new inn in Tisbury, one that had the locals in an uproar.

Trudy came through the door first, followed by the other two cousins. Mildred offered them cheesecake, and then the conversation got under way.

Trudy raised her hand. "I just want to start with a question: Can you even imagine what it must've been like to turn up pregnant in 1919?"

"That's some way to kick this off, Trudy." Priscilla laughed. "But I suppose we should start there since it's probably going to turn out to be key to the investigation."

"Investigation?" Gail took the seat that Mildred offered her. "Is that what this is? I thought we were just trying to solve a mystery that involves our family members."

"Call it what you like," Priscilla said, "but it's feeling more like an investigation to me now."

"As far as my question goes, I was just trying to make a point," Trudy interjected. "It wasn't so very long ago that girls who got pregnant out of wedlock hid the pregnancy so that others wouldn't know."

"Yes. When we were young, unmarried girls in the family way either got married quickly or went off on an extended visit to a matronly aunt or something." Mildred took the seat across from Gail. "You know?"

"Right." Priscilla thought it through. "I can't imagine what must have been going through Josie's heart and mind as she faced that situation. I'm sure she was terrified."

"Terrified that her boyfriend would figure out he wasn't the father or terrified that her family would kill her?" Joan paced the room, her words coming out in a steady stream.

"Maybe both. Poor thing." Trudy released a sigh as she took the seat at the end of the rectangular table. "I feel so sad for her."

Gail cleared her throat. "Before we canonize her and make her a saint, let's all keep in mind that she cheated on Chester Snyder, who was off fighting for his country. He came back to find that his girlfriend was pregnant, right?"

Priscilla pulled a notebook from her bag and placed it on the table in front of her. "So we've speculated. Or maybe she got pregnant after he returned home. There's only one way to know for sure."

"What's that?" Mildred asked.

"We have to find the baby. Joan and I searched online yesterday to see if we could locate any birth records, but came up short."

Joan raised her hand, much like a kid in school would do. "We did learn something else, though, ladies. Josie Bingham passed away six months after David Pearson died."

"Whoa. Not sure how I missed that in my research." Mildred shook her head. "And we're absolutely sure she had a child? How can we pinpoint that if there are no records?"

"I think we should begin with the assumption that she did. Otherwise, why was the rumor started in the first place?" Priscilla scribbled the words *Josie's baby* on to her paper. "So here's the most important question at the moment: What month was the baby born and where? If we can locate birth records, we'll be in a better position to guess who the father was."

"Unless she delivered early." Gail pursed her lips. "That happens sometimes. Not every pregnancy lasts nine months."

"Finding out when is important," Priscilla said. "But I'm more convinced we need to know where. Where was the baby born?"

Mildred shrugged. "This is just a guess, but I would imagine she went away to a home for unwed mothers and the baby was given up for adoption. If that's the case, those records might be sealed."

"Or maybe, as you said, she went to live with an aunt, someone on the far end of the island, or even maybe on the mainland. If that's the case, could be the family member took the baby in. Things like that happened all the time." Gail pulled out her phone and set it on the table in front of her then typed something into it.

"I might be able to help with this," Mildred said. "I've been able to locate evidence in the past to support documents at the museum. It's not always easy, but with a little research, maybe we'll figure this out. And just for the record, if we can locate the county that recorded Josie's death, we might narrow the search. If she died during childbirth, I mean."

"We checked the ancestry site yesterday," Joan explained. "Don't recall seeing the name of the county on her death certificate, but maybe I overlooked it."

"Do we know for sure that she didn't marry Chester Snyder after he came back from the war?" Trudy asked. "Maybe he discovered she was pregnant with someone else's baby and married her anyway."

"After killing the man who got her pregnant?" Gail asked. "I don't think so."

"And wouldn't Tilly know if her grandfather married Josie Bingham?" Joan added.

A reflective look passed over Gail's face. "Maybe not, if Josie died early in the marriage and he went on to marry Betty after the fact."

"Who's Betty?" Priscilla looked up from scribbling notes on her paper. "I don't know that name."

"Betty Snyder, Chester's wife," Mildred explained. "Or at least she was the only wife that I ever knew of."

"But was Betty Chester's first wife or second?" Trudy rose and paced the room. "That is the question."

Priscilla thought that through. "Here's what I'm thinking. If Chester married Josie first, we can assume he did *not* kill David Pearson. A man cold-blooded enough to murder his girlfriend's lover probably wouldn't be the same sort of fellow who would step up and make a decent woman out of her. Right?"

"Right. So if Josie married someone else, then Chester's still a suspect."

"But if she married Chester…"

"I'm inclined to think Josie never married at all," Joan said. "I wish I'd thought to print her death record, but I'm pretty sure her name was still Bingham at the time of her death."

"Oh." All four women spoke in unison.

"So back to the drawing board." Mildred rested her elbows on the table. "I'll do some research and see if I can find out what happened to that baby. I'll research records in all of the surrounding counties to check the location of Josie's death while I'm at it. I'm sure she didn't go far."

Trudy sighed. "Maybe she died completely alone, having given up her baby and her one true love."

"There we go, canonizing her again." Gail jabbed the table with a finger. "And which man, exactly, was her one true love? Chester Snyder, whose back she stuck a knife into, or David Pearson, the scoundrel who probably stole her innocence?"

Mildred cleared her throat. "Excuse me, ladies, but David Pearson is still family to me. If we could avoid the name-calling, it would be helpful."

"Oh, sorry." Gail put her hand over her mouth. "Just talking without thinking. I'm sorry, Mildred. I've let myself get caught up in this story. These folks are like fictional characters to me now. It's easy to carry on about someone who's not real."

"Well, they're very real to me," Mildred responded. "At least my great-uncle is. I could show you pictures if you'd like."

"Actually, pictures would be a great idea." Priscilla looked up from her notes. "Where can we find photos of townspeople just after the first World War?"

"Where you find all good things in Tisbury," Mildred said with a smile. "Right here at the museum."

She led the way to her computer. Minutes later, Mildred scrolled through hundreds of photos of Tisbury, going back over a hundred years.

"Here we go. 1919." She located a folder labeled Post WWI and clicked it. A wonderland opened up to them. After a bit of searching, she paused at a photo of a handsome fellow with dark, wavy hair and a well-groomed moustache.

"I've always loved this picture of my great-uncle David." Mildred sighed. "He was only in his midtwenties when he passed away. But you know what I notice? My own son looks a bit like him."

"Sure does," Joan agreed. "Carl even wears his hair like that, doesn't he?"

"Most of the time, yes." She squinted and leaned closer to the computer. "It's the dimples though. All of the men in the Pearson line seem to have those same boyish dimples. Look." She pointed at the screen. "I daresay my uncle David was a handsome fellow."

"Which might be why Josie Bingham took to him so readily," Trudy said.

"Do you think you can find any pictures of Josie?" Priscilla asked. "I would feel better snooping around in her business if I could just catch a glimpse of her."

"I'll look." Mildred spent the next fifteen minutes scrolling through photos. She managed to find several of her great-uncle and even a couple of Chester Snyder. Priscilla was absolutely delighted when they stumbled across a slew of photos of her great-grandfather James Latham dressed in full regalia, right down to the sword. She and the cousins squealed with delight as they took in photos of his homecoming after the war.

Just when they thought no photos of Josie were to be found, Mildred stumbled upon one. Priscilla gasped as a beautiful woman with upswept hair filled the screen.

"Oh my."

"Wow." Gail gave a little whistle. "She was quite a beauty, wasn't she?"

"Sure was. Wowza." Trudy's eyes widened. "If she'd been born ten years later, she could've been a film star. She reminds me of a young Greta Garbo."

Priscilla couldn't quite believe how exquisite Josie Bingham had been. Her slender neck put one in mind of Audrey Hepburn, but that curving regal figure looked like someone else entirely. Marilyn Monroe perhaps? No, Josie was definitely more slender than Marilyn, right down to her delicate wrists.

"Any more photos of her?" Priscilla asked.

"Let's see." Mildred kept scrolling until she landed on a photo of Josie standing with a crowd of people at the Welcoming Our Soldiers Back Home Parade. Behind her, the sign for Ortmann's Mercantile loomed large and welcoming.

"I've done a lot of research over the years about this particular parade," Mildred said. "Getting our boys back from battle was quite the ordeal."

"What do you mean?" Priscilla asked.

"Well, the war ended in 1918, but with hundreds of thousands of troops to return home, it took an exorbitant amount of time. Even the largest ships of that time could only carry five or six thousand at once."

"Wow." Trudy looked stunned. "How awful would it be to know your loved one was coming home, but then to have to wait even longer?"

"Something else complicated their return," Mildred added. "The wounded were returned first. Not only that, but many of our men had been exposed to the Spanish flu. Some were carriers. The last thing they wanted to do was bring it back with them."

"I feel so bad for our fighting men and their families," Gail said and then sighed. "They went through so much just to serve their country."

"Which is why so many of them held such serious grudges against people like my great-uncle who were unable to serve." Mildred shrugged. "Though most truly were unable from a medical or psychological standpoint."

"I feel for the servicemen's loved ones back home too," Gail said. "What a difficult wait that must've been."

"Sounds like some—like Josie—chose not to wait." Trudy pointed at the photograph on the screen. "Hey, does Josie look pregnant to any of you?"

Mildred enlarged the photo. "Not to me. That's a pretty narrow waistline, accentuated by her belt. But maybe she wasn't very far along."

"Right." Trudy nodded. "Good point."

"I can't get over her hair." Joan let out a whistle.

"Me either." Priscilla found the thick, dark hair mesmerizing. In this photo, it hung in long graceful curves over Josie's shoulders. "Gorgeous."

"I liked it better up," Gail said. "Looked more like the other women of her day."

"I like it better down," Trudy chimed in. "Looks more natural."

"Up or down, she was still a beauty queen," Priscilla observed. "It's rare to find historical photos of women who look like they could've stepped off a contemporary magazine cover, but she does."

"And this explains why David was drawn to her." Trudy paused and then snapped her fingers. "I know. Maybe she was a siren."

"A siren?" Mildred looked Trudy's direction and laughed. "First a saint and now a siren?"

"Sure, that would explain it. She wooed David until he could no longer resist. That's a possibility."

Joan rolled her eyes. "Trudy, you're grasping at straws now."

"Sorry." Trudy's gaze shifted to the floor. "This is why no one has ever hired me as a detective. I'd end up making all the suspects' families feel bad."

"I'm doing a fairly decent job of making the suspects' families irritated myself," Priscilla said.

Gail gave Trudy a stern look. "The reason you haven't been hired as a detective, Trudy, is because you don't have the qualifications. Plain and simple."

"None of us do," Priscilla reminded them. "But it has been rather adventurous to play the role of sleuth. Before long we'll all have our credentials. Of course, half the people in town won't be speaking to us, but we'll be qualified."

This got a laugh out of the ladies.

They looked at several more photos together, chatting about a wide variety of possibilities.

"Tell me everything you know about the Bingham family, Mildred," Priscilla said as an idea took root. "I really don't feel like we've learned all there is to know."

"I know the Binghams were farmers. They lived in the interior of the island. From what I can gather, Edward was about five years older than Josie. So if she was twenty-three at the time of David's death, Edward was twenty-eight. Their parents were killed in a house fire—actually, a barn fire—in 1918, just a year before my great-uncle was killed. Edward and his wife Susan took Josie into their home here in town, far away from their former life."

"Wow. How did you hear about the fire?"

"Same place I hear about everything." Mildred pointed to the computer. "Research. In this case, newspaper clippings from 1918. I did a search for the name Bingham, and it led me to a story about the fire. Would you like to see for yourself?"

"Sure."

Mildred typed in the name Bingham along with the year 1918 and then scrolled until she found the article in question. "There you go. Quite the write-up."

Priscilla leaned in and read the headline: "Fire Takes the Lives of Beloved Family."

"Sounds like the Binghams were well-loved."

"Yes, respected members of the community. Old Mr. Bingham was an elder at the community church."

"Did he have his own pew?" Priscilla snorted. "Sorry, couldn't help myself."

"Actually, he probably did. All of the pews in our local churches were paid for with family donations, and many have plaques you can read."

"I see." Priscilla skimmed the article, surprised by the details and the overly dramatic wording. "Wow, so Josie survived because she happened to be in the house, not the barn?"

"Yes."

"I'm sure she was devastated." Priscilla paused as she thought about how tragic that must have been for a young woman to lose both parents at once. It had been hard enough for her own daughter to lose a father. What if she'd lost a mother too?

Just as Mildred attempted to shut down the photo program, Priscilla remembered something. "Stop!" she called out.

Mildred pulled her hand away from the computer. "What is it?"

"That photo of Josie at the parade. Go back to it."

Mildred scrolled back and stopped when she reached the photo in question. "What about it?"

Priscilla pointed at the screen. "That man, the one standing next to Josie. Any idea who he is?"

Mildred enlarged the newspaper clipping to read the print below the photo. "Oh, that's Edward Bingham, Josie's brother, the one who took her in. Kind of a foreboding fellow, isn't he?"

"Yes. He does look a bit on the stern side," Priscilla observed. "So Josie's parents died, her boyfriend Chester was off to war, she was forced to live with this very austere-looking brother, and she turned to David Pearson, the only remaining person from the trio of musketeers she'd always hung out with, for comfort."

Mildred sighed. "There's no way to prove that conclusively, but it's looking more like it."

"I'm sure David was going through a lot of depression at that time too," Gail chimed in. "So it was probably a natural inclination for these two friends to end up in each other's arms."

"Right." Mildred shrugged. "Maybe we'll never know."

"Or maybe we will," Priscilla said, her hopes rising. "Yes, maybe we will."

CHAPTER FOURTEEN

On the morning after meeting with the cousins and Mildred, Priscilla went out to the dock. She couldn't stop thinking about the phone call she'd received from Mildred earlier that morning, filling her in on some of the gossip going around the island. Apparently this investigation really had folks in an uproar.

Jake bounded through the reeds along the coastline, oblivious as always as she repeatedly called his name. After several attempts, she finally gave up. She took her usual spot at the end of the dock and pulled off her sandals. Time to think. And pray.

Priscilla glanced at the calm morning waters and observed the angle of the sun. Off in the distance, puffy clouds hung like wispy balls of cotton candy. Interesting how different everything looked in the morning. How peaceful. How still. Priscilla couldn't help but think of Teresa and her whale-watching tours. It might be fun to take a boat ride out to the whale sanctuary to see them up close. From her dock, Priscilla rarely caught more than a glimpse and from too great a distance to snag a photo.

She stared out at the ripples perfectly aligned on the water. How did they know to line themselves up like that and to move in orderly fashion toward the shore? Surely they were drawn by an invisible hand above, one that orchestrated such beauty in all of creation.

Off in the distance, a couple of sailboats vied for her attention as they played along the shore. There were no fields in her current view—no wheat, corn, or soybeans anyway. But the bliss of staring out at the water made her move to Martha's Vineyard feel right and nearly as comfortable as the old farmhouse. For a moment, she felt a bit wistful about her old home, but those bittersweet feelings passed quickly. Who could argue with the family environment on Martha's Vineyard? If you didn't count the people who were irritated at her over this latest investigation, she'd made quite a few new friends.

Oh well. She would use the silence to collect her thoughts and spend some time with the Lord. Maybe He could give her a better perspective about folks like Tilly Snyder, Katie Ortmann, and some of the other locals who'd recently decided to turn against her. Hadn't He already smoothed the waters with Mildred and her father?

Priscilla had never been one to pray out loud, but out here it came quite naturally. Her gaze shifted to the sky as if to see Him face-to-face. She started by thanking Him for all He'd done for her and then gave extra effort to praying for Rachel. After that, Priscilla turned her attention to her cousins and friends on the island. When she'd covered every person in the lineup, she decided to rise and walk the beach.

"Lord, I have a few things on my mind. Maybe You could help me straighten them out?" She paced back and forth, giving the Lord quite a long list of things related to her investigation.

"Priscilla, aren't you cold out here?"

She turned as the familiar voice rang out. Gerald O'Bannon stood on the beach.

She smiled and waved him down to join her. "To what do I owe the pleasure of this visit?"

"After we talked about that sword, I did some checking. Not sure you'll like what I discovered."

"Oh?" That didn't sound promising.

Off in the distance Jake started barking. He ran down the beach and headed straight for them then jumped on Gerald with his muddy paws.

"I'm so sorry." Priscilla stared in disbelief at the mess her dog had created. "Please forgive Jake. He's on a learning curve. If you'll come to the house with me, I'll help you get the mud off your shirt."

"Throw in some coffee, and it's a deal."

"Of course. And I've got some breakfast Danish too. I've been keeping it since Tommy and his crew started. They'll never complain about going hungry, not as long as they're working at the cottage."

"I'm sure they appreciate that."

Gerald settled into an easy pace beside her as they walked back toward the cottage. "I stopped by to let you know that I spoke to a friend who works in forensics," he said. "He's from Boston. Asked him if they could test an item as old as the sword."

Priscilla paused and looked his way. "But he said no?"

"It's not a matter of saying yes or no. It could be tested. They could swab it and run it through a series of machines to detect and isolate DNA. They do that with older objects all the time, even ones that have been damaged over time."

"Then what's the problem?"

"It's just tougher on something that old that's been handled by dozens of people, including everyone in your whole family. And let's say they go to the trouble to locate a DNA profile, and it leads back to your great-grandfather. So what? He owned the sword. It's only natural his DNA would be on it."

"Right. But what if, say, Chester Snyder's DNA turned up?"

Gerald's brows slanted into a frown. "Sure, let's say the forensics experts actually manage to piece together a profile. How do you trace it to a man who's been dead for years?"

"By testing his rela—" She stopped short. "Oh."

"Exactly. Do you really want to test Tilly Snyder so that you can prove—or disprove—a crime her grandfather might—or might not—have committed? Can you even imagine the ruckus that would create? Half the island would turn against you in a New York minute, especially those who love Tilly and her inn."

Priscilla sighed. "When you put it like that, no. And I'd be banned from the inn for the rest of my life." She felt a catch in her throat. "There go my watermelon pickles."

He laughed. "That's all you're worried about? I could sneak you some watermelon pickles."

Priscilla brightened at this news. "You would do that for me?"

"Of course."

She led the way up the steps to her front door. After he tossed his hat on the front hall table, she put the coffee on to brew and they settled at the kitchen table. From the look on his face, Gerald had something on his mind.

His expression grew more serious. "Back to my point: any samples they find would probably be compromised anyway. They can't analyze a compromised sample."

"Okay, okay. To keep the peace, we won't question Tilly or ask her to give a DNA sample."

"Wisdom."

"But her grandfather is still number one on my suspect list." She got up and reached into the cupboard to pull out her favorite Kansas City Royals coffee mug. She grabbed a second mug, this one with a Christmas theme. Oh well. "Then again, I have a few other suspects too, so he might not be in the number one spot for long." She paused as she set a mug in front of him. "Do you think I'm ridiculous?"

"Ridiculous?" He gazed at her with such intensity that she immediately regretted asking the question. "What do you mean?"

"Asking you to talk to forensics experts about a hundred-year-old sword."

"Of course not. I didn't know the answer myself. And if we're going to start taking polls on who's most ridiculous, I'd win."

"Why is that?"

"Have you ever seen me with my grandson? When Max is around, I revert back to my childhood."

"I think that's rather endearing."

"And ridiculous." There was a trace of laughter in his voice, one that drew her in.

Just as she finished cleaning Gerald's shirt, the crunch of tires sounded from the driveway. Through the window, she caught a glimpse of Joan's car pulling up.

Priscilla bit back a smile and rose to greet the ladies at the front door. Gerald followed her.

"Come inside, ladies. Happy to see you." Priscilla gestured for them to enter.

Trudy's right brow arched as she stepped inside. "Hope we're not intruding."

"Not at all. We were just enjoying a cup of coffee."

With a look that was half amused and half skeptical, Trudy said, "We need to speak with you, Priscilla. In private, if you don't mind. Family matters."

"I can take a hint." Gerald smiled. "But if you ladies are covering up a crime, just remember—I work for the government."

"Please." Trudy rolled her eyes. "You work for the Coast Guard. You guys don't prosecute murderers."

"Are you saying there's a murderer to prosecute?" Priscilla's heart skipped a beat. "You found out something?"

"Nothing concrete." Trudy patted Gerald on the back and said, "Thanks for stopping by," then pulled open the front door.

Priscilla would've scolded her, but Gerald seemed to find her actions funny. "I've been booted from worse places than this, ladies. Don't think I'm going to hold this against you." He gave Priscilla a nod, grabbed his hat, and then turned to leave.

Priscilla turned to face her cousins. "Coffee, anyone?"

"No thanks, I've already had three cups. If I drink any more, I'll be able to thread the sewing machine with it running." Trudy giggled again. She did seem overly caffeinated.

"I've had plenty as well." Joan's expression grew more serious. "Priscilla, we really do need to talk. We have news. We've found something you're going to be interested in."

"We?" Trudy shot Joan a stern look. "I found it, please and thank you." Trudy reached into her bag and pulled out a small journal. "I know you're not going to believe it, Priscilla, but I found Great-Grandpa's journal, the one he kept after the war."

"What?" Priscilla stared at the small book. "Are you serious?"

"Yes. Aunt Marjorie passed several of his things down to me before she died. Anyway, I remembered she'd given me a large box of his things way back when, so I spent the morning looking through them and stumbled across this journal."

"Did you read it? Anything interesting in there?" Priscilla asked.

"Did I!" Trudy clutched the book as if her life depended on it. Then she gingerly opened it, flipping the pages until she arrived at one that drew her interest. "Here. Here it is. Look at this." She passed the book into Priscilla's hands.

Priscilla glanced down at the book, amazed by her grandfather's perfect handwriting. "People don't write in cursive like this anymore. This is lovely."

"Read it."

"Okay." She ran her finger along the words: *July 16, 1919: And by thy sword shalt thou live, and shalt serve thy brother; and it shall come to pass when thou shalt have the dominion, that thou shalt break his yoke from off thy neck. Genesis 27:40*

Priscilla went back and read the date again. "July sixteenth? That's the day after David Pearson was found dead."

"Really?" Joan fanned herself. "Is it getting warm in here?"

Priscilla paced the hallway, book in hand. "This is the same Scripture that's on the picture in my bedroom. Come see." She led the ladies into her room and pointed at the framed painting, which still clung to the wall. "See?"

"One and the same." Joan pursed her lips. "Maybe our great-grandfather isn't really off the hook after all, ladies. Maybe it was just wishful thinking on our part to try to remove him as a suspect."

"Maybe," Priscilla echoed. She glanced down at the open page in the journal once again. "So with that in mind, what are your suspicions?" She ran her finger across the words, stopping when she got to the word *sword*. "And what's up with the 'break his yoke from off thy neck' part? Is that the King James way of saying you're getting rid of someone?"

"Maybe not." Trudy sat on the edge of the bed. "It's a Bible verse, that's all. Lots of people write down Bible verses."

"Perhaps it had some special significance to him because of the war?" Joan suggested.

"Really? Is that what you two think?" Trudy shook her head and laughed. "I should've been a prosecutor. This journal would give me plenty of evidence against Great-Grandpa for sure. I could make my case right here and now, and we'd have him locked up in the pokey for life."

"Against a family member?" Joan asked. "Really? We are flesh of his flesh, bone of his bone."

"*Hmm.*" Trudy's nose wrinkled. "Well, when you put it like that, maybe it was just a verse that meant something special to him."

"Pretty sure a murder conviction would get you more than prison time back in 1919," Joan said. "And if our great-grandfather had gone to prison for murder, they would have executed him." Her eyes widened, and she seemed to disappear into her thoughts. "None of us would be here today."

"Good point." Priscilla paused. "So now what?"

"Now we wait on Gail. She's on her way over with the photo albums Aunt Marjorie left her. Looking at all of those photos at the museum put us in the mood to go back through family photos. You game?"

"Sure."

Before leaving the bedroom, Priscilla gave the Scripture in her great-grandfather's journal one last glance. Maybe James Latham wasn't the man he'd been made out to be after all. Maybe, like so many others of his day, his story was riddled with secrets. She would keep searching until she knew for sure.

CHAPTER FIFTEEN

Gail arrived with her arms full of photo albums. She eased them onto the coffee table and released a breath, clearly worn out.

"Whew. That was an armload. Brought as many as I could lug."

"Why so many?" Joan asked.

"I dunno. I thought they might be useful."

Priscilla walked over to the stack of albums and picked up the top one. "Great idea. Find anything interesting?"

"Oh, a thousand things, but none of them related to this case. I got so caught up in looking at our relatives that I almost forgot the point of it all." Gail plopped down on the sofa. "That was quite a workout. Can't believe how many I had."

Priscilla sat next to her and opened the album in her hand. She paused on the first picture, which happened to be one of Aunt Marjorie standing in front of the cottage. "Oh, I love these old photos. It's even more fun when they're your relatives."

"Aunt Marjorie was always so sweet," Trudy observed.

"Sure was." Priscilla sighed as a flood of memories from childhood washed over her. She pointed to another picture of a funny-looking little boy diving naked off the dock. "Crazy to think that's the same dock that's there today." She held the photo album a little closer to get a better look. "Who do you suppose that is?"

Gail snorted. "It's my dad. Can you believe it?"

"No way. Uncle Hugh?" Priscilla clamped a hand over her mouth. "Oh my. He was a precocious kid, wasn't he?"

"Still is, in his own way. Some little boys never grow up."

They kept flipping through the album until they landed on another photo of Aunt Marjorie.

"She was always such a beauty." Joan sighed.

"Even in her later years," Gail added. "She had the most gorgeous hair. Like silk. And her skin was perfect."

"That's what island living will do for you." Trudy looked at Priscilla then back at the photo. "You favor her, Priscilla."

"I do?" She gazed at the photo to see if she could find the similarity. Aunt Marjorie did have the same eyes and similar cheekbones.

"You do, and not just in looks. Marjorie was someone everyone gathered around. And look at you, living in this house. We're perfectly at home here, gathered around you, just like we used to be with her."

"I'd like to think I have the gift of hospitality." Her mood darkened. "Only I don't think most people in town would agree."

Trudy looked perplexed by this notion. "What do you mean?"

"The list of people who are irritated at me is growing," she explained. "That's what I mean. Apparently I'm not very hospitable if half the town can't stand me."

"Can't stand you?" Gail shook her head. "I can't imagine anyone not liking you, Priscilla. You're the sweetest person to grace this island in quite a while."

"Then you haven't talked to Alma Whitaker lately." She sighed.

"Alma Whitaker?" Gail looked puzzled.

"She's mad at Mildred because she thinks Mildred and I are in cahoots."

"Seriously?" Trudy snorted. "Alma and Mildred have a long-standing feud going, so you can hardly count her. Who else is mad at you?"

"Well obviously Tilly and Katie Ortmann, but also Eldora. I heard she's been going around town spreading rumors about me."

"Eldora's a gossip," Trudy countered. "Always nosing in where she doesn't belong. So I don't think you can count her either."

"And then there's the owner of the Lobster Shack."

"What?" Joan looked aghast at this notion. "Henry? Why is he mad at you?"

"I think Fred Pearson got to him with some story about how I was out to hurt the businesses on the island by destroying reputations."

"I thought you and Fred had kissed and made up." Trudy bounced a few times on the sofa. "Or did I misunderstand?"

"We've spoken, but apparently he still doesn't trust me. He must've made the rounds to the businesses right after he found out I'd located the sword. I don't know." She paused. "Oh, and the Monaghan sisters have apparently started some sort of campaign to remove the cottage and lighthouse from Teresa's tours."

"What?" Gail shook her head. "That's crazy. What do the Monaghan sisters have to do with the tour?"

"No idea. I just know they've petitioned her to remove my place as a stop." Priscilla sighed. "Not that I really care. I'm a little overwhelmed with folks coming and going every Saturday anyway. But the idea that the locals have turned against me shows just how put off they are. I need to tread carefully here before I'm booted from the island."

Joan sat up straight and gave Priscilla a tender look. "Honey, I'm sure things will simmer down. And you have plenty of folks who love you. We're all on your side after all."

"I just hate that there have to be sides."

"The waters will calm after you've figured out who's really to blame. And remember, the list of those who adore you is much longer than the list of those who don't. You've won Mildred over, and that's really saying something since her father has held a grudge against our family for ages."

"And Teresa's crazy about you too," Gail added. "Tours or no tours."

"And let's not forget Candy," Trudy threw in.

"Candy's like Switzerland," Priscilla countered. "She has to remain neutral for the sake of her customers."

Trudy shook her head. "She's anything but neutral. She's nuts about you."

Priscilla relaxed a bit. "You think?"

"I know. And think of the men working on your home—Beau, Tommy, and the others. They're happy you're here, in part because you're bringing in work."

"True."

"And Clara Lopez, the librarian, was overheard telling Candy how proud she is of you for holding your own with Tilly." Gail leaned back into the sofa. "So don't get too worked up, Priscilla. Folks on the island tend to pick sides. This just happens to be a side-picking situation."

Priscilla sighed. "I've never been accused of being divisive before. This is all so foreign to me."

"Oh, speaking of foreign, did you hear there's a new Thai restaurant in Edgartown?" Trudy's eyes lit up. "I can't wait to try it."

Joan laughed. "That's our Trudy, always thinking of others."

The conversation shifted back to where it began, talking about all the things Priscilla had in common with Aunt Marjorie.

"For sure, you have the gift of cooking, just like she did." Trudy turned the page and laughed at a photo of a little girl with chicken pox. "Pretty sure that one is me."

They continued to turn the pages, laughing and talking. Book after book, photo after photo, they enjoyed every moment as they walked down memory lane.

Finally, they reached the bottom album.

"Are you worn out, Priscilla?" Gail asked. "Ready to be rid of your uninvited guests?"

"You're always invited," she said. Priscilla grabbed the last photo album. "Might as well look at this one too. Then we'll be done." She opened the final book and thumbed through the first few pages. "Oh, this one is older. All of these have that antique look about them, rather sepia-toned." She kept looking until Joan gasped.

"Stop." Joan pointed at the page. "It's Great-Grandpa."

These pictures were different from the ones they'd seen at the museum. Not as posed or stiff. In these photos, she got to see her great-grandfather surrounded by friends and family, completely at ease.

"He was handsome," Priscilla said after a few moments. Indeed, James Latham was tall with an ingenuously appealing face. Even in the more relaxed photos, he somehow managed to carry himself with a commanding air of self-confidence. "That chin though."

Trudy nodded. "All the Latham men have that chin. Uncle Hugh has it."

"Guess so. Never really paid much attention before. What do they call that?"

"A strong chin." Trudy ran her hands across her own. "Mine is weak in comparison, but the sagging skin on my neck is more what I'm worried about."

"You're beautiful, Trudy."

"Humph." She turned her attention to the album.

Priscilla turned the page, and they all gasped at a photo of their great-grandfather standing at attention in his full Army regalia with his beautiful bride beside him.

"Oh, Great-Grandma Lila was a beauty, wasn't she? I don't think I've ever seen their wedding photo before, but she looks gorgeous. That dress is a work of art."

"Homemade too, I'd guess. We come from a long line of seamstresses, you know."

Priscilla noticed the date that had been written above the wedding photo. December 25, 1919. "Wow. They got married on Christmas Day. Less than six months after David Pearson was killed. Interesting." She lost herself in her thoughts for a moment.

"What are you thinking?" Joan asked.

Priscilla pointed to her grandfather's side. "The sword. He's wearing the sword at his wedding."

"Oh, right." Joan squinted and gave the faded photograph a closer look. "Well, since the police gave it back shortly after the murder, they clearly didn't consider it—or him—suspect."

"Right." Priscilla nodded. "I can't imagine he would wear it publicly if he'd used it as a murder weapon just a few months prior. You know? Seems too daring, if you think about people gossiping and all that." She closed the album and leaned back against the sofa. "He doesn't look like a man who would kill a one-time friend on the cliffs of Aquinnah."

"I agree," Gail said. "And obviously the police agreed, or they wouldn't have returned the sword. But what an accusation to have to live with all your life. You know it had to bother him that people pointed fingers behind his back. Gossip can be such a terrible thing."

"I'm sure it was hard on him and Great-Grandma." Joan's nose wrinkled. "But what can you do? Sometimes people talk, whether you want them to or not."

Priscilla found herself unable to focus on Joan's words. Her imagination had taken her somewhere else entirely. "You know, I keep talking about the cliffs of Aquinnah as if I actually know something about them, but I have only the vaguest memory of

Aunt Marjorie taking all of us for a picnic at the Aquinnah lighthouse. I just remember that the terrain is different there. And the lighthouse too. A different color, right?"

"Right. It's a darker color. Not white. Everything about Aquinnah is different," Joan said. "It lends itself to the mysterious because of the cliffs and that amazing view of the water. You can actually see the point where the sound and the Atlantic merge."

"It's breathtaking," Trudy concurred. "The landscape is extraordinary. Cliffs. Water. Reeds. Amazing. It's almost as if God took His fingertip and ran it along the edge of the Vineyard and pulled up this beautiful place just to take our breath away."

A lovely silence filled the room as the description left them speechless. In that moment, a terrific idea occurred to Priscilla. She sat up straight and stared at her cousins as she made her announcement. "I want to go. I want to see the spot where David Pearson died for myself. It's been ages since I've been to the Gay Head cliffs at Aquinnah, and I want to get a visual for where the event took place."

"People aren't allowed out on the cliffs anymore," Trudy said. "They put a stop to that when I was a kid. It's just too dangerous. These days I can only think of one reason a person would actually sneak past the barricades to the trails leading out there. Well, two, actually."

"What's the first one?" Priscilla asked.

"If you wanted to do yourself in, you could take quite the swan dive from the cliffs into the sound."

"Horrible way to go. What's the other reason?"

Trudy's eyes narrowed. "If someone cornered you and you had no choice. And I'm guessing that's what happened here. Someone enticed David Pearson onto the cliffs and then cornered him. And I'm guessing the killer chose to do the deed with a sword instead of a gun because if you fired a gun over those cliffs, people would hear it for miles around. Can you even imagine how that would echo?"

"Maybe not, if the waters below drowned out the sound," Joan said.

Gail shook her head. "I think it's time we stopped this, once and for all."

"Stopped what?"

"This investigation, or whatever you call it. We've taken this far enough. I've already been worried about losing friends. I don't want to lose my own cousin."

"I'm not talking about going out onto the cliffs," Priscilla threw in. "Just viewing them from the scenic overlook. I just want to see the spot for myself. Is that so bad?"

"I say go for it," Trudy said. "You're a super sleuth, Priscilla."

Priscilla pondered Trudy's words. "I've never considered myself a sleuth by any means."

"Strange things like this didn't happen to you in Kansas?"

"Oh, once in a while there would be a riddle to solve, but I think everyone goes through that. You gals have had to drag me into this mystery-solving thing kicking and screaming because I'm a bit of a scaredy-cat, living here alone."

"I love a good mystery." Trudy's eyes lit up.

"I think I'm intrigued by riddles that need solving because they remind me so much of my own life," Priscilla said. "Do you ever think back to when you were young? Remember what you wanted to be when you grew up?"

"I had the whole thing planned out," Gail said. "I was going to be a female astronaut. I guess that came from watching rocket launches as a kid. Instead I became a dental hygienist."

"I wanted to be an actress." Trudy spoke with flair. "Make it big on Broadway." She paused for a moment, and her nose wrinkled. "But my biggest accomplishment was the starring role in the Edgartown mystery dinner theater production of *A Love to Die For*."

"You were very good, Trudy. Everyone said so." Gail gave her an admiring look.

"I always felt I had potential, but being up on the big stage would have given me an opportunity to spread my wings and fly. One never knows unless one tries. But I always had that secret longing."

"I always wanted to be the first female cop on the island," Joan said. "But they wouldn't have me." Her smile quickly faded. "Back then it was a lot harder to break into a man's world."

"My point is, when we were young, we didn't know what the future held. We thought we did. We hoped. We dreamed. But in the end God gave us different paths, mysterious and new. Unexpected." Priscilla smiled. "Kind of like a mystery."

"And He's still working out the ending of the story," Trudy added.

"Don't call it the ending, Trudy!" Gail looked horrified by this notion. "Speak for yourself. I've got plenty of life ahead."

Trudy glanced Priscilla's way. "You just carry through. Do what your heart tells you."

"Right now it's telling me to go to Aquinnah and take some photos of the cliffs." Her gaze traveled from cousin to cousin. "Are you ladies free tomorrow?"

Gail shook her head. "Not me. I have to take Dad to the doctor. He has a post-op appointment to have his knee looked at."

"And I have to work at the clinic," Joan threw in.

Trudy shrugged. "Tomorrow's not good for me either. I'm having lunch with Teresa."

Tiny creases formed between Joan's brows as she looked Priscilla's way. "If you go to Aquinnah alone, promise me you'll stick to the paths. Don't be too daring."

"I'll be careful. I'm not overly adventurous."

Trudy snorted. "You're not? Of course you are. You've already proven that since arriving on the island."

"Anything I've done has just been a fluke. Back on the farm I didn't go around solving crimes. I fed cows, sure. I managed a combine. But I don't recall trying to vindicate a dead relative."

"God knew your skills were better served here in the Vineyard." Gail gave her a little wink. "So He brought you to us."

"To solve crimes?"

"That, and to cook for us. I am forever grateful to the Lord for your amazing cooking skills."

When her cousins left, Priscilla gave a great deal of thought to what they'd said. She would travel to Aquinnah tomorrow and have a look at those cliffs. She would avoid the off-roads and stick to the paved ones. And perhaps she would get a few answers along the way.

CHAPTER SIXTEEN

The following morning dawned with clear skies. Perfect for photographs. Priscilla dressed in comfortable clothing and put on her sturdiest tennis shoes. She didn't plan to do any climbing, but the shoes might come in handy getting to the scenic overlook. Just as she prepared to leave the house, the phone rang. A familiar voice greeted her.

"Priscilla? This is Teresa. Do you have a minute?"

"Good morning, Teresa. Just heading out to . . ."

"Aquinnah, I know. I'm with Trudy, and she told me."

"Oh, I see." News sure traveled fast around here.

"Priscilla, I've called to talk to you about that sword you found in your wall."

"Wait . . . what? How do you know about the sword?"

"Tilly Snyder. I was having lunch at the inn a few days back, and she must've overheard me talking about your house being on the tour now. She came up to my table, and next thing I knew she was telling me all about how you think her grandfather killed Mildred's great-uncle with your great-grandfather's sword, which you found in your wall."

"Oh, for pity's sake. I never said her grandfather killed him. His was just one of many names that have come up. And I can't believe Tilly was gossiping about this."

"It's not really gossip if it involves you—at least that's what I've always heard." Teresa cleared her throat. "And this most assuredly involves Tilly, since her grandfather has been accused."

Priscilla did her best not to groan out loud.

"But listen, Priscilla, I got to thinking about something. I know you're facing big expenses with the cottage. If that sword really belonged to your great-grandfather, and Mildred seems to think it did..."

"Wait, you talked to Mildred too?"

"Oh, don't be upset with her, Priscilla. I brought it up when I stopped in at the museum the other day, not the other way around. But anyway, she seems to think that sword is worth a pretty penny. You could sell it at an auction and make a fortune, more than enough money to pay for all of the repairs. Isn't that a fine idea?"

This notion stopped Priscilla in her tracks. For a moment she didn't say anything. She finally managed a curt, "I don't think so."

"I understand it has sentimental value, Priscilla, but if it was used in a murder, you probably don't really want it hanging around, right? And the fact that it was used in a murder will make it even more intriguing to a potential buyer. See what I mean?"

"The sword was returned to my great-grandfather after the investigation, so I really don't see..."

"Not an accusation, and I certainly didn't mean to offend. I'm sure the police would never have returned it if they'd found any evidence incriminating your grandfather. I'm of the opinion that someone else used it and tried to pin it on him. But don't you see? The sword has more value because of the story. That's all."

Priscilla gripped the phone, her emotions taking hold. "I've already written Tommy a check for the repairs, Teresa. It was a bit of a sting, but I did it. So I appreciate your suggestion but..."

"You want me to butt out?"

"It's not that, exactly. I'm just not used to people knowing so much about my personal business." Priscilla paused to consider Teresa's suggestion that she sell the sword. If she used up all of her savings, there would be little way to bring in an income. It wasn't like she could harvest the field and sell the crops.

She swallowed hard and tried not to give it much thought. She couldn't sell the sword. She just couldn't.

"I'm grateful for the call, Teresa, and I know you care. I'm sorry Tilly dragged you into this."

"Dragged me into it?" Teresa paused. "You're my friend, Priscilla, despite those not-so-pleasant things Tilly said about you. I want to make sure you have everything you need. That's all. So don't be upset. I'm sorry I butted in. I have a tendency to do that." The tone of her voice softened. "Forgive me?"

"There's nothing to forgive." Priscilla felt bad for blurting out her feelings. Teresa was just trying to help. They all were. Well, all but Tilly Snyder perhaps. Sounded like she still had a few issues.

Priscilla ended the call with Teresa, her thoughts in a whirl. Sure, the sword was worth a lot of money, but did folks really think she would sell it? Did they see her as that desperate? Was she?

As much as she longed to fix up her new home, the idea of selling off a piece of the family's history brought a wave of guilt with it. How could she let go of her great-grandfather's sword, murder weapon or not?

But then, what if the cottage needed more repairs in the future? She had to think long-term. While her bank account was still healthy, it wouldn't last forever. She didn't think she could bring herself to sell her ancestor's sword, but there was something she could sell. Something she'd been putting off for a while.

But she wouldn't think about that right now. Instead, she'd hit the road and put all of this out of her mind.

Priscilla decided to take the long way to Aquinnah, heading straight into the interior of the island, where the terrain changed completely. In this area, rolling hills and farmland replaced cliffs and ocean views. She passed a particularly lush area, part of the national forest, and sighed at the beauty. Here one might just forget they were on an island at all.

She drove past a horse farm, and something prompted Priscilla to pull off the road. She enjoyed the view of ducks and geese in an oversize pond. Beyond the pond, livestock grazed on a spacious slant of land, horses in one pasture and cows in another. Was this what Josie Bingham's life had been like? Did she enjoy peaceful days on the family farm, surrounded by horses and cattle? Did Chester Snyder travel to this place to romance her before he left for war?

After sitting for a while, Priscilla decided to get back on the road. She put the car in gear and pulled out onto the Edgartown highway, pointed toward Aquinnah and the Gay Head cliffs. The GPS on her phone led her straight to the shops at the scenic overlook.

Priscilla parked her car in the parking lot and climbed out, ready to stretch her legs after the lengthy drive. A quick glance to her right revealed the beautiful lighthouse, towering above the rocky shore. How different it looked from the one she saw every day. This one was darker in color and had a foreboding look about it. The light spun red and white, a beacon to ships to avoid the rocky cliffs below.

She walked along the sidewalk to the visitor's center, split-rail fences protecting her from the cliffs on the other side. Historical plaques shared the story of the legend of the area. Priscilla paused to read them and tried to imagine how much of this area had changed since the night of David Pearson's death. When she arrived at the visitor's center, she picked up a brochure, which she read as she made her way to the scenic overlook. When she finished, she tucked the brochure into her purse, trading it for her phone. She would use the camera to snag some great photos once she reached her destination.

A few more steps, and the view took her breath away.

"Oh my."

In many ways, the scene in front of her looked like an amazing watercolor, almost too magnificent to be real. She extended her hand, as if to touch the canvas, but only came up with air. Priscilla squeezed her eyes shut and then opened them quickly to see if the view had in any way changed. No. The cliffs, the waters, the tall grasses all merged together to form a picturesque scene unlike any other. She loved her corner of the island in Misty Harbor, but she had to admit there was something unique about Aquinnah. It wasn't just the staggering elevation from atop the overlook, though that took her breath away. What really captivated her was the water.

She set her gaze out toward the vast blue expanse of waves as they pounded the shore. To her left, the waters from the sound were one color, and the deeper waters of the Atlantic another. She could almost see the point where the two colors merged.

That was how her life had been, wasn't it? She'd come from a place of safety, much like that water along the shoreline. Once in Martha's Vineyard, she'd ventured out into the deep, had traveled into waters of a different color. And now her worlds were merging.

She took several photos of the water, trying to capture the two different variations of blue as well as the white waves breaking across dark rocks. Her gaze shifted to the white sand—almost Caribbean-white—and the cliffs in varying nuances of gray. Off in the distance, trees, green as a children's crayon, swayed in the breeze. She snapped picture after picture then stepped back to look them over.

"Wow." It was the only word she could manage. The pictures almost did the area justice. Not completely, but almost. She turned her gaze to the waters once again. The sunlight hit with radiant beams, and the whole area sprang to life, a Technicolor image only God could paint.

More photos followed until a rapid movement at her feet caused Priscilla to glance down. She almost jumped out of her skin as a sand rat scurried by and then disappeared beyond the split-rail fencing into the tall grasses on the other side.

"Sorry. Didn't mean to disturb you, little guy." She glanced around to see if any other tourists had approached. No point in letting total strangers see her chatting with a sand rat. But the overlook was devoid of tourists this morning.

She walked to the north side of the overlook and gasped as she took in the cliffs on that side, just beyond the tall grasses. "Whoa."

What kind of person would venture out there, even to do another harm? You'd have to be crazy to risk your life on such jagged peaks. Why was David Pearson out on the trails in the first place? Had his killer drawn him there, perhaps? Baited him?

Off in the distance another sand rat caught her eye, and she tried to photograph it. Unfortunately, the angle was wrong. Priscilla leaned across the railing and bent as far as she could without falling. A gust of wind caught her by surprise, and the phone tumbled from her hands into the grassy area just beyond the railing.

"Ugh." She knelt down and did her best to reach it by sticking her arm underneath the bottom rail, but fell short by several inches. "Now what?"

She tried a couple more times with no success. Really, there was only one way to fix this. She'd have to climb over the railing, grab the phone, and climb back onto the paved overlook. She took a moment to assess the situation. There were several feet of grassy area before the steep slope began. The risk was minimal.

With hands shaking, Priscilla slung her leg over the waist-high top railing. "Oh boy." Thank goodness there were no other tourists about. She could almost picture total strangers posting photos of her backside to their social media sites. What would the captions read? She shivered just thinking about it.

Getting the first leg over the railing turned out to be the easy part. Priscilla got hung up, straddling the fence like one would ride a pony. It took greater effort to heft the second leg over, now that her thighs had turned to gelatin. They wobbled this way and that as she finally swung to the far side of the fence.

Maybe the grassy area wasn't really enough for one to stand on when one had nothing but cliffs behind her. Priscilla shifted from foot to foot in an attempt to balance her weight. Icy fear twisted around her heart as she glanced down at the waters hitting the cliffs below. Panic like she'd never known before welled in her throat.

Perhaps the cousins had been right to worry after all.

Finally feeling a bit more secure, she gripped the railing with one hand and knelt to snag her phone, which almost slipped out of her trembling hand. Just as she stood aright, Priscilla heard a man's voice.

"Ma'am?"

She turned with a start to discover an older fellow in a Coast Guard uniform. "Oh, you scared me."

"I scared you? Let's just say it's the other way around." He spoke in a quiet, steady voice, his hand extended in her direction. "Let me help you back over. You're not allowed over there. It's too dangerous."

"Oh, I know. I just dropped my phone. You see? I had to get it."

"We would have helped you with that. Next time just ask. The cliffs have been closed to the public since 1962."

"Ah. Looks like I got here a half-century too late." Priscilla forced a smile and then handed him her phone. She accepted his outstretched hand and before long found herself on the right side of the fence once more, her knees threatening to buckle as her feet hit the overlook's solid pavement. Her stomach clenched tight for the first few seconds, but she finally started to relax after several long, slow breaths.

The officer gave her the phone along with a fatherly lecture. "We've lost more than one person that way. I'm sure your children would hate to get the message that Mom perished on the cliffs at Aquinnah."

Perished on the cliffs at Aquinnah. She shivered as she thought about David Pearson's family and how they must have felt getting the news of his death.

The Coast Guard officer continued to lecture as he led her away from the overlook, back toward the visitor's center. "Good thing I was there to help. The winds are so strong today they might've pulled you past the grassy area onto the cliffs."

"R-right."

"Would you like me to walk you to your car?" He gave her a not-so-subtle look.

"Okay, okay, I get your point. I'm leaving. I promise I won't go back there. I got the pictures I needed anyway." She lifted her phone in triumph.

"Hope they were worth it."

"While I have you here, could I ask a few questions? I'm investigating a family story from over a hundred years ago. It involves my great-grandfather."

"What sort of story?" The Coast Guard officer put his hand over his eyes to block the sun, which streamed down on them from overhead.

"Rumor has it he murdered a man on these cliffs." She put her hand up. "I don't buy that story, mind you. And neither did the police back in 1919, when the murder took place. They gave him his sword back."

"Sword?" The officer's eyes narrowed. "Wait a minute. Are you talking about the infamous Pearson murder?"

"Yes." She put her hands on her hips. "You know about it?"

"Everyone around here knows that story. It's legendary. I've always wondered who really killed him." He narrowed his gaze. "Are you saying you're related to the fellow who stabbed him?"

"No. I'm related to one of the people *suspected* of stabbing him. There's a difference. I just came out here today to get a visual. I wanted to see the spot where the murder took place."

"In order to see that spot, you'd have to venture out onto the trails, and I can't let you do that, as I said before. Closed to the public."

"Right." She sighed. "I guess I'll never know how the real murderer enticed him to come out here that evening."

He paused, and his gaze traveled beyond the pathway to the clay cliffs. "Back in those days, this was the perfect place to view the sunset. Lots of young lovers would rendezvous on the cliffs, at least from the stories I've been told. You should see the colors of the cliffs when the sun goes down. Breathtaking."

"I'd imagine." She stood in silence for a moment as an idea took root, one that would not leave her alone. "Oh, I think I know how he did it."

"How the murderer enticed his victim?"

"Yes." She snapped her fingers. "I'm guessing it was a setup. Maybe David thought he was meeting Josie, his beloved. She was pregnant with his child, you know."

"Um, sorry. Don't know anything about a Josie or a child." The officer shrugged.

"Lesser known points, I suppose. But there was a Josie, and she was pregnant. So maybe the murderer sent David a note—in Josie's name—and asked for a rendezvous, as you said. See? Then maybe David came here expecting his girlfriend only to find..."

"A murderer?"

"Yes." Excitement took hold of her. "That's it exactly. He came to meet the love of his life, and someone ended up taking his life instead."

"Makes sense to me. But we'll never know for sure now, will we?"

She deflated a little then shrugged. "Guess not."

"Just don't go beyond the barricades to look for any clues. Not that you would find them anyway." He nodded and then headed in the direction of the shops. "Have a good day."

"Same to you. Thanks for saving my life."

"You're welcome."

After he left, Priscilla looked toward the cliffs again and suddenly felt weak in the knees. It was all she could do to get to her car. Her thoughts flashed back to that tummy-sick feeling she'd had on the wrong side of the railing. Maybe her cousins were right. Maybe researching alone wasn't such a great idea after all. Hadn't she promised them she wouldn't do anything foolish?

Priscilla released a slow breath and thought through the day's adventures. She couldn't stop imagining David Pearson's trek to the cliffs. Had he really come thinking he would see his sweetheart? Had the murderer baited him, drawn him here to take his life?

Priscilla shuddered. The scenario made perfect sense. Suddenly she could hardly wait to get back home and call the cousins together to share her thoughts. She unlocked her car and climbed inside, ready to head home. When Priscilla put the key in the ignition and turned it, a couple of clicks followed. She turned the key again, this time hearing nothing. Absolutely nothing.

Great. Now she would have to call one of the cousins to come and rescue her. But which one? Joan and Gail would fret, so Priscilla did the only thing that made sense.

She called Trudy.

CHAPTER SEVENTEEN

Gerald?" Priscilla said through the open window as he approached the car with long, purposeful strides.

He leaned in the window, his jaw tight and concern etched in his brow. "Priscilla, are you all right?"

"Yes, of course. It's just my car. It won't start." She opened the door and climbed out.

"I know. Joan called me."

Priscilla closed the car door. "Joan called you? What happened to Trudy? I thought she was coming to get me?"

"Well, she was, but then she ran into a snag of some sort, so she called Gail, who was at the doctor's office with her dad. Post-op visit."

"Right."

"So Gail called Joan, who was at the clinic."

"Right. And Joan called you?" Priscilla groaned. "Good grief." She felt her cheeks go warm. "I, um, have no idea what's wrong with the car. It acted like it didn't want to start the other day then ran fine. Same thing this morning."

"Could be your battery or maybe the alternator." He reached inside through the open window and popped the hood. "We'll know momentarily."

"We will?"

"Yep. Just let me get my jumper cables. I know this old trick, you see. It solves riddles like this in less than a minute."

"Does it solve all riddles or just car riddles?"

He laughed. "Just car riddles. And specifically, just battery and alternator riddles. But first, let's see if it'll take a jump." He grabbed some cables from the back of his SUV and got to work hooking them up to her battery. After a few moments, he had her try to start her car. Worked like a charm. The warm rumble of the engine gave Priscilla hope.

"Now to make sure it's just the battery."

She got out of the car and watched him in action, admiring his steady hand as he unplugged the positive connection of the battery. The car died at once.

"Well, that's it then." He turned and shrugged. "It's your alternator."

"Are you sure?"

He nodded then walked over, opened the front door of her vehicle, and peered inside. "Your lights are starting to fade, which is usually a sign of an alternator problem as well. So I think we need a tow truck to solve this particular riddle."

She sighed. "Isn't there some other sort of trick for the alternator?"

"Yes. It's called a mechanic." He laughed. "And I happen to know a good one. But first we need to call for a tow. Do you have AAA?"

She pulled out her card and handed it to him. He made the call. Though she hated to admit it, it felt mighty good to have a man take care of this car situation for her. If she'd been alone . . . no, she didn't want to think about that. God had sent just the right person.

Less than fifteen minutes later, the sound of an approaching truck caused Priscilla to turn. "Tow truck's here."

Gerald waved to the driver, who parked and joined them. After a bit of discussion, the driver got to work, hooking up her car. She watched with a sigh as he headed off toward Tisbury and the mechanic's shop. Gerald made a quick call and gave the mechanic instructions then looked her way. "Ready to head back home?"

"Yes, thank you."

In true gentlemanly fashion, he opened the passenger door of his SUV for her. She climbed in, her legs feeling a bit wobbly, and looked up to offer him a thankful smile for all he'd done. Instead, Priscilla found herself distracted by the swath of wavy hair that fell casually on his forehead. It made him look like a boy, one who'd just come in for dinner after a rowdy playtime with his friends.

As they pulled out of the parking lot and back onto the road, Gerald glanced her way, a concerned look in his eyes. "Priscilla, do you mind if I ask what you were doing out on the cliffs at Aquinnah?"

"Technically I wasn't on the cliffs."

"Interesting. I heard a call go out that a woman matching your description was seen climbing over the railing."

"Ah." She paused. "Well, I didn't go out onto the cliffs. I just dropped my phone. It had some really great pictures on it."

"This story could've had a far different ending. The Gay Head cliffs are no place to get risky. Promise you won't do that again."

She sighed. "What if I can't promise? What if I go on climbing over railings and getting stalled out and finding swords in walls? What then?"

"Then . . . " He released a slow breath. "I'll pray for your safety."

"It's likely I'll give you a lot to pray about. But I'll do my best not to get into pickles anymore." She paused. "Speaking of pickles, I sure miss Tilly's watermelon pickles."

"Want to swing by the inn?" Gerald asked. "It's time for my lunch break anyway."

Priscilla pursed her lips. "I would say yes in a heartbeat, but I don't have a table at the inn, remember? Tilly gave me a not-so-subtle hint that I wasn't welcome there."

"Surely she didn't mean it. I say we risk it."

"Pretty sure she'll flip out if I go in there."

"C'mon. Everyone has to eat. And if Tilly tries to shoo you off, I'll come out swinging." He paused and then grinned. "Well, not swinging exactly, but you know what I mean. I'll rush to your defense." He turned on the SUV's left turn signal and slowed down. "Remind me what you did. To set her off, I mean."

"Oh, nothing really." Priscilla sighed then turned her gaze to Gerald's. "Just accused her grandfather of possibly murdering someone."

"Oh, is that all?" Gerald made the left turn with ease. "Surely she'll forgive a little ole thing like that."

"One would think." Priscilla paused. "Speaking of accusing folks, I have a new theory."

"New theory?"

"About David Pearson's death."

He groaned. "Don't you think it's time you let that go?"

"I can't." She pulled down the visor to check her appearance and gasped as she saw her windblown hair. "Why didn't you tell me I looked like this?" Priscilla tried to smooth out her hair with her hands.

"Like what?" Gerald seemed perplexed.

She gave up on her hair and pushed the visor back up. "Here's my theory: the murderer—and let's say it was Chester Snyder, Josie's original boyfriend—sent a note to David Pearson in Josie's name, asking for a romantic getaway on the cliffs at sunset."

Gerald shrugged. "Makes sense, I guess."

"Right. So David comes to the cliffs expecting Josie…"

"And meets up with the grim reaper?"

"Exactly."

He shrugged. "Possible. But I still don't know how you're going to prove it. Or how you'll pin it on Chester."

"I could be wrong about Chester. It might've been Harrison Ortmann."

"Harrison Ortmann?"

"Yes. Or Josie's brother, Edward. I'm sure he hated David too."

Gerald released a sigh. "If you keep naming suspects with familiar surnames, you'll have the whole town of Tisbury against you. That's not a good thing."

"I could already give you a list of people who aren't speaking to me, thanks."

He sighed. "Well, let's go back to what you were saying about Tilly Snyder's restaurant at the inn. I just happen to have a table reserved with my name on it. And no one can tell me who can or can't join me at my own table."

"So this whole reserved-table thing is true? Like reserved pews at the church?"

He laughed. "No, I don't literally have my name on a table. And the pastor would laugh if he heard you say anything about reserved pews at the church. He's all about welcoming newbies. But as far as the restaurant goes, Tilly does manage to seat me in pretty much the same place every time I show up. The point is, we islanders are creatures of habit. And you . . . " He turned to give her a quick glance. "You have disrupted our habits."

"I have a tendency to do that to people."

"You have a tendency to stir things up." He glanced her way with a smile. "Not saying that's a bad thing."

"Ah." She hardly knew how to respond. Priscilla tilted her head to one side and stole a slanted look at him. He didn't seem to notice, a fact for which she was suddenly grateful.

He looked her way, and his eyebrows arched mischievously. "Did I do something wrong?"

"No, not at all. What makes you think that?"

An easy smile played at the corners of his mouth. "You had that same look my mother used to give me when I was in trouble."

Laughter bubbled up. He thought she looked like his mother?

She turned her gaze to the window, her thoughts in a whirl. Minutes later they rounded the turn in front of Tilly's historic inn, and Priscilla's thoughts shifted to watermelon pickles. And to Tilly, who would probably refuse to offer service. Then again, with Gerald O'Bannon at her side, who could refuse her?

He parked the SUV and came around to her side to open the door. She followed his lead inside the inn, hoping against hope she wouldn't be turned away.

The hostess at the front of the restaurant didn't say anything unusual. Instead, she seated them in a booth near the side window and passed a couple of menus their way.

"See?" Gerald gestured around the quiet restaurant. "No problem at all."

"Maybe Tilly's gone for the day." Priscilla opened her menu. "Hopefully."

"Don't fret."

"Easier said than done."

Her thoughts shifted back to the scene of the crime. If her great-grandfather's sword had really been used to murder David Pearson, then perhaps she should sell it—get rid of it once and for all. It might bring in a pretty penny, enough to cover the expenses of the cottage thus far.

On the other hand, if he hadn't committed the murder—and surely he had not—getting rid of the sword would dishonor a good man's memory and diminish his legacy as a serviceman.

Priscilla sighed and glanced down at the menu.

"You do that a lot, you know." Gerald's voice startled her back to attention. He sat forward and looked at her intently.

She remained motionless for a moment, finally managing a quiet, "What?"

"Fret."

She put the menu down. "It's a habit I'm trying to break."

"If you need any help, just ask. I'm a former fretter since I joined Fretters Anonymous."

"Very funny."

"No, I'm serious." He gave her a pensive look. "After my wife left, I was paranoid about, well, everything." He pointed to his brow. "See these?"

"These... what?" she asked.

"The wrinkles. I earned every one of them. And lately I've spent way too many hours fretting over my daughter's pregnancy. She's had some bumps in the road."

"I'm so sorry. I didn't know."

"Unlike most stories on the island, we've managed to keep this one under wraps. Point is, I've had no choice but to let go and let God, as they say."

"Okay, okay, I've got your point." She put her hands up as if in defeat.

His expression softened at once. "Sorry, didn't mean to preach."

"It's okay." She forced back the sigh that threatened to erupt. "I'm probably due a long sermon right about now."

"Well, good." He glanced across the restaurant and then back at her. "Because here comes Tilly Snyder, and judging from the look on her face, she's ready to take the pulpit."

CHAPTER EIGHTEEN

Fortunately, Tilly Snyder did not kick Priscilla out of the restaurant. She did, however, give her the expected sermon. This, of course, made lunch with Gerald a bit awkward, though he handled it with ease.

Still shaky from her time on the cliffs and the run-in with Tilly, Priscilla just wanted to go home and soak in a bubble bath. Gerald drove her to the cottage where she found Tommy and Beau working outside hanging the new shutters.

Priscilla thanked Gerald as she got out of the car, and he responded with a tip of his hat. As his car pulled out of the drive moments later, she had one thing on her mind: to get inside and run water in the tub.

Unfortunately, someone else had a different plan.

Beau approached, his eyes narrowed. "Mrs. Grant."

"Beau."

He pulled off his baseball cap and twisted the brim around to the back before putting it on again. "What's this my mother tells me about a murder?"

As if the day hadn't been tough enough already.

Priscilla cleared her throat. "This conversation was inevitable, I suppose."

"I guess, but would you enlighten me before I tackle the rest of the work on the cottage? If there's some reason to think I don't need to be here, I'd like to hear it."

"No reason at all." She paused and then dove right in. "In 1919, a young man on the island was murdered, probably with a sword—my great-grandfather's sword, to be precise. And the story is somehow tied to your great-grandfather's store, which at one time, I believe, had a . . . well, a . . . "

"Betting parlor." He wiped the sweat from his forehead with the back of his hand.

"Right. A betting parlor in the back of the store."

He laughed. "My parents have denied that rumor for years, but we all know it's true."

"You do? For sure?" A wave of relief swept over Priscilla. "Thank goodness at least one part of the story is written in stone."

"Still don't know how the store ties into a murder though." He scratched his head. "Want to fill me in?"

"From what I understand, some have speculated that the young man who was murdered—David Pearson—possibly owed your great-grandfather a large sum of money."

"Whoa." Beau released a whistle. "I see. So my great-grandfather killed a man who refused to pay up? Is that how this story goes?"

"I'm not saying that." Priscilla swiped at her brow with the back of her hand. "It's just speculation. We're grasping at any and every straw. Your great-grandfather just happens to be . . . " Her words drifted off.

"A straw?"

"A person of interest," she countered.

"*Hmm.*" Wrinkles formed between Beau's thick brows, and he leaned against his truck. "Now I see why my mother was so perturbed that I took this job. She and Tilly Snyder had quite the conversation about you in the store this morning. And for whatever reason, she's mad at Mildred Pearson."

"Oy."

"She doesn't want me working for you, you know."

"I didn't know, but I do understand." Priscilla did her best not to sigh out loud. "Well, thank you for your time. Do you have anyone else you could recommend?"

Beau put up his hand. "I'm not saying I won't do it. I need the work. But you've got to promise me you won't get my mom stirred up. She's dealing with some health issues right now."

Priscilla gave him a compassionate look. "Would you like to come inside and have some lemonade? We can talk at the kitchen table."

"I'm kind of sweaty."

"Doesn't bother me one bit."

Moments later they both took a seat at the breakfast table, and Priscilla offered Beau a glass of lemonade and one of Candy's crème horns.

"No thanks." His nose wrinkled. "Not my favorite."

"Really?" Priscilla handed him a napkin for his glass. "I've never met anyone who didn't like Candy's crème horns."

"Well, I used to eat them all the time when she and I were dating."

"W-what?" Priscilla almost dropped her glass of lemonade. "I had no idea."

"It's old news. We broke up over a year ago." He shrugged. "Or, rather, she broke my heart a year ago. We've both moved on, but crème horns have never tasted the same since then. So thanks but no thanks."

"I'm so sorry, Beau." Priscilla placed a hand on his arm. "Let's change the subject then."

He nodded. "Tell me more about why you suspect my great-grandfather."

"Oh, I don't. Someone else mentioned his name in passing." Priscilla took a sip from her glass.

"Let me guess. Mildred Pearson?"

Priscilla reluctantly nodded.

"I guess that explains why Mom's upset at her too."

"I stopped in your family's store a while back and visited with your mom. I asked her about your great-grandfather's ledger. I don't think she was terribly happy to see me."

"She's not happy to see anyone right about now." He paused and took another sip of his lemonade then put it down. "She was diagnosed with MS a few months back. It's hit her hard."

"Oh, Beau." Priscilla rested her elbows on the table. "I'm so sorry to hear that. I should be befriending her, not needling her about your family's history. Please forgive me. And tell me how I can help."

"It might take some unraveling to make her your BFF, but I think she'll come around in time if you let this thing go." A thoughtful look came over him. "So here's what I'm going to do. I'm going to help you."

"Help me? How?"

"I'll find that ledger and look it over. If anything suspicious pops up, I'll bring it to you. I promise. I'm pretty sure there won't be anything to cause concern, but you'll be the first one to know if there is."

"Wow." She gave him a thoughtful look, grateful for his kindness. "Why would you do this, Beau?"

"I like you, Mrs. Grant. You seem like a good person." He took another swig from his glass then rose. "And you make a mean glass of lemonade too."

"Thank you."

He lifted his cap, turned it back around, and tipped it. "Better get back to work. It'll be quitting time soon, and I don't want to leave the job half done."

She walked him to the door and thought about all he'd said. What kindness he'd shown.

"You're a fine man, Beau Ortmann."

So fine, in fact, that she had to wonder why Candy Lane had broken his heart.

That would be a mystery for another day. Right now she just wanted to do one thing: fill that claw-foot tub with warm soapy water and climb in for a long, delicious soak.

Minutes later, with the sound of hammering outside ringing through the house, she settled into the tub. After a while the pounding—both inside her head and outside of her cottage—stopped.

She relaxed under the bubbles, ready to put this day's woes behind her. After a few moments, her eyes fluttered closed. Priscilla found herself imagining what David Pearson must have been thinking as he walked the trails onto the cliffs that infamous day. Had it been a day just like any other? Did he expect to find his beloved waiting for him under a brilliant sunset? Suddenly images of a shadowy figure, sword in hand, interrupted her thoughts. She could almost picture what David must have seen as his attacker lunged his way, weapon in hand.

She sat up so fast, water splashed over the edge of the tub. Her heart thumped madly. After a few long, slow breaths, she rested against the back of the tub once again. Priscilla was almost afraid to close her eyes for fear the images would return.

Her thoughts eventually shifted to the painting of the sword on her bedroom wall. She climbed out of the tub and toweled off. Something about the painting still troubled her, but she couldn't put her finger on it. Someone had gone to a great deal of effort to create the trap door, but who? James, perhaps? If so, then maybe he was trying to hide something.

After slipping on her robe, Priscilla walked into the bedroom and went straight to the painting. She stared at the color combinations, mesmerized by the intricacy. What fine brushstrokes. What mesmerizing detail. Though foreboding, it was a true work of art.

The longer she stared at it, the more intrigued she became. The painting had a familiar feel to it, and not just because it mimicked the actual sword. The artistry itself felt familiar.

She studied every square inch of the painting, hoping, praying, she would find something to squelch the nagging suspicions that now gripped her.

Just about the time she was ready to give up...she did.

CHAPTER NINETEEN

The following morning, Priscilla received a call from Gerald.

"Just wanted you to know your car will be ready this afternoon. I've already asked Ivan to bring it to you. He can take care of the payment at your place if you like."

"Wow, that's curb service."

"No, that's Vineyard service. How are you today?"

"Just resting after my adventure yesterday. Having the cousins and Uncle Hugh over to lunch."

"That should be fun." He paused. "Don't know that this is the best time to share this news, but I did a little digging and came up with something."

"Digging?"

"Yes. I went back through old police records from 1919 and found out that a police report was filed the night before David Pearson was killed. Want to guess who filed it?"

"I have no idea."

"Your great-grandfather, James Latham. He reported his sword missing."

"Whoa. So he couldn't have murdered David Pearson if the sword was missing."

"Right. Though some would argue that the timing of the report was a bit too convenient."

"Ah, I see. He might've filed the report to turn suspicion to someone else."

"Right." Gerald shrugged. "I just thought you might like to know. And I've also come across the autopsy report for David Pearson. It confirms that his cause of death was stabbing."

"Wow, can I see it?"

"I don't see why not. I'll bring a copy by later on."

"I'm grateful." She paused so that she could craft her next words carefully. "In fact, I'm grateful for your support, no matter how this thing turns out, Gerald."

"Glad to offer it. I don't mind a little mystery. In fact, if you're not busy, I could swing by now with that autopsy report."

"Of course."

He arrived a short while later, paperwork in hand. They looked it over, sitting side by side on the sofa.

"See what I mean?" Gerald pointed to a particular line in the autopsy report. "He died of blood loss after a stabbing. Pierced him clean through too."

Priscilla shivered. "Confirms what I read in an article Mildred pulled up. What a horrible way to go. So was the sword used or not?"

Gerald shrugged. "I guess? The entry point was in the back, and the exit point was near the naval."

"In the back? So the murderer caught him unaware. That's awful."

"The whole thing is awful." Gerald folded the paper and handed it to her. "But maybe this will help you guys figure out what really happened." A call came through on his radio, and he rose from the sofa. "Sorry, but I've got to run."

She thanked him for stopping by and then waved as he headed out to his car. She then went to work prepping lunch for her family. They arrived at eleven thirty, Uncle Hugh leading the way.

"Hope you've got some good grub over here, Priscilla. I haven't had a decent bite to eat in weeks."

"Here we go again." Gail sighed. "Hi, Priscilla. Thanks for having us."

"My pleasure." She felt the edges of her lips tug upward in a smile as she thought about the news she was about to share.

"You're up to something," Uncle Hugh observed.

"Yes, I agree." Gail gave her a probing look. "What are you hiding, Priscilla?"

"I do have something," Priscilla responded, her heart pounding a bit faster. "I think I've figured out who hid the sword in the wall."

"You have?" Gail clamped a hand over her mouth and pulled it away. "Who?"

Priscilla squared her shoulders as she responded, "Aunt Marjorie."

"Aunt Marjorie?" the cousins and Uncle Hugh repeated in unison.

"What makes you think that?" Joan asked.

"Follow me, and I'll show you." She led the way into the bedroom and pointed at the painting. "I've wondered for ages why Marjorie, who decorated all other areas of the cottage with a beach theme, would leave this rather foreboding painting on the wall. It just didn't make sense. But she obviously wanted it here for some reason, right?"

Joan shrugged. "I guess."

"Anyway, I gave it a closer look, and guess what I found?"

Trudy, Gail, and Joan leaned in close to look at the painting.

"Just looks like the same old painting I remember seeing all my life." Trudy shrugged. "Nothing has changed."

"Check out the initials at the bottom, where the artist signed it." Priscilla pointed.

Gail gasped. "Oh my goodness. ML."

"Marjorie Latham," Trudy and Joan spoke together.

"Aunt Marjorie painted the picture?" Gail asked.

"Yes. I believe she wanted to honor Great-Grandpa's legacy but couldn't bear to look at the sword because of the accusations against him."

"I guess that makes sense." Gail gave the picture another look.

"And the Scripture makes sense too if you think about it. Marjorie was never one to hold a grudge, as I recall. Look at the verse again with her in mind."

"'And by thy sword shalt thou live, and shalt serve thy brother,'" Trudy read aloud. "'And it shall come to pass when thou shalt have the dominion, that thou shalt break his yoke from off thy neck.'"

Priscilla offered the explanation that had come to her after serious contemplation. "I truly believe she wanted to break the yoke of guilt and suspicion that had hung over our family because of the sword. That's my take on it anyway."

Uncle Hugh let out a whistle. "Good work, Priscilla. And I can confirm that your aunt Marjorie was a painter. There's a garden scene that hangs above our mantel. She painted it just a few years before she passed away."

"And she painted the prettiest seagulls too," Trudy added. "I remember as a child receiving one of her paintings."

They all stood and stared at the painting of the sword as if seeing it for the first time. The mood in the room was intense... until Uncle Hugh's stomach gurgled.

He rubbed his belly. "Can we finish all of this over lunch?"

"Of course." Priscilla led the way to the kitchen, where she set out the lunch items: chicken salad, croissants from the bakery, fruit, and chips. And her favorite, sweet tea. She'd never seen Uncle Hugh so happy.

As they ate, Trudy quizzed her about the trip to Aquinnah. Priscilla deliberately left out the part where she'd climbed the railing to snag her phone.

"I hear you almost went headfirst into the Atlantic," Joan said when she finished the story.

"What? Who told you that?"

"Candy. She heard it from Sheila." Joan took a bite of her sandwich. "This is delicious."

"Cranberry Sheila?"

"Yes. She heard it from someone at the Coast Guard station."

"Not Gerald, I hope."

"No." Joan shook her head. "One of the younger guys who stopped by to check on her after she took a tumble in the bog. You heard about that, right?"

"No, definitely didn't hear that one."

"Oh, Sheila's got some real war stories." Trudy laughed. "One of these days you should sit down with her and let her share a few of them. They'll have you in stitches."

"Hey, speaking of war stories…" Gail turned to face her father. "Dad, I was thinking this would be a good day to share a few of your grandpa's stories, the ones you used to tell when I was young."

"That long ago, eh?" He chuckled and then leaned back in his chair. "What do you want to hear?"

"Any of his battle stories you can remember."

"I remember nearly every one." A delighted look came over him, and he appeared to drift away in his memories. "As a boy I reenacted most of them, so they're forever etched in my memory."

"Wow. Tell us," Priscilla said. "Please?"

"Well, let's see." He appeared to be thinking. "You know, battles during the first World War weren't like now. The Allies worked in trenches, not above ground. It was safer."

"Right." Priscilla looked around the table to make sure no one needed seconds.

"There were no cell phones, no e-mail, no way to get information other than Morse code. So many times they were working blind. Grandpa Latham was stationed near the French-Swiss border. He saw artillery exchanges and sniping. Things like that."

"Did he ever get wounded?" Priscilla asked.

"Yes, but not badly enough to return home. Happened in the winter. The weather was taking a toll on both sides, as you might imagine. Especially those closest to the front lines."

This certainly caught her attention. "Is that where Great-Grandpa was?"

"Yes. Chester Snyder too."

"Wow. The front lines." Priscilla paused. "No wonder folks were so angry with men like David Pearson who didn't have to serve while others were risking their lives at the front of the line."

"Yep. There was a particular bombardment that did in some of the trenches, as I recall. And they also battled flooding down there."

"Flooding, icy cold, and continual artillery fire from the other side." Priscilla picked up her empty plate and carried it to the sink. "Puts my woes in perspective. I thought I'd lived through hard times."

"I see now why they call it 'in the trenches' when you're going through something hard." Joan stood and gathered the rest of the plates then joined Priscilla at the sink.

"Imagine being soaked most of the time and terrified for your life too." Uncle Hugh's voice grew more animated. "Then, just about the time you think you can relax a bit, one of your buddies is hit by a sniper."

"Was Great-Grandpa hit too?" Trudy asked, now sitting on the edge of her seat.

"He always considered it the biggest miracle of his life. He was grazed on the left ear as a bullet whizzed by but wasn't injured at all. Well, other than a scratch anyway."

"Wow, how did we not know this?"

Uncle Hugh seemed a bit more reflective now. "I remember Grandpa saying he went to war a boy and came back a man."

"And Chester?"

"*Hmm.*" Uncle Hugh paused and appeared to be thinking. "I remember Chester Snyder, though of course I only ever referred to him as Mr. Snyder. He was my elder and a serviceman, a good friend to Grandpa Latham."

"So they remained friends." Priscilla pondered that notion as she filled the sink with soapy water.

"For as long as I can remember."

"Interesting."

Gail rose and carried the empty tea glasses to the sink. "Let's think this through. If Great-Grandpa killed David Pearson and Chester Snyder knew about it, he would have turned on him. Right? I mean, you don't stick with a friend who commits murder."

Her father shrugged. "Depends, I guess."

"And if Chester did the deed and Great-Grandpa knew about it, he would've told the police." Gail set the glasses in the soapy water. "He would've ended the friendship then and there, I'm sure."

"I've got to believe that," Priscilla said, "based on all the stories I know about him."

"Here's a tidbit I'll bet you didn't know." Uncle Hugh struggled to get out of his chair. "Grandpa Latham really did come back a hero. He saved the life of one of the men in his unit."

"How?" Trudy asked as she rose to help Uncle Hugh.

"The fellow took one in the leg and was bleeding out. Grandpa took off his shirt and tore off strips of fabric to tie off the bleeder until the medic could arrive."

"Who was the man? Do you know?" Trudy slipped her arm underneath her uncle's and helped him stand.

Once he was standing, Uncle Hugh shrugged. "No idea. Wasn't Chester, if that's what you're wondering."

"Any such exciting tales with Chester?" Priscilla asked. "Was he a hero too?"

Uncle Hugh gripped the back of his chair and looked her way. "Honey, they were *all* heroes in our book. I wasn't born until years later, but I saw the photographs my mother had clipped from the paper."

"We need to go back to the museum and give the newspapers a closer look, factoring in what we now know. I'll bet we find lots of clues." Priscilla got excited just thinking about it.

"You'll find war heroes being paraded up and down the street. But I doubt you'll find out more than that." Uncle Hugh snapped his fingers. "Actually, I do know a story about Chester Snyder. I'm sure Tilly could tell you more, but it seems he worked as a medic. Grandpa said sometimes the shells from the Germans were like rain pouring down behind the trench. I think Chester had a hard time dealing with the numbers of wounded."

"Are you saying Chester came back to the States with psychological problems?" Priscilla asked.

"Girl, every soldier comes back from war with issues. Every man who offers his life in service of his country needs time to rehabilitate his heart, his mind, and his body. Ask me how I know."

"Dad served in the Vietnam War," Gail explained.

At once, Uncle Hugh's smile faded. "And came back a broken man. It did something to me. This knee issue of mine really is an old war wound. That's not just a phrase to me."

Priscilla looked at him with an admiring gaze. "Thank you for your service, Uncle Hugh."

His eyes misted over as he managed a strained, "You're welcome. Don't hear that very often."

"I can't even imagine what it was like to try to acclimate to a normal life after living on the edge of terror day and night," Trudy said.

Uncle Hugh brushed at his eyes with the back of his wrinkled hand. "Not easy. We'll just leave it at that. And it has had lasting effects on many of us."

This changed everything. Her great-grandfather wasn't the only one who'd come back to the island a hero. So had Uncle Hugh. Sure, he was a bit of a curmudgeon, but who wouldn't be after surviving a war?

The conversation carried on as Priscilla and Joan washed dishes. Then Trudy offered to brew a pot of coffee, and before long they were all seated in the living room, cups in hand. Priscilla remembered that she hadn't yet shared the news about the autopsy, so she passed the paper around to her cousins.

"Gruesome." Gail shivered. "And the fact that the autopsy report clearly shows a stabbing makes me wonder...about everything."

Everyone sighed in unison.

"Did you learn anything new in Aquinnah?" Gail asked. "Besides staying on the correct side of the railing, I mean."

Priscilla nodded. "Yes. I've been trying to figure out what David was doing out on the cliffs in the first place. The Coast Guard officer I met told me the cliffs were often used by young lovers to, well, meet."

"Perfect place to watch the sunset," Uncle Hugh added. "Took my sweetie there, back in the day. We called it Lover's Lane."

"You took Mom to Lover's Lane?" Gail asked. "Wow, Pop."

His cheeks flamed red, and he coughed. "Wasn't exactly talking about your mama, girl. I did have a girlfriend or two before I met her, you know."

Gail put up her hand. "I've heard enough." She turned back to Priscilla. "You're saying that David went out there to meet Josie?"

"I'm guessing the killer—whoever he was—sent some sort of note to bait David." Priscilla sighed. "Of course, it's just speculation. I still have so many unanswered questions."

"Me too." Joan nodded. "Like, what really happened to Josie Bingham before she died?"

"Dad, did you ever hear anything about her?" Gail asked as she set her cup down. "All we know is she passed away shortly after David Pearson died."

Uncle Hugh took a sip of his coffee then, with a shaky hand, set his cup back on the table. "I don't recall hearing about anyone named Josie, at least not from Grandpa."

"Guess I'll have to keep searching to learn what really happened to her." Priscilla paused. "I only hope things don't get too complicated."

"It's unavoidable," Joan said. "This story is filled with twists and turns, and we're not the only ones making guesses. Mildred Pearson accused the Ortmanns, after all."

Priscilla shrugged. "Well, not really accused, but she's the one who let me know that Harrison Ortmann had a betting parlor behind his shop."

"Which complicates the story," Trudy chimed in. "Because Tilly Snyder and Mrs. Ortmann are friends."

"And now they're both angry at Mildred," Uncle Hugh spit out. "And you."

Priscilla sighed. "I hate that it's really come to that."

"Me too. The rumors around town are getting crazy." Her uncle shook his head and then raked his fingers through his hair. "Before long we're going to have to paint a line down the center of Tisbury and put one group on one side and the other group on the other."

"Oh my, I certainly hope not."

"It might." He gave her a knowing look. "Eldora has been spreading stories all over the town."

"I heard that Mildred and Alma had an actual tiff at the grocery store the other day, and Katie Ortmann got involved. Wasn't pretty." Gail sighed. "I never dreamed islanders would get so worked up."

Uncle Hugh looked Priscilla's way, a pleading look in his eyes. "Can I ask a favor?"

"Sure, Uncle Hugh."

"Don't stay mad at Tilly for long."

"I'm not mad at her, Uncle Hugh. Truly."

"Good. Because the idea of Tisbury being split down the middle, half the people on her side and half on ours only means one thing."

"No watermelon pickles?"

"No hummingbird cake." He licked his lips. "And I can't live without hummingbird cake."

"You can always get it at Candy's bakery, Dad," Gail said.

"Yes, but what you don't know is this: I go back and forth between the inn and the bakery, eating hummingbird cake as I please. When Candy scolds me and sends me away, I just toodle on over to Tilly's, and so forth."

"Uncle Hugh! Your blood sugar must be off the charts." Joan looked flabbergasted. "How long have you been pulling these shenanigans?"

"Oh, for years. And I'll have you know my blood sugar is perfect. Probably the exercise. All that walking back and forth has kept me in shape. Wore out my knee, but kept my blood sugar down."

Gail looked stunned at all of this. "Here I am, feeding you healthy food, making sure you get your rest and take your vitamins, and you've been living on a steady diet of hummingbird cake?"

"*Mm-hmm.* And I'm a happier man for it." He rubbed his belly. "And please don't say anything about the extra five pounds I've put on. I'll work it off." He gave her a grudging nod.

"Me? Fuss at you?" She rolled her eyes.

"You're like a nurse, only dressed in regular clothes. Always telling me what to do."

"C'mon, Dad. You know you love me."

"You're kin."

"Well, that's not much of an answer, Dad." Gail shook her head. "Of course I'm kin, but that's not the same thing as saying, 'I care about you.' I show you every day with my actions, and I say it with my mouth too. But I rarely hear anything in response but a few grunts and complaints."

His brows furrowed, and an awkward pause followed.

Gail rose and grabbed her empty cup. "I'm going to make more coffee. Priscilla, care to join me?"

"Of course." Priscilla rose and followed her into the kitchen then went to work making the coffee herself. Gail looked too rattled to be working anyway.

Neither of them said a word until a male voice broke the silence.

"C'mon, Gail. Don't hold a grudge against your old pop. I've never been one to voice my emotions out loud. You know that."

Priscilla looked up from the coffeepot to see Uncle Hugh had joined them.

Gail turned to face her father. "Right. I know that." She lowered her voice. "And I'm sure Marigold Townsend would agree. She'd probably like you to work up the courage to speak your thoughts out loud sometimes too."

A sad look came over Uncle Hugh. "We all get along fine, don't we, Gail? Aren't things great the way they are?"

"Yes, we get along fine." She turned her face to the window, and Priscilla felt sure she saw tears in her cousin's eyes. "But maybe Tommy and I would like to get along finer. Did you ever consider that possibility?"

Fine lines formed between Uncle Hugh's eyes as he gazed at his daughter. "What do you mean?"

"I'm still young and healthy, Pop," Gail said.

"And you have all your teeth." He shook his head. "What's your point?"

"Pop, really?" She put her hands on her hips.

Uncle Hugh coughed and then lifted his cup. "That coffee gonna be ready anytime soon, Priscilla?"

"Always avoiding the question." Gail released a slow breath. "At least you're consistent."

"Thank you. I'll take that as a compliment. Now, when is someone gonna fill my cup with hot coffee? I need a jolt of java."

"Just hold your horses, Uncle Hugh," Priscilla countered. "It's almost ready."

"Hey, speaking of horses..." He lit into another story, this one involving warhorses. His overly animated tone sounded forced, at best. Priscilla tried to pay attention but found herself distracted by the mist of tears in her cousin's eyes.

Poor Gail.

Before Priscilla could give it another thought, Gail grabbed her dad's mug, filled it with hot coffee, slid it his way, and then marched back into the living room.

"If looks could kill, I'd be dead right now." Hugh took a sip of his coffee, and a smile tipped up the corners of his mouth. "Oh, but what a way to go, girlie. What a way to go."

CHAPTER TWENTY

On Saturday afternoon Priscilla and Gail decided to meet for an afternoon treat at the bakery. Priscilla waved at Candy, who greeted her with a "Hey, you!" before turning to finish up an order with a customer at the counter.

Priscilla found a table and waited for Gail to arrive. She entered a short time later, and then they placed their orders. Priscilla sipped a glass of blackberry tea and leaned back in her chair, a couple of yet-unanswered questions floating through her mind.

"While I have you here, Gail..." Priscilla looked across the bakery and watched Candy at work behind the counter. "I'm dying to know something."

"What's that?" Gail took a sip of her water.

"You know Beau Ortmann is working on my home."

"Right. He's one of Tommy's best workers. Does great work. What about him?"

"Beau mentioned in passing that he and Candy..." She lowered her voice so as not to be heard. "Well, that they were once an item."

Gail put her glass down, eyes now wider than before. "More than an item. We all felt sure they were headed to the altar."

"Right. So that's why I wonder: did she really break his heart? He implied as much." Priscilla fixed her gaze on Candy. A ripple of laughter came from that side of the room as a customer said something funny to her. "She's such a sweet thing. I can't imagine her breaking anyone's heart."

"Ah." Gail shifted her position in her chair. "Well, it's not what you think. She didn't fall for someone else or anything like that." She lowered her voice and leaned forward. "See, Candy was a caregiver for her mother, who had cancer."

"Oh, I'm so sorry to hear that. Sounds a bit like your story, doesn't it?"

"Yes, but with a different ending. Her mother passed away some time back. We were all sad when it happened. Ruth Lane was a shining light on this island. But my point is, Candy's relationship with Beau came at the most awkward time, when her mother was really bad off. I think something inside of Candy just couldn't handle the mix of joy and pain at the same time. He proposed—and she's told me herself that she wanted to say yes but couldn't. Not at that time. She asked for space, and he gave it to her. It's been over a year now."

"So he said. But I wonder why she doesn't just reopen that door and let him walk through it?"

"I've often wondered the same thing myself."

Candy chose that very moment to arrive at their table. "Glad to see you went with the cupcakes, ladies. Let me know what you think about the addition of the dried cranberries, okay? Sheila's been after me for ages to add them, and I think they're wonderful."

"Sometimes doing something new and unexpected is a good move." Priscilla flashed a broad smile.

"Right. Well, since you brought that up..." Candy took a seat at the table and looked Priscilla's way. "Let's chat."

"Sure."

"You ladies know that folks on the island love my hummingbird cake." Candy beamed with obvious pride.

"Uncle Hugh in particular," Priscilla said.

"Well, I've come up with a new recipe. It was all Sheila's idea, to be honest. I've added cranberries to the mix."

"Bananas, pineapple, and...cranberries?" Gail looked perplexed.

"I know." Candy chuckled. "Doesn't sound like they go together at all, but you be the judge." She disappeared for a couple of minutes and returned to the table with a slice of cake on a plate. She handed them each a fork. "Give it a go, and let me know what you think."

Priscilla took a little nibble of the cake and found herself mesmerized by the taste. "Wow, Candy," she said after swallowing. "I'd say you have a real winner here."

"You think?" Candy nearly glowed.

"It's amazing," Gail added then took another bite.

"I never would've guessed that cranberries would work in the mix, but I was wrong." Priscilla stabbed her fork into the slice of cake and took a big bite this time. "*Mmm.*"

"What are you calling it?" Gail asked.

"That's the best part, and that's what I wanted to talk to you about." Candy pulled up a chair and sat down again. "I'm calling it the Tisbury Tizzy."

"Tisbury Tizzy?"

"Yep. A cake so good it's guaranteed to put an end to the divisions in town."

"Put an end to divisions?" Gail took another bite. "What do you mean?"

"I had this idea that I'd throw a debut party, offer everyone in town a slice of the Tisbury Tizzy for free. I'll get the whole town in here with the promise of cake and coffee…on me."

"Sounds nice. But what if people start dueling inside your bakery?" Gail asked.

"Impossible. Once they fill up on cake, dueling will be the furthest thing from their minds."

"I hope you're right about that." Priscilla took another bite. "It is awfully good."

"Thanks. Now, here's my plan." She began spilling all of her ideas for the cake debut party.

Priscilla stared at Candy, wondering where all this excitement and energy was coming from. Something was stirring in Candy-land right now, something she wasn't admitting. What had put the sparkle in her eye and the zeal in her conversation? Priscilla had her suspicions. "And all of this is going to transpire because of a cake?" she asked.

"Every once in a while I hit on a recipe that really resonates with the people, and I believe this is the latest, greatest one." She pointed to the plate. "Ladies, the Tisbury Tizzy is not a cake to be taken lightly. I honestly believe it will calm the waters once we gather folks together."

"I would never take an excellent cake lightly," Priscilla chimed in, "and this one does seem to have amazing powers. I can't stop eating it."

"It's the combination of cranberries and cream cheese." Candy put her finger over her lips. "But I'm not telling because I don't like to give away trade secrets."

"I see." Priscilla didn't, but was happy to let Candy carry on.

"Now, we'll have to figure out the details, of course. Send out invitations and so on. You gals help me spread the word. I'll supply the cake, coffee, and maybe a few other sweets, and let the chips fall where they may."

Gail did not look convinced. "I'm not sure about this. You've seen how grumpy folks are these days. What if we get them here and things go south? Let's say we put this whole thing together and it implodes? Things could end up worse than they already are."

"That's the beauty of doing it in a group setting," Candy explained. "Folks like Alma and Eldora would never react negatively in front of their friends and family. They would be forced to play along."

"That's what you think." Gail picked up her near-empty water glass and swallowed the remaining liquid. She then popped a piece of ice into her mouth and chewed it.

"I love everything about this idea," Priscilla said as the plan took root in her heart. "I really do. And while we're at it, let's invite Tilly Snyder."

"Of course," Candy agreed. "She's at the top of the list, right there with Fred Pearson."

"If this Tisbury Tizzy is as powerful as you think it is, then we've got to invite Katie Ortmann too. All of the people in town who are angry at us should be here. That way we'll kill two—er, three or four—birds with one stone."

Gail snorted. "I hope the only thing that ends up dead after this get-together is those figurative birds you speak of, not the guests. They could turn on each other in a heartbeat."

"And when they do, I will hand them a slice of cake," Candy declared. "Easy-breezy."

"You're forgetting one thing, Candy." Gail leaned forward and lowered her voice. "And it's an important thing."

Candy's brow wrinkled. "What's that?"

"Tilly Snyder has already told everyone on the island that her hummingbird cake is the best. She's going to flip when she learns you've come up with a newer, better recipe."

"Here's an idea," Priscilla suggested. "Ask her to bring her hummingbird cake so folks can enjoy both versions. We'll eat until we're sick."

Candy took a moment to respond to this one but finally nodded. "Okay. Might bring down walls between Tilly and me if we do that. We've long had this rivalry, you know."

"We know," Gail and Priscilla spoke in unison.

"Sounds like a wonderful party—half the people upset at the others and the other half nauseated." Gail shook her head. "But I'm game. I'll help you spread the word."

"Me too," Priscilla agreed.

"Perfect! Let's set the date for next Saturday, shall we?" Candy rose and clasped her hands together. "Oh, I have so much to do! I can hardly wait." She flitted away, greeting a couple of other guests as she made her way into the kitchen.

Priscilla looked Gail's way, her curiosity growing. "Why do you suppose Candy is suddenly interested in everyone making up? That might be an interesting thing to investigate."

"Yes, I suspect there's more to that than we know." Gail pushed her chair back and stood up. "She had quite the sparkle in her eye, didn't she? Haven't seen that kind of life in her eyes since she and Beau broke up. But that's her business. It's not my story, so I wouldn't want to speculate."

"I'm the queen of speculations," Priscilla said. "And my mind is reeling right now."

"I pray this plan of hers works." Gail paused and then shook her head. "The Tisbury Tizzy. What a name."

"Guaranteed to calm the waters and squelch rumors." Priscilla wanted to stand up, but with cake left on the plate, she couldn't seem to. She jabbed her fork back into the sweet treat one more time and took a big bite. "*Mmm.*"

Maybe God was up to something here. And maybe—she pondered as she licked the fork—He planned to use a cake to work an honest-to-goodness miracle for the people of Martha's Vineyard.

CHAPTER TWENTY-ONE

After leaving the bakery, Priscilla decided a stop at the museum was in order to see if Mildred had stumbled across any additional information that might be relevant to the case. She found the curator in the nineteenth-century room polishing the silver. Priscilla couldn't help but notice the tears in her friend's eyes as she greeted her.

"Mildred? Everything okay?"

Mildred turned away from her work to look at Priscilla. She shook her head and said, "Not really."

"What's happened?"

Mildred put the silver teapot down and remained silent for a moment. "We just got word this morning that my dad has lung cancer."

"Oh, Mildred!" Priscilla rushed her way and wrapped her friend in her arms. "I'm so very sorry."

"We've seen the signs of a lung infection—or something anyway—for a while now. He's had a never-ending cough and a few other symptoms. But I never dreamed it was cancer." Mildred shook her head. "It's just surreal. Things can change so quickly."

"They can." Priscilla thought about Gary and the abruptness of his death. "I'm so sorry, Mildred. What can I do to help?"

Her friend shrugged. "The church is putting together a meal train to bring food to his house daily. I guess you could sign up for that." She pursed her lips. "You know my mom's living in a care facility, right?"

"Yes, I remember. Dementia, right?"

Mildred nodded. "It's just too much to fathom—Mom and Dad both facing their own crises and they can't even be together." Tears filled her eyes. "I honestly don't know how much more I can take."

"I'm so sorry, Mildred." Priscilla rested her hand on her friend's arm.

"Dad hasn't come to grips with the reality of his diagnosis yet. To be honest, he hasn't even come to grips with the fact that Mom isn't in the house anymore. This is all going to take time."

"Yes, and probably lots of it." Priscilla squeezed Mildred's arm. "But I will be praying, I promise."

"Thank you."

"I'm also going to work double-time to find out who really killed your great-uncle. Maybe knowing will help with your dad's healing process."

"Maybe." Mildred shrugged. "Is anything new stirring on that front, other than folks not speaking to one another?"

"Candy has an interesting solution for the town split."

"So I heard. She just called me."

"Do you think your dad will come?"

"Who knows. Maybe. Anything else stirring, besides a new cake recipe?"

"I can't stop thinking about one avenue we haven't traveled down," Priscilla responded. "We've discussed Edward Bingham a few times, but I haven't really done much in the way of investigating him. What if I called his son in Falmouth?"

"And asked him . . . what? If he knows whether or not his father committed murder? That would be a delightful conversation."

"No." Priscilla fumbled around in her purse until she came up with her phone. "Just, you know, chitchat." She pulled up the search engine on her phone and typed in the words *Bingham Inn Falmouth*. Half a second later, her phone's tiny screen filled with photos of the inn, which appeared to be quite lovely. She quickly located the phone number.

"Can I use your office to make the call?" she asked. "I don't want to wander through the museum on a call."

"Of course."

Priscilla followed Mildred into the small office then called the number of the Bingham Inn. While waiting for someone to pick up on the other end, she paced the small room. A gentleman answered with a rushed, "Hello?"

"Hi there. I'm wondering if I could speak to Edward Bingham."

"Eddie? Hold one second and I'll get him." The gentleman disappeared, and another man picked up the line a moment later, this one with a frail voice.

"This is Eddie."

She swallowed hard then dove right in. "Mr. Bingham, you don't know me, but my name is Priscilla Grant."

"Mrs. Grant." His voice trembled as he spoke. "How can I help you?"

"Well, I know this might sound odd, but I'm in the process of doing some research into my family tree. I've learned that our families' paths crossed."

"How so?"

"Ah." She paused. "Well, my great-grandfather grew up in the same town as your father."

"That so?"

"Yes. I believe they were acquainted, especially during the period just after the war."

"I see. So how can I help you?"

So far, so good. "I'm wondering if you can tell me whatever became of your aunt Josie."

He paused and then responded with, "Who?"

"Josie Bingham. She was your father's sister, so your aunt."

"I'm sorry, who did you say this is again?" He sounded flustered.

"I'm Priscilla Grant from Tisbury, the town where your dad, Edward, and his sister, Josie, grew up."

"Sorry, but I don't know what you mean." The level of confusion in his voice rose. "My dad was from Tisbury, yes, but he never had a sister. He was an only child."

"Oh no," Priscilla said. "His sister was Josie. She was quite a few years younger than him, but she definitely existed. We know that your dad moved to Falmouth and opened an inn, and we..."

"Who is we?"

"Oh, several of us . . . history buffs here on the island. I'm making this call from the history museum where we're trying to piece together your father's story."

"Look, I don't know what you're up to, but this isn't funny. My dad died when I was in high school, and I can assure you there are no other living relatives on the Bingham side. I'm guessing you have the wrong number. Try some other Binghams."

"But . . . "

The call ended, and Priscilla stared at the phone.

"What did he say?"

Priscilla turned to discover Mildred standing in the office doorway. "He said I had the wrong number, that his father was an only child."

"Whoa."

"He didn't seem to have any notion that he'd ever had an aunt named Josie. Don't you find that odd?"

"Very. We know she existed. We saw her photos in the paper. She was there at the parade, standing next to her brother."

"Who had a son, Eddie. That's how he answered the phone. So we're talking about the same Bingham family. He runs the inn in Falmouth. Pretty elderly, based on the voice."

"I guess he'd have to be. Are you *sure* he said his father was an only child?"

"Positive. He said those very words. But we all know he wasn't."

"You know, Priscilla, we're talking about a man who's got to be in his late eighties or older. Maybe he's just losing his memory."

"He sounded sharp as a tack." Priscilla paced the room. "There's only one conclusion to be drawn. Edward was so ashamed of Josie that he wrote her out of his life and never spoke of her again." She paused and faced Mildred. "Was Eddie Jr. an only child?"

"I believe so, but I can confirm it with census records."

"Then that's it. Josie disappeared, never to be heard from again, and Edward moved to Falmouth, where he—for whatever reason—let people think he had no family at all."

"He didn't have a family. No parents. No sister."

"He had a wife. But maybe he gag ordered her. You know?" Priscilla plopped down in a chair.

"Right. Wonder whatever happened to that wife?"

"I don't know." Priscilla slumped down in the chair. "One thing's for sure. I never considered Edward Bingham a suspect. Throughout this whole ordeal, I'd never tagged him as a whodunit character." She paused as she remembered the photo of the sour-faced man standing next to Josie at the parade. "That is, until now."

CHAPTER TWENTY-TWO

I can't get over how much nicer everything looks," Priscilla observed as she looked over the cottage's exterior. "New windows, new clapboards, a fresh coat of paint, and it's springing to life once again."

"Thanks." Beau pulled off his baseball cap and wiped perspiration from his forehead. "I think it's coming along nicely. Glad you agree." He put the cap back on and stared at the cottage for a few moments in silence.

Priscilla's heart swelled with pride at her home. "Well, you've surpassed my expectations, that's for sure. I didn't really expect such a marked difference."

"Thanks." He looked her way. "You owe most of your thanks to Tommy. He's the mastermind behind all this. Hey, speaking of old things looking new, I found something you might be interested in."

"Oh?"

Beau nodded. "Yes. It's my great-grandfather's log of who owed what to the store."

Priscilla gasped. "Really? Are the transactions from his, um, side business listed alongside folks who owed him money for flour and eggs and such?"

"Yep." Beau cleared his throat. "It didn't take me long to figure out his coding for the gambling patrons. They were all chickens, by the way."

"Chickens?"

"Yep. There are hundreds of entries for folks who owed him for chickens. Found that odd. Odder still, that all of 'em were men." Beau shrugged. "What can I say? The island was filled with chickens in 1919. Lots and lots of chickens."

Priscilla laughed. "Wow."

"Right? At first I was kind of startled by how many chicken purchasers owed my great-grandfather money. This, of course, made me more than a little suspicious. I mean, the logbook was filled with lots of other purchases too, of course. But that many men owing him money for poultry? I don't think so."

"I see your point."

"And it says a lot about how he felt about those men, I guess. He didn't see them in the best light if they were all chickens to him." Beau laughed. "Anyway, I thought you'd want to know. Oh, and by the way..."

"Yes?"

"Ortmann's didn't even sell chickens back then."

"Ah-ha. Interesting." She paused for a moment, then something occurred to her. "Just want to make sure I'm understanding this correctly. You have the names and dates of all so-called chicken purchasers"—she cleared her throat—"with their real names, right?"

"Correct."

"So you would know if David Pearson owed a large debt to your great-grandfather and when that debt occurred?"

"Sure. Forgot to look at that though."

"Can you bring me that ledger, Beau? Please? I promise not to let a thing happen to it, but I'd love to peruse it and see if I can read between the lines. Or if I can discover any big purchases by any other islanders just before the time of the murder."

"I anticipated this question. Ledger's in the truck, and I'll be happy to loan it to you. But let's keep this between us, okay?"

"Please do. Maybe I was grasping at the wrong straws. Maybe David didn't owe your great-grandfather a penny—for chickens or otherwise." A nervous chuckle wriggled out. "You know?"

"Might be funny to clear his name with a chicken order." Beau laughed. "This is a strange conversation we're having."

"Indeed. Do you mind if I pass this information on to my cousins? I know they will be interested."

"I'm sure my mother's blood pressure will go up if she knows people are talking, but it's only right that your family should have this information. I'll be right back with the ledger." He walked to his truck and returned moments later, book in hand. "Hope you're able to find what you need."

"Me too. And thank you, Beau. You've been great."

"You're welcome."

"By the way . . . " She reached over and placed her hand on his arm. "I've been praying for your mom. Every day. I hope that one day she and I can be friends. I really do. I'm already working on a plan for that actually."

"A plan?"

"Yes. It involves hummingbird cake."

"Ah, Candy's party." The edges of his lips turned up in a smile.

"Yep." Priscilla couldn't help but laugh. "Reconciliation through sugar."

"Heard all about it." For whatever reason, his cheeks flushed pink. "It has healing properties."

"I'm living proof. I had a piece the other day, and the world is looking much brighter now."

"Interesting. Can't wait to see what you ladies have up your sleeves." He gave her an admiring look.

"Can't wait to see what you've got up yours either." She left those words as a teaser, hoping he'd take the bait and share a tidbit about Candy. Unfortunately, the sound of tires in her driveway distracted them. Tommy Townsend pulled in with more supplies in the back of his truck. She waved and then headed back inside.

At lunchtime, Priscilla decided to take her sandwich and fruit outside, where she sat at the picnic table facing the water. Jake sat at attention next to her, probably hoping she would drop a piece of lunch meat. Priscilla made it easy on him and tossed him a piece of turkey. "That's for not tearing up my garden today, boy."

"Spoiling him already?" A male voice sounded from behind her. Priscilla turned and saw Gerald. "Sorry, didn't mean to startle you."

"Oh, it's fine." She gestured for him to sit across from her. "Are you hungry? I have plenty more inside."

"Just finished my lunch—a tuna sandwich. I always bring my lunch on Wednesdays." He shrugged. "What can I say? I'm a creature of habit. I eat at the inn on Mondays, the bakery on Tuesday, bring my lunch on Wednesday, and so on. Saturdays I take my grandson to have burgers and ice cream."

"Sounds like quite the routine."

"Yeah." He rubbed his belly. "Trust me, I need to stay away from Candy's bakery and those crème horns."

"Trust me, I'll be in new clothes before winter if I keep eating sweets at the current rate."

"I wouldn't worry too much about that if I were you." His warm smile was pretty convincing. "Hey, I saw Beau pull away as I rounded the turn in the road. How are the renovations coming along?"

"Great. They've finished the front completely. What did you think of the paint job?"

"Looks great." He paused. "So what's the latest?"

"The latest?"

"You know...the latest. You always seem to know the goings-on around here these days."

She paused before asking, "Do you think I'm a gossip?"

"A gossip?" He looked perplexed by this.

"Yes, a gossip. Like Eldora and some of the others. I've spent a lot of time lately talking about other people on the island as I've tried to iron the kinks out of this story involving my great-grandfather."

"Someone once told me that it's not gossip if it involves you."

"Don't tell my uncle Hugh that, okay?" She sighed. "I don't mean to hurt people by talking about them behind their back. I'm truly sad that Tilly Snyder's upset at me. But I don't know any way around the fact that her family is somehow involved in this. And I think Katie Ortmann's a wonderful person too. I didn't write this particular piece of history, you know? It's writing me. Or rather, it's writing the plotline in my current situation, if that makes sense."

"Not much about this makes sense to me."

"I hate that the town of Tisbury is so divided over all this, and I feel like I'm partly to blame."

"What we need is something to pull all of us together, something that will make everyone happy."

"Oh, trust me, Candy's already working on that. She's hosting a party to celebrate the release of her newest cake, the Tisbury Tizzy."

"Funny name."

"*Mm-hmm*. And the point of the party is to bring people together. She's just using the cake as a way to draw them in."

"Interesting. Well, speaking of Candy, I have a little tidbit for you. You might be able to accuse me of being a gossip after you hear it though."

"Oh?"

"Beau and Candy. They're back together."

"What?" Priscilla felt her jaw drop. "How did you find out?"

"I stopped in at the bakery for a cup of coffee early this morning before heading to work. Who do you think I saw sitting at the counter, eating a crème horn?"

"A crème horn?" Priscilla suddenly got a case of the giggles. "Oh my."

"Yep. And he looked pretty cozy. So did Candy. She fixed him a cappuccino. That was always his beverage of choice when they were together."

"I knew something was up." Priscilla laughed. "I thought I saw a certain sparkle in her eye. His too."

He quirked a brow. "A certain sparkle, eh? Is that how you can tell if someone's falling for someone else?"

"Oh, definitely." Priscilla paused, deep in thought over his news. "Could I interest you in a cup of coffee?"

"I'd love one."

"Great. Follow me to the kitchen." She reached down and picked up her leftovers and almost forgot about the ledger. "Better get this inside."

"What have you got there?"

"Oh, the ledger from the Ortmann's store, circa 1919."

"Really. What are you looking for?"

"I just need to figure out one thing—whether or not David Pearson was a chicken."

Gerald's brows creased. "Excuse me?"

"I know that some people accused him of being a chicken as far as fighting for his country was concerned, but was he a chicken in the way that Harrison Ortmann was concerned?"

Gerald laughed. "Is this going to be a one-cup-of-coffee story or two?"

Priscilla laughed. "Probably two."

"Well, good. Take as long as you like. I just happen to be on a break right now." He gave her a warm smile, and they walked along the garden path together toward the cottage.

CHAPTER TWENTY-THREE

The following morning, Priscilla invited the cousins over for breakfast. She couldn't wait to show them what she had discovered. After explaining that Beau had given her the Ortmann's ledger, Trudy gasped.

"God bless that sweet boy. I always liked him."

"Love his mama too," Gail said. "She's really a sweetheart. Such a shame about all she's going through."

"I'd like to talk with you ladies a little later about how we can help her." Priscilla opened the ledger. "But first I want to share some things with you. I'll start by showing you everything that Great-Grandpa Latham purchased from the store in the month prior to the murder." She flipped the pages of the book, going back to the weeks leading up to David Pearson's death. "Looks like he bought soap."

"No crime in that," Joan said. "Everyone buys soap."

"I would hope so." Trudy's eyes lit up. "Maybe he planned to murder David Pearson and then use the soap to clean up afterward."

"That would be a stretch, Trudy," Gail said. "Besides, we're not looking for reasons to incriminate our own great-grandfather."

"Oh, right." She shrugged. "It's like a game to me now. Solving it is fun."

"And remember," Priscilla interrupted them, "David's dead body was found on the cliffs. There was no clean-up."

This seemed to let the air out of everyone's speculation.

"Now let's switch gears. I took a good, long look at David Pearson's purchases. I needed to know whether or not he owed the Ortmanns any money for chickens."

"Chickens?" All three cousins spoke in unison.

"Was there a run on poultry in 1919 or something?" Gail asked.

"No." Priscilla chuckled. "I'll explain that later. I went on a search for chicken debts…" She ran her finger along the various names, pausing every time she saw David Pearson's. "And…voilà. No chickens."

"Looks like he bought the usual supplies and food a person would buy in 1919," Joan said. "But I see no reference to chickens."

"Which lets Harrison Ortmann off the hook." Priscilla closed the book and grinned.

"Wait…what?" Trudy scratched her head. "Ortmann is no longer a suspect because David Pearson didn't owe him money for chickens?"

"That is correct." Priscilla did her best to explain Harrison Ortmann's gambling code, and before long all of her cousins were nodding.

"Oh, I see." Trudy grabbed the book from her. "Well, let's see who *did* owe him money for chickens." She opened the ledger and ran her finger along the list of customers until it landed on a name that caused her to gasp. She tossed the book aside.

"Trudy, what is it?" Priscilla asked.

"Great-Grandma Latham. She owed Mr. Ortmann money for a chicken. See it for yourself: July 12, 1919."

Joan laughed. "I'm sure that was a real chicken, Trudy. Don't get excited."

"Ortmann's didn't sell chickens back then." Priscilla gave it a closer look. "She didn't buy a chicken, Trudy. She bought chicken *feed*."

"Whew. For a minute there, I thought our grandmother was a closet gambler."

Gail sighed. "Where were we?"

"I think we've cleared Mr. Ortmann."

"And I've already made up my mind that Great-Grandpa didn't do it," Joan said.

"Which leads us to Chester." Gail tapped her fingers on the table. "Any strange purchases there?"

Priscilla took the book back and continued to peruse it, hoping something would jump out at her. Her finger trailed the names until she landed on a familiar one.

"Joan, look at this, will you?" She pointed at a line in the logbook. "This is a purchase made by someone named Bingham just two days before the murder."

"What is it?" Joan drew near.

"Farming tools."

"Well, he was a farmer, right?" Joan asked.

"His parents were, but then that barn fire happened. The census we located online from 1919 showed Edward's address in town by that time. He lived with his wife, Susan."

"Interesting. So he gave up farming."

"Right. Or so I thought." She gave the book another glance. "Very interesting indeed." In her heart, Priscilla knew what she had to do. "Ladies, I need to make a quick trip to Falmouth."

Joan shook her head. "No one makes a quick trip to Falmouth. You have to have a ticket to take the ferry, and that has to be arranged in advance. Unless you have a pass. Even then, you need a time slot."

"Why do you need to go to Falmouth?" Gail asked.

"I just have to see something for myself. Eddie Bingham refuses to acknowledge that he has an Aunt Josie. I want to see him face-to-face just to settle the issue in my mind, once and for all."

"What issue?"

"That it's the same Bingham family."

"Well of course it is. We know that Edward opened the inn, and now his elderly son runs it. What more do you need?"

"I have no idea, but I have to go there."

Joan sprang to life, reaching for her purse. "Take my car." She reached inside her bag for the keys and tossed them Priscilla's way. "And show my pass. If there's an opening on one of the ferries, they'll take you onboard. We'll be praying it goes well. I would go with you if I didn't have a dinner commitment."

In the blink of an eye, Priscilla found herself in Joan's car headed for the ferry landing. She managed to get the last spot onboard the ten thirty ferry headed to Woods Hole, just a hop, skip, and a jump away from Falmouth. As they crossed the waters of the Atlantic, seagulls circled the ferry. Off in the distance, Jet Ski enthusiasts raced alongside them.

Less than an hour later, Priscilla drove Joan's car off the ferry at the Woods Hole landing. Five minutes later, she found herself in the heart of Falmouth. She'd loved this town when she drove through it on her way to her new home. Now, though, she saw it through different eyes altogether.

The GPS led her straight to the Bingham Inn, right on the square. She pulled into the parking lot and found a spot. As she looked over the gorgeous building, Priscilla noted that it had a rustic feel about it. "Let's get this show on the road," she said to no one but herself.

Priscilla climbed out of the car and walked inside the spacious lobby, decorated with more rustic items that put her in mind of an old-fashioned farm. How sweet and quaint it looked.

"Is Mr. Bingham here?" she asked the young man at the front desk.

"He's in his apartment." The boy, who looked about twenty, glanced her way. "Would you like to speak to him?"

"That would be great, thanks."

She couldn't help but feel compassion for the hunched man with the silver hair who hobbled her way moments later, leaning heavy on his walker. "Can I help you?"

"Yes, thank you for seeing me. Could I have just a few moments of your time, please?"

"Sure. Why not." He led the way into his apartment just beyond the lobby and gestured for her to sit on the floral sofa. "Pardon the decor. My wife, God rest her soul, was into flowers. I didn't have the heart to redecorate after she passed."

"I think it's wonderful that you stayed on here at the inn."

"This is my home. Where else would I go?" A hint of tears brimmed his lashes. "Who did you say you are again?"

"Priscilla Grant from Martha's Vineyard. I called you from our local museum a few days ago about your father because I thought you might be able to help us with a history project."

His kind expression immediately shifted. "You're not bringing up that nonsense again, are you?"

"I have no choice." She pulled the photos of Josie she'd asked Mildred to print and handed them to Mr. Bingham. "Does she look familiar?"

"Where did you get these?" he asked as he thumbed through them.

"From the museum. Her name is Josie Bingham." Priscilla reached over and pointed at the photo of Josie and her brother standing side by side the day of the parade. "She's the sister of Edward Bingham."

"That's my father." The elderly man gazed at the photo, his hand trembling.

"Correct."

"This is the strangest thing..."

Eddie rose and hobbled to the bookshelf then returned with a photo of a beautiful young woman with dark hair. "This picture of my daughter was taken when she was in her early twenties." He held the picture of his daughter next to the photo of Josie and gasped. "She's a dead ringer."

"Yes."

His hand continued to tremble as he placed his daughter's picture on the coffee table. "It's getting harder to ignore you, Mrs. Grant. But why would my father have kept my aunt's existence a secret? Makes no sense."

"I'm sure he had his reasons. She passed away in 1920. We believe she died during childbirth."

"Childbirth? So there's another relative out there that I've not met? A cousin?"

"Possibly, though I suspect he or she would have passed on by now."

Eddie ran his fingers through his thinning silver hair. "You know, when you called, I thought you were crazy."

"I don't blame you one bit." She felt the edges of her lips curl up in a smile.

He picked up the photos again and thumbed through them, stopping when he reached the one of his father along the parade route. "I knew my father came from the Vineyard, but we rarely spoke of it. Whenever someone brought it up, he would say that was his former life. He came from a long line of farmers, you know."

"Oh, I know. I've done my research."

"It would seem you have, though I still don't know how I can help you."

"You have already," she said. "More than you know."

She spent the next several minutes sharing the things she'd learned about Josie and Edward's parents, but never hinted at the real reason for her visit. No point in letting Eddie know that she suspected his father of a crime. They carried on an easy conversation, and then he struggled to stand.

"If you're interested, I'll show you some of the things my father passed down, Mrs. Grant. We made a display of them in the lobby."

"Display?"

"Sure. You didn't see the farming tools? My wife thought it would be conversational to fill the hotel lobby with all of my dad's old things from the farm. Come, and I'll show you."

He led the way to the lobby and pointed out several of the tools attached to the wall to her right.

Priscilla took in a rusty old saw. "Wow, look at this beauty. Still got all its teeth." She snapped a photo then a second one of the jagged teeth.

"More than I can say for myself." He laughed. "Rusty too. So is this old sickle, but I hung it anyway." He pointed to an impressive hand tool with a long, slanted blade.

Priscilla paused to read a plaque underneath the sickle that read Honor. Justice. Family. She took a picture. "What's this about family honor?"

Eddie ran his hand along the handle. "Pop always said this sickle was his favorite tool of the trade and brought honor to his family. These items are among the few that survived the fire, so they meant a lot to him."

"Nice." She nodded. "And this?"

"Cattle prod."

"Ah." She skipped a photo of that one. "What's this one?" She pointed to a long bar with several prongs.

"That's my favorite." He ran his hand across the bar. "A broad fork. I like to picture my dad as a boy, working out in the field with his father. They raised horses. From what I understand, most of the horses died in the fire. Sad."

She took a couple of pictures then stepped back and tried to look at the wall from Eddie's point of view. After a few moments, she thanked him for his time.

"It's been nice getting to know you," he said. "We got off to a rough start, but now I'm sorry to see you go."

"I'm sorry to have to leave. Maybe I'll come back and see you sometime. Sorry I startled you with the news about your aunt Josie."

A contemplative look came over him. "I wish I'd known her. She looked like a beautiful person."

"She did indeed."

And, as Priscilla left the Bingham Inn, she had to conclude that Eddie Bingham looked like a beautiful person too.

CHAPTER TWENTY-FOUR

On the night before the Tisbury Tizzy party, Priscilla tossed and turned all night. Images of her great-grandfather's sword haunted her. She saw it over and over again in various dreams.

Priscilla finally crawled out of bed before the sun rose and made her way to the kitchen table for a cup of coffee and some time in her Bible.

She went back to the book of Proverbs, looking for some comfort and direction. She found an applicable verse in the third chapter, the sixth verse: *In all your ways submit to him, and he will make your paths straight.*

She paused and thought about those words.

Path.

Straight.

"*Hmm.*" She stared at the words again, and an idea tugged at her mind. It took root and began to grow, finally morphing into a full-fledged possibility.

Time to go over all the records one more time, this time with a fine-toothed comb. She started with the autopsy report Gerald had given her. Everything looked pretty straightforward. It confirmed the cause of death as a stabbing. As she read it, something new jumped out at her. Why she hadn't noticed before, Priscilla could not say, but there it was, in black and white.

"That's it!" She rose and paced the room. "I've got it!" She glanced down at Jake, who'd risen at her shout. "Looks like I'm on to something here, Jake. Just need to confirm one last thing…"

She grabbed her computer, opened an Internet browser, then typed in the words: *Adoption Records 1920 Massachusetts*. One of the options that presented itself was an adoption database for the state of Massachusetts. Priscilla only had one name to go on, so she entered Josie Bingham as the birth mother. At first she had no date of birth to enter, but then it hit her.

What date had Josie died again? January 2, 1920.

Priscilla pulled out the manila envelope that held all her documents related to the investigation and confirmed the date then quickly entered that as the date of the baby's birth.

Nothing.

She entered the day prior, January 1.

A whole new world opened up to her. Priscilla stared in amazement at the file, complete with time and date of birth for Josie's child. What really threw her, though, was the infant's name.

"Oh my goodness."

Priscilla's heart began to thump harder than before.

She looked over the rest of the document, honing in on the words *Catholic Charities, Falmouth, Massachusetts.*

She was just about to press the Print button when something else jumped out at her. For the first time, the column that read *Adoptive Family* caught her eye. When she read the name, she almost jumped for joy. For in that moment, a thousand questions were answered at once. Suddenly, Priscilla could hardly wait to gather her friends and family to share the news.

She flew into action, dressing as quickly as she could while putting in a call to Joan.

"Can you meet me at the bakery a half hour before the party starts?"

"Sure. I planned to go early anyway."

"Good. I think I've stumbled across something."

"Can't wait to hear about it. You want me to call the others?"

"Yes, please." Priscilla put on her shoes. "And Mildred too, if you don't mind. Oh, and Tilly Snyder."

"Tilly Snyder?"

"Yes, trust me, she'll want to be there."

"I'm sure she was up all night working on that hummingbird cake of hers, but she'll probably come."

"Good. Oh, and you might as well invite Katie Ortmann. We need to clear the air with her as well. Try to get a table in the corner of the bakery where we can talk while Candy's setting up for the party. Okay?"

"Sure. Can't wait," Joan said.

They ended the call, and Priscilla patted Jake on the head. "I think I've done it, boy. Pretty sure I've got this thing figured out."

He wagged his tail as if to say, "You go, girl!"

Unlike her usual drives around the island, Priscilla didn't pay a bit of attention to the scenery as she headed out minutes later. She had one thing on her mind and one thing only. Getting to the bakery and sharing her news with the others.

Ten minutes later, she pulled into the parking lot and brought the car to a halt. She reached for the manila envelope that held the items she needed then bounded from the car.

As Priscilla entered the bakery, she lifted her hand to wave to Candy and froze.

Beau was working behind the counter, wearing a bakery apron. She took several quick steps in his direction.

"Beau?"

"Can I help . . . ?" He glanced up from the glass case he'd been filling with pastries to face her. "Oh! Hi, Mrs. Grant."

"*Oh* is right. What in the world?"

He laughed. "Candy's in the kitchen icing cakes. I knew how busy we were going to be today, so I offered to help out."

"We?" Priscilla quirked a brow.

"*Hmm*." The edges of his lips turned up in a playful smile. "Did I say 'we'?"

"You did."

He nodded and leaned forward, putting his elbows on the glass case. "Okay, okay. I guess the secret's out."

"Ha! It was out days ago. Gerald told me you and Candy were back together."

He laughed. "Who needs the Internet when you've got islanders?"

"Right? But even he didn't know you were helping out at the bakery."

"It's just for the party, that's all." He smiled. "I won't be giving up my day job, if that's what you're worried about." A pause followed. "On the other hand, the construction business is really slow in the winter, so maybe you'll see me at the bakery more. Who knows."

"Who, indeed?" Priscilla winked. "Anything else brewing?"

"Yeah. Vineyard Blend. Can I get you a cup?"

If he'd been any closer, she would've slugged him. "Good grief, no. I mean, yes. I'd love some coffee. But no, that's not what I meant. Just being nosy."

He reached for an empty coffee cup and then turned to fill it from the large coffee maker behind him. His cheeks flamed red, but he kept his mouth firmly shut.

Priscilla laughed. "Never mind, never mind."

She looked around the restaurant to see if any of her family members had arrived. It looked like she'd gotten there first. She set her sights on an empty table in the back corner and was about to make a beeline to it when Candy emerged from the kitchen, her apron covered in powdered sugar. Or flour. Or both.

"Beau, would you mind…?" Candy shifted her attention to Priscilla. "Oh, hey, Priscilla! Great to see you."

"Great to see you too. Baking up something new, I hear?" She quirked a brow.

Candy didn't seem to pick up on the innuendo. "Yep. You wouldn't believe how many layers of Tisbury Tizzy I've made. Folks are going to flip. I hope." She glanced at the clock on the wall and gasped. "Oh, I have so much to do before the guests arrive." She turned and headed back into the kitchen.

Priscilla wanted to offer to help, but she had to take care of something first. When her cousins arrived, she gathered them at an area in the far corner so they could be alone. "Anyone seen Tilly?" she asked. "And Mildred?"

"Mildred's on her way." Gail pushed two tables together and adjusted the chairs. "Tilly? Not sure if she'll come. She seemed kind of standoffish."

"Hope she does," Priscilla said as she took her seat. "Boy, do I have some news for her."

By the time Mildred arrived, the ladies had already ordered coffees and then settled in to talk. Just when Priscilla thought Tilly and Katie would be no-shows, they entered together and slowly made their way to the table.

"I don't know what this is about." Tilly stood behind an empty chair as if refusing to sit.

"Neither do I," Katie added as she rested her hand against her cane.

"Please join us, ladies," Priscilla said. "I promise, you won't be sorry."

"Humph." Tilly pulled out the chair and took a seat then eased it forward. Katie took the seat next to her. "I've got a car filled with hummingbird cakes, so make this quick, before they melt."

Beau approached the table and gave the women a nod. "I'll get those for you, Tilly, and put them on the cake table."

She tossed him her keys and grunted a thank-you then looked Priscilla's way. "So?"

Priscilla passed cups of coffee their way and smiled. "So we have a lot to talk about."

Tilly refused the coffee. She leaned back in her chair as though in defiance of this whole thing. Katie took a cup of coffee and gave Priscilla an inquisitive look.

"Priscilla, tell us what's happened," Trudy said. "We're on pins and needles over here."

"Okay." She smiled and plowed forward. "It's been quite a journey to figure this out, but I've taken all the evidence, examined all the clues, and then, by process of elimination, drawn some conclusions."

"Conclusions?" Tilly's gaze narrowed. "Is this the part where you tell me that my grandfather was a murderer?"

"No, it's the part where I tell you without hesitation that he was not."

Tilly looked stunned. "Really?"

"How do you know?" Gail asked. "Conclusively, I mean?"

Now for the fun part.

Priscilla rested her hand on Tilly's arm and smiled. "I've stumbled across a piece of evidence that has convinced me that Chester Snyder was an amazing man. Not only did he forgive David Pearson and Josie Bingham, he showed them the greatest act of love a human being can offer."

Tilly's eyes filled with tears. "What do you mean?"

"After David Pearson died, Josie disappeared. We knew from her death certificate that she passed away a short time later, presumably after giving birth. We couldn't prove the existence of a child at the time though."

"Are you saying the baby was just a rumor?" Tilly asked.

"Hardly." Priscilla shook her head and lifted her hand from Tilly's arm. "But I'll get to the baby momentarily. First, a little backstory. A couple of years after David's and Josie's respective deaths, your grandfather met and married a wonderful woman."

"My grandma Betty."

"Yes. And they had three children."

"Actually, they had four," Tilly countered. "My pop, his brother Chip, and his sisters, Maddie and Paula."

"Correct." Priscilla took a sip of her coffee, which was already growing cold. "Three of their own, and one they adopted."

"Adopted?" Tilly shook her head. "I never heard anything about one of the kids being adopted. Are you sure?"

"Very." Priscilla pushed her coffee aside and reached for a napkin. "See, I got to thinking about Josie's baby. I just couldn't let go of the idea that her baby really did exist. It just made sense that she was pregnant if she disappeared and then passed away so quickly. So I did some research online and located an open adoption database for Catholic Charities."

"I searched several databases too," Mildred chimed in, "but came up short."

"This was just a God-wink," Priscilla said. "I was working on a whim and actually found something concrete."

Gail leaned her elbows on the table. "The suspense is killing me."

"It's not like today, of course. Most adoption records are sealed now. Back then, most unwed mothers went to homes like the Catholic Charities to have their babies, and those records are slowly becoming available online as modern-day relatives search for long-lost ones. We're talking a hundred years ago, after all."

"Makes sense, but I'm still confused." Tilly crossed her arms and leaned back.

"Let me show you something I just printed from the Catholic Charities site, Tilly. And, just for the record, this is a game changer." Priscilla opened the folder with the adoption paper inside and pushed it toward Tilly.

"Tell me what you see here."

"In March of 1923, Chester and Betty Snyder adopted a young child from the Catholic Charities by the name of . . . " She stared at the page and then looked up at Priscilla before glancing down again. "John David."

Priscilla nodded as a collective gasp went up from all in attendance.

Tilly bristled then gave Priscilla a wary look. "That's my father's name." She paused, and her eyes flooded with tears. "Are you telling me that my father was the adopted one?"

"Yes, evidently so. The point is, Tilly, your grandfather and his wife Betty felt such compassion for Josie, even though she betrayed him, that they took in her child after she passed away. And that child was your own father, John David Snyder."

Tilly was reduced to tears. She cried with such intensity that it drew the attention of Candy and Beau, who rushed to the table.

"Everything okay over here?" Candy asked.

Priscilla nodded. "We're just having a moment. Could you bring more coffee, please?"

Candy nodded, albeit with a concerned look on her face, then she and Beau headed toward the kitchen.

After a moment, Tilly reached for a napkin and wiped her eyes. "Priscilla, are you telling me that Mildred's great-uncle David is my real grandfather?"

"Oh my." Mildred stared at Tilly, who stared back at her.

"Biological grandfather, yes," Priscilla explained. "And it would appear that Josie named the child John David at birth. The moment I saw the name, I knew the truth: she named him after his father, David Pearson."

"Whoa." Trudy took another sip of coffee, then added, "This is better than a movie."

"With more drama, for sure," Joan added.

Tilly's eyes now sparkled with newfound excitement. "Oh, how I wish my father was still alive. I wonder if he ever knew he was adopted. Do you think?"

Katie Ortmann's nose wrinkled as she chimed in. "Maybe it's better if he didn't. You know?"

Tilly nodded. "I guess you're right, though things like that happen all the time. Can you imagine what he must have felt, though, growing up in a household with a brother and two sisters and wondering why you looked—or acted—different? Maybe he…" Her words drifted off. "Oh my goodness!" She reached inside her purse and came out with her wallet. She opened it to reveal several small photos. "Look, Priscilla." She pointed to a faded black-and-white picture of her family's historic inn. "This is a picture of my father's whole family when he was just a boy. Grandpa Chester had just opened the inn."

Priscilla leaned in to have a closer look. "Oh my."

"He doesn't look a thing like his siblings, does he?" Tilly observed. "And for that matter, I don't look like any of the Snyders either. I've got this wavy hair and such a petite physique." She gave the picture a closer look and shook her head. "For pity's sake."

"There's a reason for everything," Priscilla said and smiled as Candy returned to the table with fresh coffee. "But don't give up on me yet, ladies. The story most certainly does not end there."

CHAPTER TWENTY-FIVE

"You mean there's more to this tale?" Tilly asked. "I'm not sure if my heart can take it!"

"Much more, but we'll start with your cousin Eddie from Falmouth." She glanced at the bakery door as more townspeople entered. Before long, this party would be in full swing. She'd better spit out the story, and quickly.

"Wait. I have a cousin named Eddie?" Tilly looked perplexed by this notion.

"Yes, ma'am. The only remaining Bingham, at least on that side of the family."

"Wow." Tilly leaned back in her chair.

"And you'll be interested to know there's a family resemblance."

Tilly's eyes filled with tears again.

"Now, let's talk about the murder weapon." Priscilla leaned forward and let the truth spill out. "I went over the autopsy report several times and almost missed one thing. It jumped out at me early this morning. The bloody sword was found next to the body."

"Which points to Great-Grandpa," Trudy said.

"That same sword that was reported stolen the day prior."

"Which points to someone other than Great-Grandpa," Trudy added.

"But if you look closely at the autopsy report"—Priscilla pulled it out and set it on the table—"what do you see?"

Mildred leaned forward to give the report a closer look. "'Cause of death: blood loss from stabbing, pierced clean through.'" She shrugged. "He was pierced through with the sword, of course."

"Think so? Read the details."

"'Stab wound approximately one inch in diameter, entering the back, traveling through the heart, and piercing the abdomen upon its exit just above the naval.'" She shrugged and put the paper down. "I don't get it. Sounds pretty cut-and-dried to me."

"How wide was the wound?" Priscilla asked.

"One inch."

"And how wide is the Patton Saber at its widest point?"

Mildred's jaw dropped. "Oh my goodness. I see what you mean. It's at least two inches at its widest point, right?"

"Correct. So I've concluded the sword must have been a plant, stolen and placed beside the body to draw attention away from the actual murderer. I'm assuming the police must have concluded the same thing because Great-Grandpa James was never arrested, and there's a note in the report that his sword was returned to him one month after the incident."

"So we know that our great-grandfather didn't do it," Joan threw in.

"And my grandfather didn't do it," Tilly added.

"Which just leaves one suspect." Priscilla closed the folder and leaned back in her chair.

"Is this the part where you try to convince me that my great-grandfather killed David Pearson because of gambling debts?" Katie's eyebrows arched. "Because if you are…"

"On the contrary. We know for a fact, thanks to Harrison Ortmann's own documentation, David Pearson didn't owe him any money at all, which removes any motive. I also know that Harrison saw a miraculous turnaround in his spiritual life and went on to be a huge asset to his community and his church." She paused. "I brought you here, Katie, to apologize to you." A catch in Priscilla's throat made the next words difficult. "I'm truly sorry to have added any more agony to what you're already going through with your health. I want you to know that I've been praying for you. I truly have. And I want to go on record as saying that Ortmann's is the finest grocery store in Tisbury."

Katie reached for a napkin and dabbed her eyes. "You'll never know how much your words mean to me, Priscilla. For so many years our family has had this cloud hanging over us—not that my grandfather murdered anyone, but that he ran a gambling parlor. You'll never know how that affected my family through the years, especially when the newspaper articles from those days kept popping up over the years. Talk about embarrassing."

"Well, we're not here to point fingers." Priscilla offered her a warm smile. "Only to say that we're here for you, regardless of what anyone did or didn't do in the past."

"So my grandfather is no longer a suspect," Katie said.

"Correct. Which brings us to just one." Priscilla released an exaggerated breath. "And to be honest, I knew the answer in my gut the moment I left Bingham Inn in Falmouth on Thursday."

"Edward Bingham!" Trudy clasped her hands together. "He killed David Pearson?"

"He did indeed. And I will tell you how I came to that conclusion, even before locating the adoption records for Tilly's dad."

"How so?" Joan asked.

"Two days before David Pearson was killed, Edward Bingham made several purchases from Ortmann's."

"Chickens?" Katie asked.

"No, real purchases. Farming equipment. Which, if you think about it, was odd because he had long abandoned the family farm. He lived in town with his wife. So why buy a broad fork and a brand-new sickle and several other large items? I was curious about this, but that curiosity became suspicion on Thursday when I saw the decor in the lobby at Bingham Inn in Falmouth."

She pulled out her phone and scrolled through the pictures she'd taken while visiting with Eddie Bingham. Priscilla stopped at a particular photo and passed it around to the ladies.

"Read the inscription," she said as Joan took the phone in hand.

Her cousin squinted to read the fine print. "'Honor. Justice. Family.'" Joan clasped a hand over her mouth. "Oh, Priscilla!"

"I've been thinking and thinking about that autopsy report. The entry point was in the back, cutting through the heart and coming out above the naval. It would be very difficult for a weapon with a straight line to make that sort of angle or curve. I didn't pick up on that until I saw the real murder weapon hanging on the lobby wall at Bingham Inn. A sword isn't curved, but a sickle is."

Mildred looked as if she might faint. She dropped her head onto the table and took several slow breaths then straightened up again. "So Edward Bingham killed my great-uncle with a sickle—sick as it makes me feel to state that aloud—and tried to make it look as if someone else was to blame."

"That's my best guess." Priscilla took her phone and shoved it into her purse. "All of the evidence lends itself to that."

"I daresay your guess is right on the money." Mildred shook her head. "It's just all so gruesome."

"Indeed. Edward Bingham took revenge on the man who had sullied his sister's reputation. Then, in the end, he abandoned that sister's memory as well, never speaking her name to anyone after she died."

"And displayed the murder weapon in plain view on the lobby wall of his inn, along with a caption about family and honor." Trudy shuddered. "That's the move of a cold, calculated killer, a man who was actually proud of what he'd done."

"Precisely," Priscilla agreed.

"Wow." Mildred still looked a bit ashen. "Did you tell Eddie Bingham your suspicions about his father?"

Priscilla shook her head. "No. Eddie's in his golden years with nothing but admirable thoughts about his father. I would never do that to him."

"Good call," Trudy said.

Joan nodded. "Yes, and what a relief to clear our great-grandfather's name."

"I stumbled across something else in my research this morning," Priscilla said. "It has to do with that Bible verse on the painting."

"What did you learn?" Gail asked.

"Turns out, Great-Grandpa Latham's division held that verse dear. It was one they all shared every morning when they met to receive their orders for the day. I looked up his division online and found several references to that verse. It was their motto, I guess you could say."

"Wow." Joan nodded. "So that explains it. He wasn't trying to send some sort of subliminal message; he was just quoting a familiar verse that stuck with him all of those years."

"Yep." Priscilla nodded. "But I still believe Aunt Marjorie gave the verse a dual meaning when she added it to her painting of the sword. I honestly think she just wanted to put the whole ordeal behind the Latham family."

Gail gave her an admiring look. "You're quite the investigator."

"Hardly. I think I'm just a good guesser."

A crowd of locals poured through the door, ready to get the party underway. The noise level in the bakery rose to new heights.

"I'm so relieved to know that you Lathams no longer suspect my grandfather." Tilly's eyes flooded with tears once more as she raised her voice to speak above the crowd. "I'm so sorry, Priscilla. Truly." She swiped at her tears with the back of her wrinkled hand.

"And for what it's worth, I would be honored if you would join me this coming Sunday morning on the Snyder family pew." Her eyes grew wide, and she rested her chin in her hand. "Oh my."

"What is it, Tilly?" Mildred asked.

Her lips curled downward in a pout. "I'm not really a Snyder. That's not even my pew. All these years I've been sitting in the wrong place."

This got a laugh out of everyone.

"I'd say it doesn't matter because we're one big happy family." Mildred reached her hand across the table to grab Tilly's. "So sit with me, if you like. Or with Priscilla. Or with anyone you choose."

Before Tilly could respond, Priscilla heard Candy's voice over the loudspeaker welcoming all the guests.

"Come on over to the cake table, folks, and have a slice of my new Tisbury Tizzy hummingbird cake. And for those who don't like cranberries . . ."

"Who in the world doesn't like cranberries?" Sheila hollered above the noise of the crowd.

"Well, for those who don't, Tilly Snyder has brought several of her marvelous hummingbird cakes from her restaurant at the inn."

A cheer went up from the crowd at this news.

Tilly's cheeks flushed pink. She rose and walked over to the cake table then started carving up large slices of her cake.

Priscilla had just started to get into the cake line when something at the door caught her attention.

"Oh, Priscilla, look." Trudy's eyes flooded with tears as she pointed to Fred Pearson, who'd just entered the bakery pushing an unfamiliar elderly woman in a wheelchair. As Fred struggled to get the chair through the narrow opening, Gerald O'Bannon stepped up to offer assistance. Seconds later, they were safely in the room with the rest of the partygoers.

"I haven't seen Ginny Pearson in ages, since she went to the care facility." Trudy bounded across the room to greet Mrs. Pearson, who appeared rather dazed and confused.

"God bless him for bringing her," Joan added as she took Trudy's place alongside Priscilla. "This has to be hard on him, what with all they're both facing."

"Bittersweet," Priscilla said, her gaze never leaving the man as he tended to his wife. "I'm sure."

But, oh, what a testimony to the love these two shared. She watched how he treated her with such gentleness, such sweet pats on the shoulder and kisses on the forehead. Was this the same ornery fellow she'd met just weeks before, in this very bakery, the one with the stern expressions and accusing tone? After all he'd been through, she could hardly blame him for lashing out.

"I have it on good authority that Candy took one of her Tizzy cakes to Fred last night. I'd say it worked its magic." Joan slipped her arm over Priscilla's shoulders. "If you'd asked me a couple of hours ago, I would've said we needed that cake to perform a miracle on all of the townspeople, but you've done it, Priscilla. You solved the case and brought everyone together. We didn't need the cake after all."

"Speak for yourself! I'm getting in line."

Priscilla headed to the cake line and stepped into place behind Fred and Ginny Pearson. When she finally made it to the table, she found herself torn. Which cake should she take? If she opted for Candy's, Tilly might be upset. On the other hand, if she took Tilly's, Candy might be hurt.

Unable to decide, she took a slice of each.

When she turned back to the party, it looked as if half the town was eating both versions, and the ensuing smiles were lighting up the room.

Priscilla greeted the townspeople as she made her way through the room but kept her gaze on one special person—Katie Ortmann. Before approaching her, Priscilla reached into her purse and came out with a small gift bag. She carried it to her new friend.

"What's this?" Katie asked as Priscilla extended the bag in her direction.

"Oh, just a little something I picked up at a gift shop when I went into Falmouth. Open it and see."

Katie gingerly opened the bag and then doubled over in laughter when she saw its contents. In fact she laughed so hard, tears rolled down her cheeks.

"You're not offended, are you?" Priscilla asked.

"Offended?" Katie stopped to catch her breath. "Heavens, no. It's perfect. Just exactly what the doctor ordered. I'm so glad we're friends now, Priscilla. Truly." She gave Priscilla a warm hug, thanked her with great zeal, and then headed across the room to help Tilly at the cake table.

"What was all that about?" Beau asked as he squeezed through the crowd with a stack of dirty plates in hand. "Is my mom okay? Looked like she was crying."

"Happy tears. I gave her a little gift."

"Oh?"

"Yes. I found the cutest little ceramic salt and pepper shakers at a gift shop in Falmouth. Couldn't resist giving them to her."

"Salt and pepper shakers?" He looked perplexed.

"*Mm-hmm.* Chickens." Priscilla laughed until tears came to her eyes. Before long, Beau joined her.

This brought the cousins running from the cake table.

"What did we miss?" Trudy asked. She took a big bite of Tisbury Tizzy cake, and a delirious look came over her.

"Yes, why all the laughter?" Joan asked.

"What happened?" Gail echoed.

"Oh, I just had a moment with Katie Ortmann," Priscilla explained. "I gave her a little gift, and she enjoyed it."

"A gift?" the cousins asked in unison.

"Ceramic chickens," Beau said, and the ladies all erupted in laughter.

He wedged his way through the crowd to take the dirty plates to the kitchen.

"So that's it then? That's what's come from this investigation of yours?" Joan put her hands on her hips. "It all boils down to chickens?"

"*Mmm.* Boiled chicken. Sounds yummy." Trudy licked her lips. "Puts me in the mood for chicken salad."

"No, I got a lot more from this investigation than a lasting memory of chickens." Priscilla paused, lost in her thoughts. "Much, much more."

"What have you learned, Dorothy?" Trudy asked.

"Dorothy?" She looked her cousin's way.

"Yes, from the *Wizard of Oz*. At the end of her journey, the scarecrow asked her what she learned from her journey. She gave a list. Actually, I think it ended with, 'There's no place like home,'" Trudy threw in. "But don't let that sway you to go back to Kansas like she did, okay?"

Priscilla laughed. "Trust me, I'm not climbing into a hot-air balloon and flying back to Kansas, not for all the hummingbird cake at Candy Lane's bakery." Besides, there was no going back now.

"Well, that's a relief because I'd hate to send the flying monkeys after you." Trudy looked genuinely relieved. "But you didn't answer my question. What did you learn, Dorothy?"

Priscilla paused to think through her answer. "Well," she said after a moment of pondering, "I think I've learned that some battles are worth fighting, no matter how difficult. I needed to defend the honor of our family, but in doing so, learned a lot about my own journey to get to this new phase of my life."

"New phase?" Joan asked.

"Yes. If Great-Grandpa James could go all the way to France to become a hero, what's a little trip from Kansas to Martha's Vineyard? And if he could stay and face the criticism of his peers after David's death, then how hard can it be for me to stay and face the obstacles set before me with any additional renovations on the cottage? I don't need to sell off a piece of our family's legacy to pay my way. I'll display the sword proudly, where all can see. It will have a place of honor in the lighthouse museum when the time comes."

"Good girl." Joan gave her an admiring look. "Even the Wizard of Oz would approve of that answer."

Perhaps he would at that. "There's something else. I called a Realtor back in Wheatfield and told her to put the farm on the market. I'm selling it. It's time."

"Oh, Priscilla." Joan pulled her in for a tight hug, and Trudy and Gail piled on, squeezing as hard as they could. After a long moment, Joan shrugged them off and pulled back so she could see Priscilla's face. "I know that must have been a hard decision to make."

"It was. But it was also the right one." Priscilla smiled, fighting back tears. "This is my home now, and I couldn't be happier about that."

"Neither could we!" Trudy exclaimed.

Before she could respond, a familiar male voice came over the loudspeaker, calling everyone to attention.

"Is that Beau?" Trudy asked.

The noise in the room lowered as he spoke.

"Candy Lane, you're wanted at the counter. Candy Lane, you're wanted at the counter."

From the cake table, Candy gave him an odd look. She waved her hand and hollered, "I'm busy!"

"Not too busy for this, I hope." He crossed the room to the cake table and knelt down on one knee.

The whole room came alive as folks began to cheer.

"Keep it down, everyone," Katie hollered. "My boy's about to propose."

And propose he did—right there in front of a room filled with people. Beau delivered the words with nervous precision. Candy's "Yes, yes, yes!" left little doubt in anyone's mind where she stood. She let out a whoop as he slid the ring onto her finger. The crowd released a joyous roar as Beau stood and wrapped his sweetheart in his arms then planted a kiss on her that the folks of Tisbury wouldn't soon forget.

"Wowza." Priscilla turned to face her cousins, completely overwhelmed with emotions. "There really are healing properties in that cake."

"Then let's give Marigold and Pop each a big slice," Gail whispered in her ear. "What do you think?"

Delightful idea. Perhaps they should do just that.

Priscilla placed her hand on her heart as she watched her friends celebrate alongside one another. Off in the distance, Gerald visited with Fred and Ginny Pearson. Tilly continued to slice up pieces of her hummingbird cake and even dropped a few hints that it would make a terrific wedding cake. Katie Ortmann wrapped her future daughter-in-law in her arms and squealed with delight. Even Uncle Hugh joined in the fun, slipping his arm around Gail's shoulder and placing a kiss on her brow.

"What do you think of the Vineyard now, Priscilla?" Joan asked.

Priscilla's gaze traveled the room. She took in her new friends, her heart filled with joy. "I'd say we're one big happy family." For the first time in months, she finally felt the truth of those words.

And to think, it only took a trip from Kansas to get her here.

AUTHOR LETTER

Dear Reader,

What a blessing to share this story with you. There are few places that ignite the imagination like Martha's Vineyard, as I learned firsthand when I visited the island while writing this book. I'm not sure which I enjoyed more: touring Edgartown, where the movie *Jaws* was filmed, or getting lost in Aquinnah, after visiting the Gay Head cliffs.

No matter where I ventured, I found myself captivated by the lighthouses, the coastline, and that magnificent water. I also discovered a lot about myself while visiting and subsequently writing this book. Though I hadn't realized it until I boarded the ferry in Woods Hole, I'd allowed my years as a caregiver for my mom (who has stage six Alzheimer's) to isolate me from family and friends. I had deliberately pulled away from others, an island unto myself. Visiting the Vineyard brought respite and reminded me that staying connected with those I love is critical as I walk this difficult road.

I feel so honored to bring you a story set in such an idyllic place. Many thanks to my amazing editor, Susan Downs, who made this possible. I also owe a huge debt of thanks to Jessica Barnes, who helped me shape the story to fit the cozy mystery line. I hope you enjoy your travels to the Vineyard as much as I did.

Sincerely,
Janice Thompson

ABOUT THE AUTHOR

Award-winning author Janice Thompson got her start in the industry writing screenplays and musical comedies for the stage. Janice has published over one hundred books for the Christian market, crossing genre lines to write cozy mysteries, historicals, romances, nonfiction books, devotionals, children's books, and more. She particularly enjoys writing lighthearted, comedic tales because she enjoys making readers laugh.

Janice is passionate about her faith and does all she can to share the joy of the Lord with others, which is why she particularly enjoys writing. Her tagline "Love, Laughter, and Happily Ever Afters!" sums up her take on life.

She lives in Spring, Texas, where she leads a rich life with her family, a host of writing friends, and two mischievous dachshunds. When she's not busy writing or playing with her eight grandchildren, Janice can be found in the kitchen, baking specialty cakes and cookies for friends and loved ones. No matter what she's cooking up—books, cakes, cookies, or mischief—she does her best to keep the Lord at the center of it all.

AN ARMCHAIR TOUR OF MARTHA'S VINEYARD

The Gay Head Cliffs
Aquinnah, Massachusetts

There are many breathtaking views in Martha's Vineyard, but none compare to the scenic overlook at Gay Head Cliffs in Aquinnah, Massachusetts. In this special place, you will find the island's only non-white lighthouse. After snapping a few photos, you'll want to follow the trails to the nearby scenic overlook, where you can read about the area's rich history.

Peer down at the waters below, to the very spot where Vineyard Sound meets the Atlantic Ocean. Beautiful blue waters take on varying hues at the point of their merger, creating a picturesque view. You can almost envision the two different bodies of water shaking hands.

Don't let your gaze linger for long though. There is far too much to see on the other side of the overlook: a grassy perch tipping out on to rugged cliffs that hover over a pristine white-sand beach, begging for footprints.

In this majestic spot, one can literally feel God's presence. You can picture Him at creation, His fingertip carving out the picturesque cliffs, the whisper of His breath causing ocean waves to rise. If, with just a word, just a touch, the God of creation can make something beautiful out of Gay Head Cliffs, what can He do in your life? Perhaps a trip to the island is in order to find out?

SOMETHING DELICIOUS FROM OUR SEASIDE FRIENDS

Hummingbird Cake from Candy Lane Confectionery (Uncle Hugh's Favorite)

Cake

- 1 cup (room temperature) butter
- 2 cups granulated sugar
- 1 tablespoon vanilla extract
- 4 large eggs
- 3 cups all-purpose flour
- 1 teaspoon baking soda
- 1 teaspoon ground cinnamon
- 1 teaspoon salt
- ⅓ cup buttermilk
- 1½ cups mashed ripe banana (about 4 medium)
- One 8-ounce can crushed pineapple

Frosting

- 1 cup (room temperature) butter
- Two 8-ounce packages cream cheese, softened
- 1 teaspoon vanilla
- 1 tablespoon lemon juice
- 2 cups confectioners' sugar

Optional Toppings/Garnishes

- Coconut
- Macadamia nuts

Cake: Beat softened butter, sugar, and vanilla until light and fluffy. Add eggs, beating well. Stir in bananas and pineapple, but don't overmix.

In separate bowl, mix flour, baking soda, cinnamon, and salt. (Note: If you use salted butter, you can omit the salt.) Add flour mixture to butter mixture, alternating with buttermilk as you go.

Add to greased/floured pans and bake at 350 degrees for twenty-five to thirty-five minutes or until center is cooked. Remove from oven and cool (in pans) for fifteen minutes, and then turn out cakes on to cooling racks until room temperature. Frost and garnish.

Frosting: Combine butter and cream cheese; beat until creamy. Add vanilla and lemon juice. Gradually add confectioners' sugar until frosting reaches the desired consistency. Frost the cooled cakes using the garnishes of your choice.

Read on for a sneak peek of another exciting book in the series Mysteries of Martha's Vineyard!

Adrift

by Beth Adams

Priscilla was just climbing into her car when her phone rang. It sounded so foreign out here, on this spit of land surrounded by crashing waves, that it took her a moment to place the sound. Then she dug around in her purse to locate it before it stopped ringing. It was always buried under her wallet, her keys, sunglasses—there it was. She pulled it out and looked at the screen. Gerald O'Bannon. She answered the call.

"Couldn't wait, huh?" Priscilla was on her way to meet Gerald at the Nautilus Cafe for lunch. He'd invited her, saying he had a favor to ask of her. She was glad for the opportunity to see him and had been looking forward to it.

"I'm afraid I'm going to be a bit late for lunch," Gerald said. She could hear some voices behind him and what sounded like metal banging on metal.

"Is everything alright?"

"Yes, it's fine. It's just—something came up at work, and it looks like it might take a while."

"Oh dear." Priscilla felt more than disappointment. Gerald was a captain at the Coast Guard station just up the road. She knew that if something had come up at work, it was serious. "Do you want to reschedule?"

"No. I mean, I'd still really like to have lunch, if you have time."

"I have time." Priscilla certainly kept busy since she had moved from a farm in Kansas to Martha's Vineyard a few months ago, but this lunch was the only thing she had on her calendar today. "Do you want me to meet you in an hour?"

"I'd love that, but I'm not sure exactly how long I'll be. How about this—could you come here? And then as soon as I get this squared away, we can drive over to the Nautilus together."

"That sounds just fine," Priscilla said. She had only been inside the Coast Guard station briefly, but she'd thought it was fascinating to see what it was like inside a real military post way out here on the coast of this remote island. And, she had to admit, she was a little curious about what could have happened to delay him. It had to be something big, the way he sounded. "I'll be there shortly."

Priscilla tucked her phone back into her purse and set it on the passenger seat. As she started the engine, she looked up at the lighthouse. It stood tall and proud, guarding the craggy hillsides that gave way to the ocean below. Sometimes she still couldn't believe she lived here.

Priscilla backed the car around and pulled out onto the narrow old lane that led to the main road. Trees arched over the road.

The first of the leaves were just starting to turn orange and gold. She couldn't wait for her first New England fall. Sure, she'd seen plenty of trees change color back in Wheatfield, Kansas, but everyone said she hadn't seen anything like the riot of color she would witness here.

As she drove down the road, she passed small wooden houses, set right up next to the road, that had been here for centuries, and cottages sided with weathered shingles. These homes were the kind of beautiful that didn't call attention to itself. Understated and classic. She loved this place. She passed barns faded to a soft gray and fences made of stones piled one on top of each other. She turned right at the Quaker graveyard that had tombstones dating back to the 1700s. That was another thing that was different from Kansas—the sense of history that permeated this island and the pride the islanders took in their past.

As she got farther from the heart of Misty Harbor, houses gave way to marshland, and finally she wound her way around the last bend and the bay opened up before her, blue churning water all the way to the horizon. Beyond that lay Cape Cod, she knew, but she couldn't see the mainland on this hazy morning. Off to the right was a road with a big white wooden sign that read US COAST GUARD.

She turned in and drove toward the stately white buildings that made up the station. The main building was three stories and topped by a cupola surrounded by a widow's walk. She saw several cars parked in the lot and more lined up in front of the white building that served as housing for the officers stationed here, but this area was quiet. She looked around and saw people in orange suits headed down the hill, moving toward the dock that lay just past the row of old weather-beaten fishing shacks. Priscilla started moving toward the action, and as she got closer, she saw what had gotten everyone so excited.

It was a building. A floating wooden building tied up at the dock.

Drawing nearer, she saw that it was a cabin of some sort. A houseboat, maybe? But what was it doing here? There were a couple of people who didn't look like they could be much out of their teens wearing the official Coast Guard dry suits, but they didn't pay her any mind as she walked down the catwalk toward the vessel.

"Hi there," Gerald called, seeing her as he stepped out onto the dock from the cabin. He was wearing an orange dry suit over his clothes, and he gestured for her to come closer.

"Hi." Priscilla now stood in front of the floating building, and she realized what it was. "Is that the houseboat that's been parked out in the marina?"

Until a few weeks ago, the only kind of houseboat Priscilla was familiar with were the typical double-decker floating motor homes that spewed out exhaust and leaked gasoline. People liked to take them out on the lakes during the summers back home. But this was nothing like that. This was a floating wooden cabin of sorts, built on a platform that surrounded the tiny home. It was covered in wooden shingles and had a sliding door that led from the platform to the inside. It was kind of like those houseboats in the movie *Sleepless in Seattle*, only newer and with less rain.

"That's right," Gerald said. "This is the one that's been moored over in the harbor. The one that's been causing so much uproar around here."

Priscilla nodded. She'd read in the newspaper about the furor this boat had caused when it appeared in the marina a few weeks back. No one seemed to know anything about the man who had taken up residence on the harbor, and he didn't seem inclined to come ashore and introduce himself. And some people in Tisbury and the surrounding communities, it seemed, did not like the idea of a houseboat being parked out in the harbor. It ruined the view, or something. Priscilla had seen the headlines, but she hadn't really paid that much attention to the story. She didn't see what the fuss was about. A boat was a boat, right? She could see the marina from the top of the lighthouse, and it hadn't bothered her to have it there.

"Interesting." She stepped closer. Up close, she could see that it was very well-constructed, with solid wood siding and neatly painted white trim. "But what's it doing here?"

Gerald let out a sigh. "I wish I knew," he said. Then he stepped off the dock and onto the houseboat's deck.

"Captain O'Bannon," came a call from inside. Gerald turned toward the door and peered inside. "Can you come check this out?"

He smiled at Priscilla and held up a finger, asking her to wait. Priscilla stepped onto the houseboat's deck and watched as Gerald stepped in through the open sliding glass door. He crossed the small space and hunched over something on a small table, across from a young man in a Coast Guard uniform. Priscilla had met him before. Seeley? She thought that was his name.

Priscilla stood outside the door for a moment, feeling awkward. Should she just hang out here? She'd thought he was just going to duck in for a moment, but he was now in discussion with the other Coast Guard officer. The platform the boat rested on bobbed up and down, and the air carried the salty, briny tang of the sea. Priscilla waited a few more minutes, but Gerald didn't come back out. She peered through the door and saw that it was just a small space, and it was only Gerald and Seeley in there right now.

She made a decision. She hadn't exactly been invited inside, but no one had asked her to stay out either. She stepped through the open sliding glass door. No one seemed to notice. Both Gerald and Seeley were focused on something on the counter.

"The police are on their way," Seeley was saying. "I'm sure they'll run tests—fingerprints, UV scans, the works. But if we can get this unlocked before they get here..."

"Yes. Good. Focus on that," Gerald said. Then he added, "Thanks."

He turned and saw Priscilla standing inside the boat, and she was certain he was going to kick her out, but he didn't. "Be careful there," was all he said, indicating a wet patch on the floor.

"Thanks."

She looked around. So this was a houseboat. It was small—not more than ten feet by twelve feet, she guessed, but it was cunningly designed. Directly across from the glass door was a table, which she could see folded down into a bench when not in use.

Priscilla and her late husband Gary had gone on a trip to Yellowstone in an RV many years ago, and it had had the same feature, but this was built out of solid, handsome cherry. The table was crookedly hanging off its hinges now, and the blue-and-white-striped fabric that had lined the bench had been sliced open.

The front wall held a few cabinets and a narrow electric stove. The cabinets and drawers had all been yanked open, and cans of coffee and beans had spilled out onto the counter. Milk leaked out of the open door of the minifridge. Next to that was a slightly opened door, which afforded Priscilla a glimpse of the smallest bathroom she'd ever seen. A single bed was pushed up against the far wall, blankets strewn over the floor, the mattress sliced open. A dog bed was propped on its side next to the mattress, and it had also been sliced through. Most of the remainder of the small space was given over to a table and an easel and chair. Tubes of oil paints had been knocked onto the floor, and a shelf that held canvases in various stages had been knocked over, the canvases tossed this way and that.

"What happened here?" Priscilla asked. It looked like it had been ransacked.

Gerald let out a slow breath. "We got a call from Almeida Charier this morning," he said. Priscilla nodded. She had met Almeida, who drove one of the ferry boats that went back and forth to the mainland. "She was driving the first boat out this morning, and she spotted the houseboat floating in the shipping channel, headed out to sea."

"It was just floating? No one was driving it?"

Gerald shook his head. "These houseboats don't have motors. There's no way to drive them. They just float."

"So how did it get out there?" Priscilla tried to wrap her head around this. "And what happened to the guy who was living here?"

He shrugged. "That's what we're trying to find out. My crew towed it back here, but there's no sign of the man who was living here."

A feeling of dread washed over her. Judging by the state of this place, whatever had happened, it could not be good.

"Somebody was looking for something," she said, indicating the opened cabinets and the sliced upholstery.

"Looks like it," Gerald said. "But we don't have the slightest clue what."

"Who was he?" Priscilla wandered into the kitchen area and peered in the open cabinets. Some coffee, a tin of sugar, coffee filters. A half-empty box of granola bars and a few packages of beef jerky.

"We don't know that either." Gerald sighed and turned to Seeley.

Priscilla studied the canvases that were strewn around. They all seemed to be abstract paintings, with lots of patterns repeated over and over but no discernible bigger shape. Not Priscilla's taste, but interesting in their own way, she supposed. The whole space had the oily, mineral smell of turpentine.

She pointed to the dog bed. "He had a dog, right? I remember reading that in the paper. What happened to the dog?"

Gerald just shrugged. "No idea. Any luck, Seeley?"

"No. It's password protected."

Priscilla noticed that he was hunched over a small silver laptop computer. He must be trying to get inside.

How odd, she thought. Someone had gone to a lot of trouble trying to find something in here. But whatever it was, it wasn't the guy's laptop. She would have thought that would be the most valuable thing on this boat.

She turned back toward the open cabinets in the kitchen. What had the person been looking for?

She crouched down and peered in the open lower cabinet. The pans it had contained were now scattered across the floor, and only a couple spare lids remained inside. A few large-handled knives had come out of the butcher block and were splayed across the counter. Had one of these been used to slash open the furniture?

Someone had come on to this boat looking for something. She wondered what it was, and whether they had found it. They certainly had done their best. The guy who'd been living here must have done a good job of hiding it. Whatever it was.

She thought for a moment. If she had been hiding something on this boat, where would she have put it?

She didn't even have to think. She knew exactly where she'd always hidden important things. The same place her grandmother had hidden the farm's papers when her grandfather threatened to sell in the darkest days of the Great Depression.

The same place Priscilla's mother had also hidden her cash. Where Priscilla always kept emergency funds, just in case. In the last place anyone would ever look: taped to the underside of the silverware drawer.

Still crouched on the floor, Priscilla looked up.

"Gerald?" she called. "I think I found something."

FROM THE GUIDEPOSTS ARCHIVE

"Respite Journey" by Janice Thompson of Spring, Texas, originally appeared in *Guideposts*.

Wow," Crystal said. my friend was clutching the white railing of the ferry taking us to Martha's Vineyard. We had come a long way to see this island. Flying from Texas to Boston. Spending a night in Cape Cod before catching the 6 A.M. ferry. Now, at long last, the island was coming into view. Sailboats dotted the coastline, sails snapping in the breeze. Wooden piers and green cliffs jutted out over the water. Crystal turned to me and smiled before looking back toward the island. "It's beautiful."

"Uh-huh," I said and walked back to the covered portion of the deck. The glare from the sun was making it hard to read my text messages. I scrolled through them, wondering how things were going back home. Had my daughter Megan remembered how to use the video monitor in the bedroom? Had I explained to give Mom her chai tea first and *then* a glass of cranberry-grape juice for breakfast?

Mom had been diagnosed with Alzheimer's in 2010. There'd never been any question of who would take care of her. I moved in immediately. Raising four daughters had been hectic, but it was nothing compared to caring for Mom 24/7. She had always been as sharp as a tack. Quick to laugh or make a joke. She fought the disease at first, but soon she was forgetting names, dates, and details of her personal history. It wasn't just memory either. When she spoke, it was in monosyllabic, nearly unintelligible phrases, and she became so attached to me that I couldn't leave the room without her crying. Her dependence only grew as the disease progressed.

Mom still loved to travel though. We took several trips that summer of 2016. Went on a cruise, drove across Texas, spent a week at the beach. It was the only way I was able to keep my sanity. I needed the breaks from our routine, and Mom seemed to enjoy the change of scenery.

So when I had the opportunity to write a book set in Martha's Vineyard, going there seemed perfect. Mom would get to see Cape Cod, and I would get to do what I love most: write. I booked tickets for a fall trip.

But by September, Mom was fighting a series of infections. Then she suffered a bad fall. There was no way she could travel. Which meant there was no way I could travel. And if I couldn't travel, I couldn't write my book.

Writing wasn't just my passion; it was my livelihood. I churned out as many as eight books a year. Though taking care of Mom slowed me down some, I still found time to write. But writing was getting more difficult. It had gotten to the point where I couldn't even go to the bathroom without my mom getting anxious about my whereabouts. Every five minutes brought another interruption. Writing might be my livelihood, but taking care of Mom was a duty, a cross I willingly bore. Something I felt God had asked me to do.

The morning after her fall, I stood in the kitchen, making Mom's cup of chai tea. Was it time to give up my writing altogether?

If I went to Martha's Vineyard now, who would be there to watch Mom? Who would want to spend a long weekend doling out medications and trying to interpret her monosyllabic phrases?

And yet I couldn't rid myself of the nagging feeling that I needed to go. In fact, it grew more urgent. With only 36 hours until my flight, I pulled out my phone and texted Crystal. "What are you doing the day after tomorrow? Want to go to Massachusetts with me?" Then I started calling family members to see if they could help with Mom.

"I know it's a lot to ask," I began when I proposed the idea to my daughter Megan.

"I'm happy to help," she said before I'd even finished. In fact, she seemed almost excited.

Four people stepped up to help with Mom while I was away. I wrestled with guilt from the moment I texted Crystal. Although I'd obsessively made lists—a timetable for each medication, the phone number for all Mom's doctors and therapists—I worried my family wouldn't be able to handle it.

If I could just make the most of this time, it would all be worth it.

The journey to Cape Cod had gone smoothly. Except for the incessant beeping from my phone. Was it okay for Mom to go to bed at 6 P.M.? Should Mom be allowed to buy whatever she wanted at the grocery store?

I was exhausted before we even set foot on the Vineyard ferry. I'd spent the night in Cape Cod tossing and turning.

"I hope Mom's okay," I said to Crystal, coming out from under the ferry's awning, phone in hand. "I feel guilty enjoying all of this while making other people take care of her."

Crystal wrapped her arm around my shoulders.

"God can take care of it. Maybe you need to let Him," she said. "Besides, you didn't make anyone do anything. They're probably enjoying the chance to spend time with their grandma. Why should you have all the fun?"

Was Crystal right? Was it time to let go? By hoarding all the caregiving responsibilities for Mom, I wasn't just robbing myself of rest; I was robbing my family of time to spend with her. I slid my cell phone into my purse and allowed myself to truly take in the view. It was stunning. Rust-colored cliffs melted into grassy pastures. White clapboard houses and wooden canoes lined the shore.

The knots in my stomach finally began to unwind.

It was hard enough to lose my mom to Alzheimer's. I couldn't lose myself too. I couldn't be a good caregiver if I didn't take care of myself. I needed breaks. Adventure. Time to write. And to do that, I needed to trust other people to look after her. Trust that the Lord was taking caring of us both.

"I'm so glad you texted me," Crystal said, her eyes fixed on the enchanting island in front of us.

"Me, too," I said. "It's going to make a big difference for the book. And for me too."

A NOTE FROM THE EDITORS

We hope you enjoyed Mysteries of Martha's Vineyard, published by the Books and Inspirational Media Division of Guideposts, a nonprofit organization that touches millions of lives every day through products and services that inspire, encourage, help you grow in your faith, and celebrate God's love.

Thank you for making a difference with your purchase of this book, which helps fund our many outreach programs to military personnel, prisons, hospitals, nursing homes, and educational institutions.

We also create many useful and uplifting online resources. Visit Guideposts.org to read true stories of hope and inspiration, access OurPrayer network, sign up for free newsletters, download free e-books, join our Facebook community, and follow our stimulating blogs.

To learn about other Guideposts publications, including the best-selling devotional *Daily Guideposts*, go to Guideposts.org, call (800) 932-2145, or write to Guideposts, PO Box 5815, Harlan, Iowa 51593.

Find more inspiring fiction in these best-loved Guideposts series!

Mysteries of Martha's Vineyard

Come to the shores of this quaint and historic island and dig into a cozy mystery. When a recent widow inherits a lighthouse just off the coast of Massachusetts, she finds exciting adventures, new friends, and renewed hope.

Tearoom Mysteries

Mix one stately Victorian home, a charming lakeside town in Maine, and two adventurous cousins with a passion for tea and hospitality. Add a large scoop of intriguing mystery and sprinkle generously with faith, family, and friends, and you have the recipe for Tearoom Mysteries.

Sugarcreek Amish Mysteries

Be intrigued by the suspense and joyful "aha!" moments in these delightful stories. Each book in the series brings together two women of vastly different backgrounds and traditions, who realize there's much more to the "simple life" than meets the eye.

Mysteries of Silver Peak

Escape to the historic mining town of Silver Peak, Colorado, and discover how one woman's love of antiques helps her solve mysteries buried deep in the town's checkered past.

Patchwork Mysteries

Discover that life's little mysteries often have a common thread in a series where every novel contains an intriguing whodunit centered around a quilt located in a beautiful New England town.

To learn more about these books, visit Guideposts.org/Shop